Hidden Heritage

Books by Charlotte Hinger

The Lottie Albright Mysteries
Deadly Descent
Lethal Lineage
Hidden Heritage

Hidden Heritage

A Lottie Albright Mystery

Charlotte Hinger

Poisoned Pen Press

Copyright © 2013 by Charlotte Hinger

First Edition 2013

10 9 8 7 6 5 4 3 2 1

Library of Congress Catalog Card Number: 2012910478

ISBN: 9781464200755   Large Print

Poisoned Pen Press
6962 E. First Ave., Ste. 103
Scottsdale, AZ 85251
www.poisonedpenpress.com
info@poisonedpenpress.com

Printed in the United States of America

Hidden Heritage is dedicated to the memory of my beloved husband, Don Hinger. His wisdom, love, and integrity inspired and sustained me throughout our long marriage.

Acknowledgments

With each addition to the Lottie Albright series there is growing list of people who have lent their expertise. Scott Foote took time out of his busy day to take me on a tour of the magnificent Hoxie Feedyard and answer my questions. It is an enormous operation and functions like a small city.

Carla Olsen, the fabulous office manager, knows everything there is to know about the feedyard. She's one of those "don't know how she does it persons" that everyone looks up to. Travis Schaffer—the head cowboy—looked like he stepped out of an old western movie. All of the cowboys were attired in western gear and there was a sensible reason for each item of clothing. Carla and Travis supplemented Scott's information and I can't thank the three of them enough.

My late husband, Don Hinger, was a bull hauler. He hauled cattle. It was a privilege to spend my life with such a good man. When we first married and even after he bought the truckline, Prickett & Son, Inc., he always referred to himself as a truck driver, never as the owner of a business that employed a number of people. I know this business inside and out, first from his perspective as a driver and my frustrations as a truck driver's wife, and later through his constant double-binds as the owner, dispatcher, and manager of a high risk business. Each day was a little like being on the Chicago commodities floor.

I would like to thank Marge Hass for answering a number of my medical questions. Her patience was deeply appreciated. A special thanks to Dr. Doug Lyle, who fields a number of weird questions from mystery writers. I thank the National Academy of Emergency Medical Dispatch for providing their Priority Medical Dispatch guide.

John Crockett and Janis Davis-Lopez proofed this manuscript. Not only do I thank them, but I'm sure my editor and agent are equally grateful. I'm dismally inept at seeing typos and detecting missing words in my own work.

In every book I praise the Kansas State Historical Society. Incredibly, it was founded in 1875, when Kansas was still wet behind the ears. Local historical societies are manned by volunteers throughout the country and I salute their unselfish efforts to preserve our country's heritage.

With this book in particular, I am indebted to Barbara Peters' keen editorial insight. She is extraordinary! A special thanks to Annette Rogers, Jessica Tribble, Robert Rosenwald, Nan Beams, and the Posse for their help and expertise.

I owe a special debt of gratitude to my wonderful agent, Phyllis Westberg, for her patience and encouragement.

Take the staff, and you and your brother Aaron gather the assembly together. Speak to that rock before their eyes and it will pour out its water. You will bring water out of the rock for the community so they and their livestock can drink.

—Numbers 20:8 (NIV)

Chapter One

The call came at two. Usually, Keith, my husband, was the first to answer the phone. No, he had dropped into bed exhausted just an hour before. Although he tells our neighbors he wants out of the vet business, he never refuses a caller panicked over a sick animal. Tonight, he had gone down the road to the Sellers, knowing they could never pay the prices of the new veterinarian. He found a kid's 4-H calf half-dead just five days before the county fair.

We have a special phone in our house when a 911 call comes into the sheriff's office. The tone is intended to wake the dead. Deciding to pull rank, I leaped out of bed. Whatever the reason, I could handle it by myself. I am the undersheriff of Carlton County and Keith is merely a deputy. I remind him of that from time to time.

"Sir, slow down, where are you calling from?" The male voice was incoherent, broken. I couldn't make sense of his garbled words.

"The feedyard. It's terrible. Just terrible."

Then I recognized his voice. "Chase? Is this Chase?" I know Chase Dudley. He is an off and on again bull hauler for our county's largest truck line. They have a liberal hiring policy. Finding drivers with cattle experience was getting harder all the time. Anyone with a commercial driver's license who knew a heifer from a steer, and could come up with an accurate head count, was looking better all the time to the owner.

"Chase. I'll be there in a flash. Just hold on."

"No. Not you. Not by yourself. Send Keith."

Keith was fully awake now, pulling on his jeans. I was close behind, cradling the phone to my ear so I could talk while I dressed. "We'll both come," I said. Chase was usually laid back, certainly not an alarmist. He hung up immediately before I could get any details. Our 911 system is informal. No need to trace locations. In this county, everyone knows where everyone else lives.

"What?" Keith was pulling on his boots.

"Don't know, but it's something bad. That was Chase Dudley. He wants you there, too." I called Sheriff Sam Abbott from the OnStar as soon as we jumped in Keith's Suburban. "Chase was terrified, Sam. He wasn't even making sense."

"I'll call Betty Central to take over the 911 line and head that way."

"Okay."

"Poor old bastard." Keith braked for tumbleweeds blowing across our path and drove as fast as he dared on the gravel road leading to the blacktop. Sam was an old man and needed a good night's sleep. "We've got to get more reserve deputies."

"Wouldn't do a bit of good for these kinds of calls. Sam would come on out anyway."

Keith said nothing. He knew I was right.

No letup from the record breaking heat this summer. Wheatland and pastures might as well have been set on Mars. Folks prayed for rain, then quit, figuring God had moved on to California.

A haze of dust dimmed the yard lights rimming the administration buildings in the feedyard. Dust mixed with the aroma of dried feed, manure, and diesel fuel seemed to draw the oxygen from the air.

Chase ran toward us as we came up the road leading to the feedyard. "Follow me," he yelled. He dashed to a pickup and we followed him along the lane that led past large cattle pens and went deep into the vast feedyard. He stopped and gestured at the cattle truck washout, the "shit pit," where the drivers used high pressure equipment to blast dirt and manure out of their possum belly trailers. The drainage from the initial pool led to one of four artificial lakes. When everything worked right, that is.

Chase parked, then loped over to the first rank lagoon and pointed. "In there. Jesus Christ."

Even in daylight one couldn't see through the water. Now despite the yard lights and spotlights we couldn't see what he was pointing at.

And then we did.

"Son-of-a-bitch." Keith whirled around and went back to the car. I stared at the spot where a body had bobbed up, then disappeared into the water.

Nauseated, I turned away. "Keith is calling EMTs, Chase. They'll be here in a little bit."

"Won't do no good. That man is dead."

"We have to follow procedures and they will take him right to the coroner's office. Sam Abbott will be here shortly and we need you to stick around and answer a few questions."

"Hell of a note." Chase stepped away and blew his nose. He was greyhound-lean with an exaggerated Old West mustache. The pearl snaps on his western shirt gleamed in the glow of the yard lights. He removed his worn old Stetson and his black hair blended into the shadows. He was an old school bull hauler who didn't hold with untucked shirts or fancy drivers who chromed up their trucks and blew all their settlement checks on LED lights. His truck was not his castle, and the lights were strictly utilitarian. He loaded on time, shunned the beer joints and arcade setups, got a decent night's sleep when he could, and by God, got 'er done.

"Do you have any idea who it is, Chase?"

"No. He never turned faceup. I finished unloading and backed up here to wash out, and the water pressure made him bob up. He went under again, so I guess it was just luck I saw him at all. If you can call this luck."

"Were you the only one unloading tonight?"

"No, some of the drivers picked up a load of feeders in Colorado and brought them here earlier in the evening. My load was in Missouri, so they were long gone by the time I got here."

"The dispatcher will tell us who the others were," I said. Then we heard the sirens from the approaching ambulance and the fire department truck. Silently, I thanked God I was not going to have to go in after this man. I'm a trained historian with a PhD, and had originally become involved with law enforcement to help our resource-poor county solve a crime quickly. I never dreamed it would become a full-time job.

My husband hadn't either. It became a bone of contention between us. Then he became a deputy to protect me during ugly situations and he, too, was suckered in. That's the way it goes in small towns. You volunteer for some little no-count job and soon discover you've sold your soul to the devil.

Other cars were coming up the drive now. I recognized the pickup driven by the owner of the feedyard. More people came. Sheriff Sam Abbott arrived before the dust from the fire truck settled.

"Everyone stay back. Every one of you," he yelled. "Go home. Get the hell out of here." The old man looked exhausted in the feedyard lights. He turned and barked at Keith. "Get the tape. We need to get on this fast. Just in case."

The "just in case" meant a suspicious death, of course. We had bumbled in the past, and decided too quickly that deaths were accidental.

Word had already spread and now feed-yard workers were driving up.

"Ah, shit," Sam muttered. But folks obediently moved behind where Keith staked the tape, and Chase stepped forward to help him.

Dwayne Weston, the owner of the feedyard, drove toward us like a mad man. He slammed on his brakes, leaped from his pickup and took charge the moment he banged the driver's door shut. "Back, goddamn it," he yelled at the growing crowd of gapers. His face was white under the lights. "Everyone stay back or I'll, by God, sue each and every one of you for trespassing."

"Thanks," I hollered, relieved that I could turn my attention to helping the firefighters. Crowd control is a nightmare for law enforcement in small towns or counties. Nevermind what is shown on TV about preserving the scene. We do our best, but we don't have the manpower.

The fire chief, Barry Whitcome, drove up and parked his pickup next to Keith's Suburban.

I hurried over. "The lagoon." I pointed. "There's a body there."

He whirled around and shouted at the responders. "You'll need wet suits." He turned back to me. "Tell Weston we'll be using his office to change in."

Three men ran over to the administration building and soon emerged wearing wet suits and masks. The fire truck backed up to the pit, and lowered a chain suspended slab.

The men went in the pit to locate the body. It had not been in long enough for natural body gases to produce buoyancy. As Chase said, it was sheer luck the water pressure from his hose had made the body bob to the surface. I shuddered as one of the men came to the surface, clutching an arm. The other fireman grabbed the platform and pulled it down into the water and maneuvered the lifeless form onto the slab and strapped it to the board. The operator in the truck winched the slab from the lagoon, rotated toward land, then lowered it to the ground.

Keith knelt and loosened the restraining straps

and carefully turned the body over. He stood up and glanced at the cluster of people forced to keep their distance, then called to the owner of the feed-yard. "Weston, we need you here."

Dwayne came over, knelt, looked at the drowned man, then rose so abruptly he nearly lost his balance.

"It's Victor. Victor Diaz, my foreman." Dwayne slammed his fist into his hand then walked back to the group, which was reluctantly complying with the order to stay behind the crime-scene tape. "It's Victor Diaz," he hollered. "Victor. Now go on home. Every last one of you. Get the hell off this property."

He took off for his pickup with angry strides and had one foot on the running board by the time Keith caught up with him.

"You can't leave yet, Dwayne. We have some questions."

Obediently, he backed down. "Damn ghouls. I need to tell his wife before she hears it from anyone else. Damn ghouls." He drew out a handkerchief and blew his nose. "What the hell was he doing here this time of night, anyway?" He choked back a sob. "Nothing like this has ever happened here before."

Dwayne is a slim man in his early fifties. He has a gorgeous thatch of bright silver hair. With his rugged good looks and authoritative manner, he wouldn't have been out of place in an old wagon-master western. His father and grandfather had passed down the feedyard, but he had greatly expanded the capacity.

"This will just about kill Maria. Victor has worked here five years and they just now bought their first house."

"I'll be the one to notify her." My mouth went dry. It's part of my duties, but it never gets any easier, this telling families that their husband, their father, somebody's son had died in the middle of the night. Hard under any circumstances, but worse to tell a woman her husband had died alone in a stinking hell hole.

"I'll go with you," Weston said. "It will make it easier on Maria if I'm the one bringing the news."

"You don't have to, Dwayne."

Tears filled his eyes. "I don't see how something like this could have happened. There was just no reason for him to be here."

"Are there usually people here in the feedyard during the night?" I dug out my notebook. I was learning fast in this thankless job that seemed to spread into unexpected areas. Sam, Keith, and I were all naturally quick studies, but Keith had been the first to see that we needed to start proper procedures right from the beginning with any unattended death. Before data was lost or overlooked. Before we started making stupid assumptions.

"Just one. He's an older man and more like a night watchman. If something comes up or there's a real emergency he calls me. Like a real bad storm. Then I start calling the cowboy crew and we make sure the cattle don't start bunching up."

"One man doesn't sound like much for a place this big." The feedyard is enormous and accommodates about fifty-five thousand head of cattle. "I thought your security was tighter than a lot of hospitals."

"They talked about it after 9/11. Everyone was worried about terrorists spreading anthrax to America's beef supply, but nothing ever came of it. As to having only one man, nothing much goes on out here at night. During the day, there's about fifty employees counting the office help." He gestured toward the rows of front loaders, tractors, feed trucks, cattle trucks, bulldozers, tank trucks, conveyor belts, hay balers, and mountains of silage. Massive silver tanks store liquid grain. Even they are dwarfed by the water tower. On the way in, I had noticed about two acres of bales of hay. The feedyard sits on a section of land and uses every foot of it to get feeder calves fattened for market.

"This is like a city."

"I can vouch for that," Keith said. "Guess I've been out here often enough to know."

My husband is a large man. People who like him find his square-shouldered stocky appearance reassuring. Those who don't, resent his success, his landholdings, and his professional status as a veterinarian. They find his foray into law enforcement a bit much. He became a deputy to protect me, but I was by turns amused and then furious by his and Sam's obvious unspoken vow to shield "the little lady."

It should not be necessary. Carlton County is a small county in Western Kansas. But after a couple of bizarre cases had spiraled out of control, the three of us became edgy. On the lookout for shadows. For menace.

Dwayne turned toward Keith without so much as an apologetic glance toward me. A man doing a man's business. Naturally, he wanted to talk to another man. I no longer smolder over such things. I took notes.

"Victor had no business here," Dwayne blurted. "None whatsoever." He pulled a handkerchief from his back pocket and blew his nose. "He's my right-hand man. My foreman. I just don't understand what the hell he was doing here at this time of night."

"And he's only worked here five years?" I broke

into the conversation. "That's a pretty good step up the ladder to become a foreman in that short a time."

"He was great. Just great. One of those employees you can count on for just about anything. No matter how trivial. He cared and worked hard and..." Dwayne choked on his words, then embarrassed at his loss of control, turned away.

"We'll talk more later." Keith clapped Dwayne on the shoulder, then walked over to the EMTs who were transferring the body to the ambulance. The solemn crowd of onlookers was dispersing and heading for their cars. Victor's identity was now known and whispered around. There was no need for anyone to stay.

Sam went over to the three firefighters still in wet suits and gestured toward the lagoon. They headed back toward it. Shocked, I looked at Keith.

"They need to make sure."

"Sure of what?"

"Sure there's not another body down there."

Chapter Two

Sam left them to their work. He walked over to where we were standing. "Mighty sorry, Dwayne. Wasn't around Victor much, but he was a fine man, from everything I've heard about him." He gestured toward the office buildings. "It's going to take the men a while. Can we go in there to talk? I need to get a little more information to send along to the district coroner."

Keith and I exchanged glances. Sam saw, and then gave a slight shake of his head warning us not to ask questions. We had them, of course. The normal procedure was to send a body to our county coroner, not the district coroner.

"Christ," Keith muttered under this breath, too low for anyone but me to hear. The three of us followed Dwayne across the lot. Sam's white hair gleamed below his Stetson. I squared my shoulders. I always did when I was around this old man who should have been enjoying a spot by the fire in his old age. But having lost his only son in Vietnam and his wife to cancer years ago he'd turned to work and was re-elected sheriff every four years.

There was no better mind for police work, but Keith was beginning to grumble about the lack of equipment and methods that were outdated. In short, Sam's unwillingness to integrate computers and data diminished his natural aptitude.

Dwayne took us back to his office, the largest of three administrative suites. He gestured toward the two chairs facing his desk. "Sorry. I'll get a folding chair."

"No need. I'll stand," Sam said. "This won't take long."

The phone rang and Dwayne automatically started to pick it up, then stopped. "Forgot. Bart's dispatching tonight."

The furnishings were Danish modern. Easy to clean in an environment dominated by dust. Keith glanced at the main server that was large enough to store data for half the state. In a couple of hours it would display a running tape of the commodities futures market. What Carlton County lacked in population, it more than made up for in computer geeks per square mile. MBAs and Agriculture Economics majors now ran corporate farms, and the beef industry was dominated by men hardwired for profits.

Opposite the hall leading past Dwayne's office are several rooms for the drivers' comfort. In them are exercise equipment and a small kitchen with a mini fridge and a microwave. Dwayne had given me a tour once and I knew the shower had a full collection of toiletries. Another room has a flat screen TV and another has four bunk beds so drivers could catch up on their sleep between loads. The tile floors gleam and there are plants galore.

I had been out here many times during daylight hours and knew that no amount of filtering would eliminate the faint haze of dust particles that permeates the air or minimizes the odor rising from thousands of cattle being fed out.

The sky was lightening. Poets can write all they want about the glories of dawn, but when there's been a death, daylight isn't welcome. Dark and shadows soften reality.

A truck entered the feedyard and Dwayne rose and went to the plate glass window that faces the road.

"They can't unload yet," Sam said. "Not until…" He faltered. Keith looked at him sharply and I knew he was mentally filling in the missing sentence. Knowing instantly that Sam had seen something when Victor's body was loaded. Knowing for some reason our sheriff thought this death was suspicious.

Dwayne's face flooded with blood. A vein on his temple throbbed. "Just a minute here, Sam. We have to unload that truck right away. Get those cattle weighed and put in a holding pen. The cowboy crew gets here right before daylight. In another hour or so, the processing crew will start coming in, too, and finish them the rest of the way. Other trucks. More cattle coming in all day long. We can't have truckloads of cattle just sitting here. They need to be inspected, and fed and watered."

He turned to Keith who was often called on to look over the cattle. "Tell him, Fiene. They have to unload."

"He's right, Sam. He can't leave them on the truck." Keith studied the whiteboard dominating one wall and listing pens and ear tag numbers. He glanced at Dwayne. "Where are you going to put them?"

"Pen fifty-one. It's empty right now. Three more truckloads coming in today with feeders that weigh about the same. They aren't custom feeders, so they will all be put in the same pen."

"Custom?" I asked, doing my best to follow the conversation.

"We buy most of the cattle at sales through order buyers. They belong to the feedyard. Custom-fed cattle belong to mostly local men who contract with us to feed them out." Annoyed at having to explain basics, he turned back to Sam and Keith. My face flamed. The menfolk!

"Have you done anything special to that pen?" Sam asked.

"Like what?"

"Disinfected? Anything like that?"

"No, just the usual. The maintenance crew comes in and cleans it up with bulldozers with a blade on front. All the manure is removed and piled and sold to local farmers for natural fertilizer. Then the ground is leveled, and the water and feeding troughs cleaned out. That pen is ready now."

"Other cattle been there in the last month?"

"No."

"Good," Sam said. He turned to me. "There's a kit in my car. Please process that pen immediately." I glanced at Keith. A surprised look flickered across his face. "Keith, go with her to record any notes."

I had become the unofficial CSI person for the sheriff's office. Keith's powers of observation were second to none, but both men accepted my intuition and my ability to sense that something was "not quite right." From time to time Keith would grumble that it was like living with a witch, but I knew what came into play was my training as a historian. I accepted the importance of documentation, but so often documents were wrong. Facts—black and white—could lead to a false conclusion.

My twin sister, Josie, a clinical psychologist and part-time professor at Kansas State University, had said last spring that personalities as high in intuition as mine were rare. She is more logical. More cynical. Together, our separate academic disciplines equaled a regular science team.

Neither of us, however, could hold a candle to Josie's spoiled little shih tzu, Tosca, whose judgment was infallible. If Tosca didn't like someone, there was something rotten in Denmark. Thankfully, she found most people neutral.

"This won't take long," Sam told Dwayne. "All we need are a few soil samples."

"Why are you doing this? Going over an empty cattle pen?"

"This is just standard procedure." Sam didn't blink.

But it wasn't standard. Keith and I exchanged looks.

"Tell me what happens when a load of cattle come in."

Dwayne went through the routine beginning with a load logged in, the cattle unloaded and sent through chutes one at a time, inspected, ear-tagged with the pen number, and moved to their base pen where they remain until they are sent to market. When he finished explaining the process, ending with the trucks backing up to the shit pit and getting rinsed out, Sam held up his hand, palm out turned like a traffic cop.

"Not tonight. They have to wash out somewhere else. You can unload, but you can't wash out here."

Sam cut off Dwayne's furious protest.

"I don't want that pit touched until we've had a chance to analyze it, too."

Now I was certain that Sam had seen something. Inwardly, I groaned. We were looking at holding pens of thousands of cattle and a lake of wine-rich manure teaming with excrement and bacteria. It was an impossible situation.

Then I understood. The unoccupied pens would serve as a control. Pen fifty-one had been empty.

"Since you've said Victor wasn't supposed to be here, we want to do things right from the beginning," Sam said. "Just in case."

"Just in case," had become the sheriff department's motto by now. Nevermind the serve and protect bit. We automatically assumed that no matter how innocent a situation seemed on the surface, whatever could go wrong usually did.

"I won't know what might have been dumped in that lagoon until the boys from KBI have taken a look," Sam continued.

My skin crawled. Keith was silent. The KBI

from the very beginning. No doubt now that Sam had seen something.

The whole feedyard was being treated as a crime scene.

"Lottie, Keith, after you process that pen, I want you to take soil samples of every tenth unoccupied pen." He turned back to Dwayne. "Send your trucks to a commercial washout. There's one in Dunkirk."

It was an order, not a request. Sam has a commanding voice that goes with his military bearing. Only a fool challenges the general.

"All right," Dwayne said reluctantly. "I'll tell the men to unload and then go to Dunkirk and wash out. But we need to go to Victor's wife right away. I can't take a chance that someone else will tell her—if they haven't already."

"Does Diaz have other family here?" Keith asked.

"His great-grandmother. A sister. And I think George Perez is his cousin. He's a welder for a heating and air-conditioning company over in Dunkirk."

"No children?"

"None. There was just the two of them."

"Goddamn it." Sam took off his hat and ran his hand through his hair. "Can't be helped. You and I can go tell his wife while Keith and Lottie make sure those empty pens don't have anything we need to know about."

"Why pen fifty-one? It's been empty for four months."

"That's why," Sam said. "I want soil samples and scrapings off the fencing in that pen as a control to compare with the other full pens."

He looked at Dwayne hard. I had been on the receiving end of Sam's zingers often enough that I should have seen it coming, but I didn't.

"Was Victor a citizen? Is everyone working here legal?"

Dwayne's face reddened. "Victor's family has always been here. He was born in America. He didn't come from Mexico. His family has always been here."

"And all the others? Do they have the right papers?

"Of course. We check that out first thing. My office manager takes care of all those details."

"Glad to hear it. It's a good idea to have everything shipshape if the Feds come around." There was a ghost of a smile on Sam's face. "Grab anything you need and let's go break the news to his widow."

Chapter Three

It didn't take much time to process the cattle pens. It was a matter of putting samples from the floor of the pens into test tubes for the KBI lab—but we didn't know why—since Victor had drowned. It had the feel of busywork. We scraped off samples from the creosote-soaked fences. Keith noted that there was nothing visibly wrong. The soil and the fencing would give an excellent sample of what clean pens should be like—provided the labs didn't find anything out of place.

When we finished, we went back to the processing area. Keith walked over to the cattle truck and beckoned to the driver, who backed up to the chute, then hopped down out of the cab to check his position. The best drivers could maneuver the exit door within inches of the opening.

I didn't know him, but Keith obviously did.

"Hear there's been a little excitement out here tonight."

"Yeah, well," Keith said. "Can't talk about it, Billy."

"Plenty of chatter about it on the CB."

"Can't help that. But none of the details came from me."

"Hear ol' Victor's dead? That right?"

"That's public knowledge. That's right."

"He drowned in the shit pit? That right too?"

Keith nodded. "The holding pen is ready to go. Best hop to it."

Cattle left standing on a truck shrink at a predictable rate of three to four percent an hour. Nothing made buyers and sellers more irate than dawdling drivers who sat too long at truck stops swilling coffee while cattle on hot stationary trucks are deprived of food and water and becoming smaller and smaller. Loads are weighed when the trucks are first loaded, then again at the end of a run. Buyers who had bought cattle weighed on the hoof weren't happy to be paid considerably less when critters arrived at their destination shedding pounds like contenders for *The Biggest Loser*.

Keith and I turned to leave and then my cell phone rang. I glanced at the screen. Sam.

"Need you to get over here, Lottie." His voice was low and terse as though he didn't want anyone to overhear. "This got ugly fast and I think you can help calm Mrs. Diaz down."

"Be right there." I hung up. "Problems, Keith. We need to get over to Victor's, or at least I do. It might complicate the situation to have another man around."

"If it does, I'll go back to the car."

"Ugly" wasn't a strong enough word. Maria Diaz had dissolved into a bitter bawling mess. My heart ached, and I could not find words to comfort her. The trite overworked one on every cop show, "I'm sorry for your loss," struck me as woefully inadequate. I bit my lip in a vain attempt to hold back tears.

It didn't help. I put my arms around this little sparrow of a woman. I only knew her by reputation. She was the go-to person when new arrivals hit the town. She helped parents enroll their kids in school and looked over everyone's paperwork. She took them to the right place to learn more about citizenship proceedings.

Hospitals in three counties were grateful when she called on patients because she was fluently bilingual and could help relay symptoms. One look at her kindly brown eyes, light olive skin, and pillowed breasts was all it took. They knew they had a friend. She had a fine sense of outrage and could do battle with city hall when it was necessary.

But now there wasn't a trace of her toughness

and resourcefulness evident. She was reduced to the most primal of all emotions. Grief. Profound grief.

I held her as she sobbed. From over her shoulder I gazed at the array of statues and candles arranged before photos standing in gilt frames. Heavy incense perfumed the small living room. Even though Sam and Dwayne had brought her the news, they clearly thought I should know how to comfort her. Even more than telling someone about a death in the family, I hate trying to figure out what to say next.

By now, I knew she might as well set a place at the table for Grief—for the shadow that would dog her heels. Prepare herself for the quick embarrassing onslaught of tears. For the bittersweet memories that would wake her in the middle of the night.

She quieted a little. "They told me he died where they wash out trucks."

"Yes," I murmured, knowing this religious woman could not bring herself to say "shit pit."

"Why was he there? Why would he be called out in the middle of the night? He didn't say when he left."

She was asking important questions and raising issues we should talk about formally. It wouldn't be seemly for me to suddenly push her away and start taking notes. On the other hand, I wasn't sure I could trust my memory to recall everything she was saying. I wanted to follow up on her "why" questions.

I gave her a final squeeze and led her to the sofa, hoping we could give her some concrete information soon.

Trusting me to know what to do and say, Sam and Dwayne had gratefully fled to the relative peace of the small lean-to porch when we arrived. Keith had stayed there with them. Their voices drifted inside, competing with the racket coming from the cheap air cooler that strained to overcome the heat in the tiny airless room. The cooler was poorly ventilated. Nauseated by the odor from the feed-yard, the stale air robbed of oxygen by the array of candles, I wanted out. Feeling dizzy, I started to rise. I needed a drink of water.

Silently, I cursed the men who had escaped this burden. Angry now, I stepped outside.

"Sam, Keith. If you have questions for Mrs. Diaz, please ask them now. I'll ask members of Victor's family to come spend the night with her. I don't want her to be alone. Don't string out anything you want to ask. Let's get this over with so she can be around people who might help her."

Sam nodded.

"I'll go on, then," Dwayne said. He shook hands with Sam and headed for his pickup. "If you have any questions, you know where to find me."

"Is she Catholic?" Keith asked, before we went back into the trailer.

"Yes, I'm sure. There are a number of icons, saints' pictures, candles."

"Father Schmidt is out of town. At a retreat."

My husband is a devout Catholic, but I'm an Episcopalian, and frankly have little or no religion compared to my husband. However, we do have an Episcopal priest in the area now: Ignatius P. Talesbury. He had set up residence in Carlton County in circumstances so bizarre they had a fairy-tale quality.

Nothing was more startling in our little Western Kansas town than to see this thin, aesthetic, gaunt-faced priest coming down the sidewalk trailed by five or six African boys, always dressed in khaki shorts and shirts. He had established an informal orphanage and through the auspices of the church had managed to dodge a plethora of regulations because he rescued African child soldiers. It was a nearly impossible job.

When I looked in the eyes of these poor shattered souls, safe now here in America, they seemed relieved to live in the middle of nowhere with their humorless protector. But even though Father Talesbury had once been a Catholic priest, I would not ask him to call on Maria. It was hard to imagine him in the role of comforter. Rescuer, yes, but not comforter.

Sam and Keith crowded inside the room.

Sam removed his hat. "We have a few questions, ma'am."

She nodded.

"According to Dwayne, your husband was not supposed to be at the feedyard tonight. Do you have any idea why he went?"

"No. He got a phone call and said he had to go. It's not like it never happens, but he didn't have a regular night shift anymore."

"Did the call come in on the house phone or his cell?"

"The house phone."

"This one?" He pointed toward a cordless handset lying beside her.

She nodded and handed it to Sam. He showed her the "most recent" list.

"I made the first one. To Estelle Simpson. The next number would be the one Victor answered. Should be from the feedyard." She glanced at the number. "Yes, from the office. I just supposed it was the usual. Too many trucks coming in for the night watchman to handle. Or some cattle down." She reached for a Kleenex. "I don't pay much attention to what goes on out there."

"When did he get the call?"

"It was about one thirty, I think. Look at the call log. The time should show up there."

Sam toggled down again.

"One thirty-five, in fact."

He just said he had to go. Nothing else. His last words to me. That's all: 'I have to go.'" She smiled bitterly. "And then he did. And I just went back to sleep. Just went to sleep like it was nothing at all. Nothing."

"Who would have keys to the office to make a call from there?"

"He didn't need one, Sam," Keith said. "I've gone out there in the middle of the night myself a number of times and checked the board to see what feed ratio cattle are getting before I go out to the pens. Anyone can get into the building and the drivers' area or look at the whiteboard information at any time. Only Dwayne's and Bart's offices are locked."

"So this number could have been dialed any-where inside the office?"

"That's right."

"Was Victor...are you, citizens?"

Keith looked at Sam sharply, his thoughts obviously mirroring mine. *Why would Sam ask such a question? Why would it matter if Victor was a Mexican national or an American or from Timbuktu? His nationality would not matter as to how or why he drowned.*

But Keith and I silently waited for her answer without taking our eyes off her face because Sam never asked idle or speculative questions. He rarely went fishing.

Her eyelids fluttered. "Victor. Victor's family has always been here. He's an American." She swallowed. "Was. He was an American. I'm Mexican. But I'm here legally." Something in her eyes flared. "My papers are in order and I am preparing for the citizenship exam."

Sam nodded and closed his notebook. "And the other men who work at the feedyard?"

"I'm sure they are here legally. Dwayne does a good job of running his business. Victor used to talk about how lucky he was to work there. The wages are fair. The hours are long and hard, but not slave hours. Not like some places."

"Anyone he had problems with? Did he talk about having fights with anyone?"

"No." She tapped her lips with her fingers. "Not really."

"Not really?" Sam pressed, his eyes steady.

"It was nothing. Some of the men made smart remarks over his being promoted so quickly. It was unusual, I think."

"Did it go beyond making remarks?"

"No," she said firmly. "Just talk. But my Victor was smart. He had a degree in agriculture economics. And he was good at math. It made all the difference. He could figure feed ratios in his head faster than most people could do it with computers. And he was an honest and a decent man."

Tears filled her eyes again. She pressed a tissue against her mouth, but could not stop trembling. "So decent."

"One more question and I won't trouble you any more tonight. Where do all the men who work here come from? This is the county's largest employer."

"A lot of the men were raised in this county. And some have come from the village in Mexico where I grew up and from other towns close by. Dwayne asked me if I knew good men who were not troublemakers or drunks and who knew how to work. He cared about helping immigrants. He knew I helped people get settled. It worked out just fine. People who had any trouble at all or didn't want to work hard, couldn't or wouldn't stay. They left."

Sam made a quick note, rose, slapped his hat back on his head, touched the brim, and walked to the door. "I'll go on back to the feedyard, ma'am. Keith and Lottie will stay here until Victor's great-grandmother and sister get here."

"No. Not them. Neither of them like me. I don't want them on my property. Keep them away." Her voice trembled. A mixture of rage and despair. "Keep that witch away from me." She dabbed at her eyes. Then her voice softened with shame. "What you must think of me. Having so little sympathy for his great-grandmother, when I know this will just about kill Francesca. Just kill her. She was so proud of Victor. Even though she's always hated me, I wish her no harm."

"Maria, we don't want you to be alone tonight." As law-enforcement officers we certainly couldn't prevent his family from coming over. And by the look on the men's faces, they were as shocked as I over her refusal to call her in-laws.

"I'm sure the whole Diaz family knows by now, but please check. I owe Francesca that much. Not to hear about this from strangers," she said softly.

"Whole family? I thought there was only his sister and a great-grandmother and a cousin here."

"Here in this county, yes. But other kin scattered around Kansas. And other states, too, I suppose."

"Still, you need someone here with you."

"Estelle Simpson is on her way. She's my closest friend. She lives in Dunkirk. Her husband is the head cowboy at the feedyard. He's bringing her and she'll stay a couple of days."

I knew Estelle by sight although I'd never made her acquaintance. A slight jangly woman with cropped blond hair and a flair for bling, her name popped up in all kinds of places. She was an effective and popular speaker on immigrant rights.

When an organization needed a program, she was the first person who came to mind. Her aggressiveness counterbalanced Maria's softer approach to problems.

"She'll be here soon."

"Shall I start coffee? Put on water for tea?"

"No. Thank you very much."

Keith knew what to do. He went out to the Suburban and retrieved the rosary he kept in his glove compartment. His religiosity was an odd trait in a man who could swear like a dockhand, and in his youth was a little too swift with his fists. When he came back inside he silently showed it to her. Tears streamed down her face and she rose and went to the bedroom and came back with her own. Then we heard a car drive up.

Estelle Simpson came up to the door. Her husband followed carrying a small suitcase. The two women hugged, wept, then Estelle led Maria to the sofa. Hugh Simpson removed his Stetson and held it across his chest. Large wet patches stained the underarms of his pearl-buttoned shirt. His oversized mustache drooped unevenly in the hot room and his tall body seemed too close to the ceiling. Deep pouches under his red-rimmed eyes said more about the depth of his grief than his mumbled "sorry for your loss."

Estelle and Maria couldn't stop crying.

Hugh fidgeted and moved from one foot to the other. "Well, goodbye. Need to get some shut-eye. Got a big day tomorrow." Then embarrassed by the crassness of words he couldn't take back, tears stung his eyes. "Shit."

Estelle rose and gave him a quick hug. "Go on now. Try to get a couple hours sleep. We'll be just fine."

"This never should have happened," he mumbled.

Keith and I said goodbye and drove back to the feedyard. I leaned my head against the headrest. Keith kept his eyes on the road and I tried to recall what I'd heard about Victor's great-grandmother, Francesca Diaz. The legendary Francesca Diaz.

So Victor came from *that* family.

Sam waved to us when we drove up to the feed-yard. Dwayne's pickup was no longer there. Sam wore latex gloves. I wondered what evidence he had found to collect. Our tiny county didn't have a team of criminalists on duty. Nor would we ever have the population necessary to sustain an effective crime laboratory. A couple of years ago, I would have said that was not a problem because there was so little crime. But our murder rate per capita has risen dramatically. We now compensate for our inadequacies by calling in the KBI right at the beginning.

In fact, I was thinking of putting them on speed dial.

"Something?" Keith asked.

Sam jerked his head toward a heel ridge in the dirt. "Maybe. I'll know when I compare it to Victor's boots."

The print was slanted to one side. The stride was wide and veered from side to side.

Keith knelt and examined the prints. "There's blood here. Just a trace."

Sam nodded.

"You saw something, Sam. When they removed Victor's body. That's why you had him sent directly to the district coroner. What did you see?"

"His throat. Someone tried to cut his throat. He didn't just drown in the shit pit. He ran for it and dove in to keep someone from killing him."

"My God." I pressed my hand against my mouth to quell the sudden surge of nausea.

"Jesus. Can't imagine anyone following him into it," Keith stared at the filthy lagoon.

'No, but I'm willing to bet they find a couple of bullets in his body, because he had to come up for air."

"There's no way to trace other footprints or

tire marks or anything else," Keith said. "Not after everyone came to gawk."

"Only reason I noticed those footprints is because they were made by a running man and ended at the edge of the pit."

"And the throat."

"I saw that when we turned him over, and covered his head right off before we put him in the body bag so no one else would see it. No one will look at him again until we get him to Hays and the KBI is there to observe."

Exhausted, I stared toward the east and the bloody gauze of rainless clouds highlighted by the first rays of dawn. Soon the merciless copper sun would explode from the horizon, and beat down on our brave, struggling county filled with good people who knew how to outlast the devil.

We had always outwitted the damned sun bent on burning us up alive.

We were getting good at ferreting out murderers, too.

Chapter Four

Keith's voice woke me the next morning. I pulled on jeans and stumbled downstairs toward the coffeepot, then headed for his office and stood in the doorway listening to his questions. He was obviously talking to Sam.

"Anything?" I asked after he had hung up the phone.

"Yes. It's just as Sam suspected. There were a couple of bullet holes in Diaz in addition to that gash on his throat."

"They were able to do an autopsy that quickly?"

He gave a wry smile. "Yes, they have a funny way of expecting the worst from out here by now."

The KBI sends a couple of observers to our county right away for any autopsies of unattended deaths when Sam calls and even hints there might be trouble.

"God, I don't want to go through this again.

But we can't *will* this away. We can't control something like murder."

Keith glanced at me. I knew I looked like hell and he didn't look any better. Our jobs were killing us. "Neither one of us can keep up this pace, Lottie. I want us to get together with Sam next week and do some serious planning. I have some ideas for overhauling the department."

"Yeah, well good luck with that."

He laughed. "Stonewall Sam will come around. You'll see. He knows we're overwhelmed."

We were interrupted by a car coming up the lane. I went to the kitchen and glanced out the window. "It's Zola," I called. "Today isn't her day. What is she doing here?"

Zola Hodson is my cleaning lady. She had come in answer to an ad when I realized I could no longer keep up my household while holding a job at the historical society and serving as the undersheriff of Carlton County. Now I couldn't do without her managing the house.

"Forgot to tell you," he muttered, "she's going to work for me a couple days a week."

"Zola?"

"Yes. Turns out her estate work included animals."

He felt my hard look. We talked most things over. Hiring Zola without so much as a word to me had a sneaky feel to it. As though he thought I might object to his working with a woman. Chagrined, I knew I had won a major victory. When we first married, Keith's sense of men's work and women's work was seared into his brain. It took a while to get him to forget gender and give competence a chance.

"That's wonderful. I'm just shocked, that's all. I shouldn't be. There's nothing she can't do."

"You think you were shocked. She answered my ad in the *High Plains Journal* for a part-time ranch hand and of course, when she showed up, I knew there was no way I could do better."

"You've needed more help for a long time, Keith. We've both needed to say 'uncle' and get our lives straightened out."

But I didn't appreciate his hiring Zola without a word to me. Did he think I would throw a hissy fit? He had run the same kind of silent maneuver last spring, when he became a deputy sheriff behind my back. I had been livid over the underhandedness of his move. It was a done deal, made by him and Sam without discussing it with me. Worse, I knew he had made the move simply to protect me. His wordless hiring of Zola brought back memories of my week of bewildered rage before I settled down and began to appreciate his quiet assistance.

We watched her come up the walk. Today she was dressed in light blue coveralls and work boots. Zola Hodson is the Eighth Wonder of the World. When she first came into the historical society office in a dazzling white shirt with starched crisp jeans and wearing black boots with silver tips that matched her silver hand-tooled belt buckle, I thought she looked like a model. She was whippet-thin and the answer to my prayers. I was drowning, going under from overwork. Her coal black hair was cut in a polished wedge. But it was her high-handed Mary Poppins attitude that set her apart.

She had nearly refused to work for me. In fact, I felt like I had to audition to get her to agree. She required nearly total control over my household including consent to call in outside persons to take care of a problem. Provided, of course, it wasn't a very minor plumbing or electrical problem. Those she took care of herself.

Slowly but surely, all the maintenance issues of our large three-story house were being corrected. Loose floorboards on the front porch were repaired. She found an excellent carpenter and a painter. When we'd first hired her, she'd said her English grandfather was an estate manager in Northumberland, the northernmost county, and he had let her follow him around when she spent summers there as a small child. Her great-great-grandparents had helped colonize the little town of Studley, three counties over from Carlton.

I opened the door before Zola could knock. "Come right on in. Keith is pulling on his boots."

She stepped inside carrying a bouquet of marigolds. "From my aunt's garden," she said. "If you don't mind the odor."

"I love it."

"I didn't have time to tell Lottie you would be working here for me a couple of days a week," Keith called from the back porch. "When she saw you pull up, she thought she had gotten her days mixed up."

"I like working here. It's a challenge," she said carefully.

"You mean a mess," I laughed.

"Not a mess. Please don't misunderstand me. It's that both of you have taken too much on."

"It's not our nature," I said. "In fact, it's making us both miserable."

"I know that. I've seen the way Keith manages his vet supplies and the way you file material. You are both organized by nature."

"It all came apart at the seams when we got involved with law enforcement. And that was accidental."

She raised her eyebrows in disbelief and walked over to the stove and turned on the teakettle with a disapproving glance at my coffeepot. Although she had never commented on the contents, she clearly disapproved of my brew, a cross between espresso and battery acid.

"And how can a decision to become deputy sheriffs be accidental?"

"Well, when I was working for the historical society and collecting family histories, I needed access to criminal databases to solve a murder quickly before a young man's political career was ruined. Then later, when I became an undersheriff, Keith became a deputy to protect me. He was afraid I'd get hurt."

Her large gray eyes widened. "And you both stayed in *why?*"

"I've stayed in just long enough to see a case through," Keith said. "I didn't want to abandon Sam. Or my daredevil wife here." He shot me his look. "We had just finished recruiting enough reserve deputies to put the department on a sensible schedule, until Victor Diaz's murder."

"I understand Sam Abbot is seventy-six?"

"Yes, but don't underestimate him. He's the sharpest law officer around anywhere. He can no longer win footraces, that's all." I was always quick to set people straight about Sam's abilities. "The

KBI got involved immediately this time, though, so we will soon wind up our responsibilities in the investigation."

"Good. It's best to stay away from that family."

"Why?" Zola was not a gossip, and consequently, I put a lot of stock in any information she passed on.

"They are so unhappy. It's like a curse that hangs over them. They've all been quarrelling forever. I mean forever."

"Over what?'

"Same thing everyone quarrels over out here. Land."

"If I stayed away from families angry over landownership in Western Kansas, I would have to reconcile myself to a life of isolation."

"The Diaz family's lawsuit is different. Truly. It's gone on forever. Suing and countersuing."

"Over land?" Keith asked.

"I don't know all the ins and outs." She went to a cabinet, found a vase, and began arranging the marigolds before she continued. "Have either of you read Dickens' *Bleak House?*"

"No." I couldn't imagine what an old English novel had to do with a man murdered in the twenty-first century.

"At the heart of the book is a legal case that went on for generations. *Jarndyce versus Jarndyce.*

Same thing with the Diaz family. I hear they have all been suing each other or the government for time out of mind. My grandfather said things would start to die down, then some cousin would rile them up again."

Keith was all ears. Then he glanced at his watch. "Guess we'd better start worming cattle," he said reluctantly. I knew he would rather be in town telling Sam about this latest bit of information.

"Do you have everything under control for this weekend?" Zola was heading for the back door. "Anything extra I should be thinking about?"

"Just one thing. Keith and I want you to come as a member of the family. We insist. After the kids start arriving, you are not to turn a hand." I smiled. "Let the girls take over. Needless to say, I'll run you ragged until then."

"With pleasure!"

"I'll take over for Sam at about two." I called after them. "What about lunch?"

"Don't bother," Keith said. "We'll grab some sandwiches. You need to focus on anything the KBI discovers."

Zola really was part of our family now, I thought as I went upstairs and changed into my summer uniform of a blue short-sleeved shirt and knee-length twill shorts. But things were a bit complicated between Zola and Keith's oldest daughter, Elizabeth.

Zola and Elizabeth. Godzilla versus Tyrannosaurus Rex. Should make for a fun weekend.

Zola had majored in archeology at Montana State University. But after graduation, she answered an ad seeking a property manager for the estate of a wealthy film family. She left for California at once and landed the job. One day after she started working for me, she drove up in a brand new van and when I stood there admiring it, she said she was paying for it through her royalties.

She laughed at my astonished look, then explained that she had created a comprehensive checklist of estate managing techniques, organized all her routines, then wrote a book. It was exquisitely detailed down to applying the right fertilizer for irises, and the right way to polish silver.

It became an immediate best seller among a rather elite circle of readers. Frustrated actors and directors now had a tool by which they could judge the competence of their help. *Zola's Way* was the bible for property management.

I'd never asked her why she hadn't applied her degree in archeology to more lofty employment, but Elizabeth did. My ste-daughter was immediately suspicious that any woman with a superior education would stoop to doing the kind of work most people considered blue-collar.

Elizabeth hadn't phrased it quite that blatantly, but she could have and usually did. Zola crisply informed Elizabeth that she was doing the work she loved, and that she found digging for bones under a hot sun quite boring.

When Keith married me—a woman twenty years younger—Elizabeth didn't hold back her outrage. Of Keith's four children, she is the only one who has not overcome negative feelings toward me. She sometimes refers to herself as "the suicide's daughter" like she's contaminated with defective genes. I think she hopes—prays—the wind and the isolation out here will get to me, too, but all her yearning is misspent.

For a historian, Kansas is the mother lode, and for someone who lives in Western Kansas, it's paradise. No one else wants to write about this region of the state, yet it's filled with enough people and stories to fill a million books.

So I gritted my teeth. No, darling stepdaughter, I'm staying. Put that in your pipe and smoke it. And yet sometimes I find myself loving the contradictions of Elizabeth, this turbo-charged girl, whose own education as a lawyer is not used to convict corporate scoundrels but to tackle horrendous women's issues.

All of Keith's children would be home for the Fourth of July parade. It was Gateway City's biggest event. Keith and I have been married eight years and although my sister Josie had been around Keith's three daughters, Elizabeth, Bettina, and Angie, her exposure to his only son, Tom, consisted of a hasty "hello, pleased to meet you" when he had been passing through.

Tom is a geologist who spends a lot of time overseas searching for oil. He's an independent contractor and if there ever were an adored older brother, he's it! His three sisters flock around him like they've never heard of women's lib. They court his approval by bringing him beers, baking him cookies. If darning socks were still in vogue, they would do it.

The first time he showed up after Keith and I were married, we both stopped in our tracks and stood studying each other. He's the second-born after Elizabeth and only a couple of years younger than I. For an instant, I thought he looked like a red-headed reincarnation of the ill-fated movie star, Jimmy Dean. Tom had stood at the edge of the patio door, carrying a duffel bag and his guitar case. I'd heard all about him. It was Tom this, and Tom that. I knew he had Keith's musical ability and also his father's carefulness. But his pictures couldn't capture the something else. A winsome achy-breaky heart that came from what I knew about his mother's legacy.

Although any mention of Keith's first wife's death was taboo, once in a while her life comes up in the form of "Mom used to string popcorn for our Christmas tree…. Mom used to braid my hair…. Mom used to embroider. Have you seen her handwork?"

It would have been unthinkable to live anyplace but Fiene's Folly—as our homestead is called—but after so many "mom used to's," one night I fled to the patio. Keith followed and put his arms around me and patted me like I was an injured little animal. He didn't speak and I didn't explain. I sat there seething until I got a grip.

But it was only through Tom that I had a glimpse of this hidden side of Regina. Tom and the few paintings she had actually finished. She had a unique style yet one reminiscent of impressionists. Tom was an engineer grounded in science, but there was a brooding quality about him that unsettled women. Made them want to fix him.

He bought things at variance with the Fiene family's behavior. Just because he could, I suspected. There was a bright red Corvette carefully housed in one of the machine sheds. Keith didn't hold with show, so his son's extravagance surely hadn't set well with him.

When Tom first uncased his guitar I gasped at the intricate veneer and the mother-of-pearl inlays. Team that blatantly showy instrument with rundown boots, jeans that were not fake torn and dirty but came by their wear the hard way, and you have one complex human being. Outwardly, Tom was funny, witty, whereas Keith was solemn, a problem-solver and a worrier.

I supposed I owed it to Josie to call and tell her that this weekend might be a little stressful. She needed to know that while neither Keith nor I would be officially on duty, we were still on call in case of emergency and she might have to fend for herself among the siblings.

But I was in no mood to be lectured by my disapproving Eastern Kansas twin.

Josie is a registered consultant for our tiny county and had become involved with more crimes in Carlton County than most large towns experience per capita in a year. She didn't hesitate to remind Keith and me about the toll stress was taking on our lives.

In the beginning, my sister had not been in favor of my marriage. To put it mildly. But last spring she had a change of heart. Her acceptance of Keith came because both are incredible musicians. Tolerating Kansas, the land, the prairie was harder. The wind, the emptiness came harder yet.

Her adjustment was helped along by Tosca, who was Mistress of the Universe out here and She Who Must Be Obeyed to the zillions of rabbits who lived in our windbreak.

Perhaps it was the lack of sleep, the horror of another murder to deal with, or the challenge of dealing with a collection of difficult personalities, but the thought of Josie meeting Tom made my stomach roil.

Chapter Five

Wednesday morning I was back in the historical society office taking advantage of the peace and quiet to lay out pages. Our office manager, Margaret Atkinson, had taken a well-deserved day off. It was pleasant to work when there was no one else around. Last spring all of the Fiene family's systems had undergone a major upheaval. The first move had been to hire Zola. The second step was to put Margaret in charge of organizing everything but the county history books. She now kept track of volunteers, ordered the supplies, did the bookwork, and helped with research requests.

When I let Margaret start bossing people around she stopped criticizing everything I did. We had even managed to come up with enough money for her to have her own part-time secretary. The hired girl was still in high school and couldn't spell "cat" without using Spellcheck, but Margaret gained a new spring in her step after she was able to drop "my secretary" into conversations.

As I cut and pasted stories and inserted little newspaper clippings for fillers, I suddenly realized we had no immigrant stories in our books. How had I been that unaware? Victor Diaz's death had set me thinking about the impact of groups coming into Carlton County.

Inspired, I began a time line of events. Carlton County was organized in the 1880s. There had been a bitter county seat fight as there was in over half the counties in Kansas. However, there had been no bloodshed—just an exchange of inflammatory rhetoric among newspaper editors. The biggest issue had been the location of the county seat, because there were only two surefire ways to create lasting towns on the prairie: attract a railroad, or establish a town as the county seat.

Restless, I got up, walked outside into the hall, and gazed out the window at the end of the corridor. Below stretched a patchy carpet of drying grass. My office is technically a windowless vault once used to store old county records. In summer, the door is open to the main air-conditioned part of the courthouse, and with the help of a strategically placed fan, enough cold air filters in to keep the room comfortable.

Back at my desk, I loaded microfilm and started at the county's beginning. There had been five towns vying for the county seat and one of the critical issues was a good water supply. Digging a well was a terrible ordeal and a regular cause of accidental deaths. Wells were dug by hand. Sometimes men died from the deadly methane gas at the bottom, or the sides collapsed, or rocks became dislodged and crushed their heads. That is if they knew where water was to begin with. And there was only one way for pioneers to find out. A sure and revered method.

They used someone who could witch wells.

Wells. Still a charged issue out here.

At the beginning of summer, my very scientific husband wanted to drill a new well to water his cattle. He had hired a geologist who traced all the logical water sources and picked the most likely spot. The only question was the drill depth before he found water.

The evening before the drilling team was to arrive, I had been sitting on the patio reading, when an ancient pickup rattled up our lane. Keith was working in the machine shed. He hollered a hello and wiped his greasy hands on a shop rag, then walked over to the vehicle. An old man climbed out, along with the ugliest brown-furred three-legged mongrel dog I had ever seen. I stared. I knew who this man was.

Old Man Snyder.

Last spring, he blew my gifted twin sister out

of a fiddle contest. She hadn't thought it possible. I used my research skills to dig up what I could about him. He lived alone on a hardscrabble farm with land that didn't look like it could produce enough to feed a chicken during its best years. Since childhood he had been tugged away from work by fiddles and footsteps. Deep down, I wondered if he hadn't chosen the best life of all. He went where he pleased and showed up when he'd a mind to and the Gods of Commerce stopped in his presence. He floated above our lives, dipping, swaying, and playing that old wrecked fiddle.

He and Keith walked over to the geologist's well site. Keith gestured and waved at the equipment already in place. The old man nodded and went back to his pickup and took out a little forked tree branch and carried it over to the site. Then he grasped the two sides of the branch with the single prong in front and began to walk back and forth.

He shook his head. Keith threw up his hands.

Then Snyder moved further away from the geologist's spot. The stick suddenly dove toward the ground. Keith shoved a stake into the spot and tied a bandana around it. He took out his wallet and peeled off some bills. The old man took the money, shook Keith's hand, and whistled to his dog who obediently jumped onto the bed of the pickup.

Snyder spotted me and lifted his battered old fedora in acknowledgment, then off he drove.

"What was that all about? " I asked, when Keith came in for supper.

He looked sheepish. "Old Man Snyder can witch."

"Witch?"

"Water," he said. "Some people can find water."

"How?"

"They use a willow stick. For some folks if they hold onto a forked willow branch with both hands and walk out, the stick just naturally turns down over water."

"And we paid a thousand dollars to a geologist, why? And you gave Old Man Snyder how much?"

"One hundred dollars."

"And that stick he put in the ground is supposed to be where we can find water?"

His mouth quirked into his little half-smile. "Pass the mashed potatoes."

I couldn't. I excused myself from the table and went into the bathroom, laughed until I cried, then composed myself. When I came out, Keith looked at me as though I were a misbehaving child.

"Don't believe in well witching do you?"

"Ahem. Well, I've never heard of it and your believing in it just surprised me."

"How do you think early settlers found water,

Lottie? They couldn't just dig a hole and expect water to bubble up."

That stopped me. "I guess I've never stopped to think how. From a historical standpoint, I've cared more about *who* found water, not *how*."

"Well, witching is the how."

"But now? Surely there's a better way? Something more reliable?"

"There is. That's why I hired a geologist. But scientists don't know everything."

"Hey, that's my line." In fact, it was nearly always Keith who resorted to stone-cold logic.

But the better way wasn't. Two days later, the drilling teams sank a dry hole, and Keith asked them to try again before they left. He led the men over to the little red flag and they set up their equipment one more time, and struck water at a depth of about twenty-five feet.

I sensed there was some sort of weird connection between this old man's affinity for music and his ability to witch water.

"Oh boy," I whispered. "I absolutely, positively, do not believe anyone has the ability to witch water."

Taking myself in hand, I consulted the few notes on my time line, beginning with the county's first failed water well, then the decision to relocate Gateway City to lower ground where a well was dug at a reasonable depth.

I thought about Old Man Snyder as I read about the furious attempts to dig a well for the Carlton County seat. It was never stated, but a well witcher had surely been brought in.

I glanced at my time line and jotted down locating the water well as an important event in county history. Then I began to focus in earnest on the arrival of immigrants. Western Kansas had usually been settled in colonies. The state's reputation as The Great American Desert was enough to keep all but the hardiest of souls away. The English, Zola's people, didn't last long as a group.

They were followed by the Volga Germans—Germans from Russia. Keith's people. They were ideally suited for the prairie. When they arrived and stepped off the trains, they took one look at its expanse. It was just like Siberia.

They were ecstatic. They thanked God, erected a large cross in the center of the site selected for their new village, and proceeded to build some of the most gorgeous churches outside of Europe. One, the Cathedral of the Plains, is famous worldwide and has a priceless rose window.

Then came the French. One very wealthy Frenchman, Ernest de Boissiere, angry because he had been criticized for giving money to black children in New Orleans, marched off to Kansas and founded Silkville in Franklin County in

Eastern Kansas. Although producing silk was a well-intended venture, it cost too much to import the worms, and de Boissiere went back to France. In Western Kansas, French Canadians founded Damar in 1880. The town had fewer than two hundred people now.

Discouraged by the sparseness of information about Damar, I realized I had better hustle before all of Western Kansas was depopulated. If the heat didn't kill folks, the failed crops might spawn a mass exodus. I smiled as I recalled a photo of a sign on a departing covered wagon: 'In God We Trusted, In Kansas We Busted."

Realizing I needed to do a lot more research on the French before I moved on to Bohemians, I listed steps for tracking down material.

All these groups were third- and fourth-generation Americans now. Some, like the Volga Germans, took great pains to preserve their heritage. They had put up with extreme prejudice when they first arrived. They dressed and talked "funny," and were accused of working cheap, depriving other settlers of needed wages until they could make a homestead productive. Through hard work, brilliant management, and intense religiosity, they ended up owning most of the farmland in Ellis County, and a good part of Sheridan County.

Now the Mexicans were enduring the same

hostility experienced by the Volga Germans, and subjected to group judgment rather than individual assessment on their merits.

Tapping my pencil against the desk, I realized I could help. All it would take was a volley of shared stories. The whole community would benefit. There was no limitation on submitting family histories. Ancestors didn't have to be wheels in the community or property owners. I continued my time line and noted the year each group had arrived.

I rose, and refilled my coffee cup. I can usually focus without my attention wavering, but the image of Maria Diaz kept crossing my mind. I leaned back in my chair, closed my eyes, then took myself in hand.

The African Americans were next. They came in colonies after the failure of Reconstruction. I jotted down the names of some of their leaders and then was interrupted by the phone.

Sam didn't bother to say hello. "We've been summoned. Dimon wants us in Topeka tomorrow."

I jolted to attention. "Why?"

"Didn't say."

It had been difficult to convince the KBI that we were not a bunch of fools out here. Although I had finally established a good relationship with a few of the members of the team, two were my favorite:

Nancy Sparks and Frank Dimon. Dimon was a severe man who seldom smiled, but he was fair.

"Talk about bad timing."

Obviously my goal of concentrating on immigrants was shot all to hell. I couldn't even remember the next group to arrive. Not Mexicans. I was sure of that.

I put my work away and drove home, mentally reshuffling preparations for a weekend teeming with stepchildren, my sister, grandchildren, and various friends in the community.

Chapter Six

Agent Dimon ushered us in and beckoned toward a chair. His tidy desktop gleamed and his office always smelled as if someone had just sprayed it with lemon wax. I was out of uniform and wore gray twill slacks and a free flowing white linen top. My feet were chilly in sandals. Combined with long silver earrings and silver bracelets, I felt frivolous in the presence of this lean, austere man who still called me "Miss Albright" as though "Lottie" would invite too much familiarity.

"I'm sure you've wondered why I asked you to come here. Would you like coffee before I begin?" He said this with the self-conscious air of someone who knew he was supposed to be hospitable when he simply wanted to cut to the chase.

I never refused coffee. He went out into the hallway and came back with a large ceramic cup. Dark-skinned, with short black hair, Dimon was handsome enough. I imagine a number of women had set out to scooch closer to his work-centered soul, and failed.

"The KBI ran into some problems when it was called in to investigate your most recent murder."

I smarted at the "most recent" jab.

"I'll put all the cards on the table at once. We don't have to resources to keep doing this. We're suffering from budget cuts like everyone else. We've had to dispatch men to your county that we needed in Johnson County."

"We can't help that," Sam said. "It's our right to call in the KBI."

"Your right, maybe. But it just isn't working. We would like to start a regional crime center."

"Regional?"

"Yes. You already have a regional coroner system out there."

The "out there" sounded like our county was located on Mars.

"That's different. Every county elects its own sheriff. It's the law."

"It doesn't have to be the law. It won't be too much of a challenge to talk the legislature into going with a regional system."

I said nothing. This was between Sam and Dimon.

"Sure this isn't personal?" Sam asked quietly.

Dimon flushed. "No. Water under the bridge, Sam."

I didn't have the slightest idea what they were talking about.

"It's not just your county, but you've got to admit you have a dismal track record. A third murder in the last eighteen months."

I jumped in. "Now wait just a minute, Frank. We can't stop murders, but you're the one who brought up track records. The bureau was called in for both of the previous cases, but it was Sam who eventually solved them."

"With your help, Lottie," Sam said.

"And the bureau had filed them under some open case file and then walked away."

"Well, what did you expect us to do? Leave a man out there full time?"

"That's the point. We're the full-time people," Sam snapped.

"Sam, I assure you there is nothing personal here. But you can't keep this up forever."

Sam's eyes narrowed at the veiled ageist remark. "Maybe not."

He was struggling to keep his voice even. He automatically patted his shirt pocket for the pipe he had left in the car. "I don't think a regional center is a workable idea, Dimon. Anything else you want to discuss with us?"

Dimon stared at Sam. The silence went on too long. Then he abruptly stood up. "Only that I want one or both of you at the Diaz funeral tomorrow. I don't want to waste valuable time and money sending one of our agents out there. Fax me a full report in the evening."

"Why?"

Dimon shot Sam a withering look.

"I want to know who attends and if you notice anything strange."

"All funerals are strange. My point is that Lottie and I would stick out like a sore thumb. We don't know anyone in the family. So we couldn't tell you if anyone is there who looks out of place. And some folks show up at every funeral. Just to see how the family is taking it."

I groaned inwardly, knowing who would be doing this. If for no other reason that I would have to send the information using the historical society's fax machine.

"And I want a copy of the feedyard's schedule for six weeks before Victor's murder. Today, if you can get there before it closes."

Sam nodded.

We all formally shook hands. As though every-thing was just dandy. But intuitively, I knew Dimon thought it was time for Sam to go in another way.

◇◇◇

I kept my eyes on the road and drove five miles over the speed limit. "Mind telling me what that was all about? What was not personal?"

Sam reached for his pipe. I didn't stop him. Putting up with a little secondary smoke seemed a small price to pay for his acceptance of me as an equal.

He took his time tamping the tobacco, then shook out the match. "Dimon doesn't trust me to run a county the way he thinks it should be run. Happened before your time here. Gave him a black eye with the immigration folks. Ever hear of proxy marriage?"

"No."

"Well, Kansas is one of the five states that allow them. A couple of men at the feedyard were from El Salvador and tried to rescue two women who were undergoing abuse in their own country. On two separate occasions, they smuggled the women in on trucks and sent them on to Denver. The weddings had already taken place by proxy and the women could legally stay in the country because they were married to a United States citizen."

"Wow!"

"It happened twice before I found out about it. I shut it down immediately. Dwayne Weston was beside himself when he learned what was going on."

"I'll bet he was."

"Problem was, Dimon blew sky high that it had ever happened in the first place. Proxy marriages aren't supposed to be fake. It's illegal to bring immigrants into this county under a ruse."

"Was money involved?"

"Oh, hell no. The women got good jobs and got a divorce—if they wanted to—in good time. But Dimon hasn't trusted me ever since."

"So that explains your grilling Weston about the legality of his employees."

"Yup. He told me it would never happen again. Just wanted to make sure."

"I'll drop you off and head on out to the feedyard and fax the info to Dimon," I said finally. "And attend the funeral tomorrow. It's only fair since you are going to be on duty this entire weekend."

We finished the trip in gloomy silence.

I drove directly to the feedyard. Dwayne was in the office. He looked up from the phone and waved at me to take a seat when I walked into the room.

"No!" he yelled at the caller. "Goddamn it. I need you in Wyoming Thursday." He slammed down the phone. "Damn drivers. Claims he needs off to take care of a home problem. He wouldn't have so many home problems if he went there at the end of his run instead of trying to keep up with two women."

I raised an eyebrow.

'Sorry, Lottie. What can I do for you?"

"I wondered if I could have a copy of your duty schedule going back six weeks."

"Sure." He pressed the intercom and yelled at the office manager and told him what he wanted. We discussed the cattle market while we waited for him to bring the information.

Minutes later, Bart Hummel came in with a printout. Bart wore the pearl-buttoned western shirts and jeans that seemed to be the unwritten dress code for bull haulers and feedyard cowboys. Rumor had it that he was one of the best paid men in town, which could have been true, but it wasn't saying much because the town's wage scale was a disgrace. For that matter, his title of "office man- ager" was an understatement. He was Dwayne's go-to person and jack-of-all-trades. Tall, thin, he was as pale as a prisoner with the sleek rounded head of an eel.

The thing that impressed me the most about Bart was that his hands didn't shake.

On the few occasions when I had been around dispatchers for trucking companies, it was evident they were all a couple of days away from a nervous breakdown. Even police dispatchers earned the public's gratitude after a 911 call that ended well. But trucking dispatchers had to put up with irate customers, drivers, drivers' wives, mad farmers, and cattle buyers. Some of this I'd learned from observation and the rest I'd put together from Keith's comments when he was called to feedyards.

Wives were mad when husbands were late getting home from trips. Farmers and cattle buyers went ballistic if cattle were delayed from reaching the packing plant. Every hour caused shrinkage and affected profit. Some cattle went to kosher packing plants and were slaughtered in accordance with ancient rituals that affected the availability of empty pens for unloading. Lease drivers kept a skeptical eye on employed drivers to make sure they were getting their fair share of loads. Wives were mad if their paychecks were short because their husbands had drawn too many advances. Ex-wives were mad if the men *hadn't* written advances. To them. And they all took it out on the dispatcher.

Sam, Keith, and I had made a number of trips to this feedyard to serve garnishment papers on drivers' wages to collect alimony.

But when I did, Bart always simply said, "Good morning, Lottie," glanced at the papers, signed the receipt form, got up, went to the right driver's cubby hole, tucked the garnishment in, and went back to his work. Knowing he would see it through to the end, I usually just tipped the brim of my hat and left.

This poker-faced nerveless man was the hub of this feedyard. Dwayne employed two full-time dispatchers and two bookkeepers and then they could hardly keep up. Second in command, after Dwayne, Bart controlled the whole operation.

I made a mental note to suggest to Agent Dimon that he call in the A team if they questioned Bart. I suspected he could pass any lie detector test because he would anticipate every question in advance and then work out answers that were plenty truthful enough. With just enough information to make law enforcement people go away so he could go back to work.

Silently, Bart handed me the monthly calendar for people working at the feedyard, wheeled around, and walked off to his office, which had a huge window facing the cattle pens. He thrummed his pencil on his desk, glanced at a piece of paper and start entering data. He hadn't allowed himself more than five minutes away from his desk.

"Thanks, Dwayne. Time for me to get on home." I rose, turned to leave, then paused in the doorway. "I guess you know you haven't seen the end of this. We'll be back to question the employees and so will agents for the KBI."

"Oh, Jesus. Why the KBI?"

"Because we had to call them in. That's our prerogative and our county doesn't have great investigative resources.

"Christ, this is all I need."

I waited for him to explain. A feedyard wasn't exactly a business affected by bad publicity. "Don't you want to know what happened to Victor?"

"Of course," he said. "But three times in two days now, I've had farmers who planned to custom-feed here, cancel, saying they were going with another place until things settled down."

I glanced at the papers, thanked him, and drove to this historical society to get them faxed before the KBI office closed.

The funeral was Thursday morning. The church was sweltering. I wore a lightweight black linen suit with low-heeled black sandals. I meant to blend in, but even though I was a stranger among strangers, I felt miserably conspicuous in this Catholic Church. Although few people in Carlton County claimed to be friends with the Diaz family, Victor was the most well-known. I signed the guest book. People had come from all over the state. There was a smattering of Spanish surnames. Several Diaz family members from Texas and a couple from Johnson County.

Once inside, as Sam had predicted, I couldn't tell the extended family from professional mourners. I didn't know enough to differentiate who had always lived in Carlton County from those who had moved here recently.

I took a seat at the back and glanced at the attendees. There were people from the feedyard, and Dwayne Weston and his wife, of course, and Hugh and Estelle Simpson, who shared front row seats with Maria Diaz. There was no roped-off family section, as though Maria wanted to emphasize her aloneness. Stony-faced adolescent girls sat next to weepy middle-aged women. Friends of Maria? I had no way of knowing. Nuns in modern dress who had donned the headdress of their order were working their way along the rosary.

There was no air conditioning. Several women pulled bejeweled accordion fans from their purses. They had come prepared. Safe to assume they were members of this church. A number of men suffering in suits looked to be Victor's age. Some were accompanied by beautifully dressed women. Others sat next to women not so fashionably attired. High school classmates who had moved on, I guessed, or perhaps friends from college.

There could have been cattle buyers present or people Victor met at seminars, if he went to any. The state conducted compliance training for truckers. Were there similar workshops for feed lot owners? I made a mental note to ask Dwayne if Victor's job required travel. A large number of men sitting in a cluster wore starched jeans and dress western shirts. A sizable showing in all.

But bottom line, Sam was right. Maria might appreciate my attending her husband's funeral— this show of support. But it was a waste of time for Dimon's purposes. How would I know if someone "suspicious" was here today?

Conspicuously absent were Victor's sister, and his great-grandmother, Francesca Diaz.

I dutifully observed, quietly moved my feet to one side and shook my head, when others in my row got up to take communion.

I went to the burial and scrutinized the clusters of people who immediately formed groups. That was a much more accurate indication of some kind of affiliation than who they sat beside at a church.

Maria shook with sobs after the last prayer. Hugh and Estelle helped her to her feet. They stood to one side while people filed by to offer condolences.

I felt like a creep. A peeping Tom.

Was there anything strange here? Absolutely. I thought about Zola's comments about the amount of division in this family. There was not going to be a church-supported community dinner with a chance for people to eat and visit. Usually, a funeral is like a mini family reunion. It's a sure-fire way of getting folks together. New spouses and kids are introduced to the rest of the clan.

Some of the mourners went to their cars and drove off. A few women fell on Maria's neck and added their tears to hers.

I moseyed among the different groups and listened in. A cluster of men I recognized from the feedyard were paying more attention to Dwayne than to Maria.

"It's going to leave a hell of a hole in the feed-yard."

"That's a fact."

If there was anyone vying for his job, I couldn't detect it.

Several women went out of their way to express their sympathy to Maria. "You've helped my family so very much when we came to this country. I'm so sorry. Victor was a good man."

In fact, the phrase I heard the most was that "Victor was a good man."

Two men broke off from their group, walked over to Maria and introduced themselves. Maria obviously didn't know either of them. They both wore jeans and sports coats accented with loose bola ties. I moved closer.

"Ma'am, I'm sorry we have to meet this way." The speaker had an alarmingly red face. The kind that makes doctors reach for their prescription pad. He removed his hat and nodded in respect. He drew a handkerchief out of his back pocket and mopped his sweaty forehead. Blood pressure, I decided. Not just the heat. His belt buckle glinted below his large belly. Huge hands and even larger thighs. The kind of man who looked like he spent most of his time swilling beer and watching NASCAR, but could knock the hell out of someone if he took a mind to.

The small man at his side stared intently at Maria. He shifted his weight from one foot to the other and fidgeted constantly. He kept fingering his moustache as though needing reassurance that it hadn't melted in the noonday sun.

"I knew your Aunt Lucia back in Mexico. In fact she's a cousin by marriage to some nephew. So I suppose that sort of makes us related."

"I don't have an Aunt Lucia."

He laughed. "Typical. Doesn't take long to forget the home folks. Or leave the old life behind."

It was a mean thing to say to a woman at her husband's funeral. I considered taking her arm and steering her toward Hugh's car.

"I have never turned my back on family," Maria said. "I have never met this woman." She rummaged in her purse for a packet of tissues. "

"Speaking of family, I'm surprised Victor's great-grandmother isn't here today. Or his sister."

I wasn't the only one listening. Everyone within hearing distance froze in place and waited for Maria's reply. She looked like a guppy gasping for air in contaminated water.

Hugh intervened. "Francesca is not well."

"Or being hateful."

"Now is not the time to discuss it."

Estelle immediately moved in protect Maria. "It's time for us to go, dear." She turned to the cluster of mourners. "The family wants all of you to know how much we appreciate your sympathy. The flowers. The cards. We are going to leave now. As you can imagine, the death, the circumstances of Victor's tragic death, have been so hard on Maria. We are going back to the house."

And that was that. No invitation for the family to join her there. No food. Just this abrupt farewell.

I faxed my report to Dimon. It consisted of an estimation of the number attending and a notation that there were no incidents at the funeral. Strained conversations did not rise to the level of reportable incidents. No people acting strange as far as I could tell.

Since the KBI wasn't interested in speculation about the importance of what was not right before their eyes, I did not mention that Victor's great-grandmother and sister did not attend. That the extended family was obviously barely speaking. That not having a funeral dinner following the burial was practically unheard of in a rural community.

There was no point. Dimon was only interested in the facts.

I had missed Tom's arrival.

"You're early!" He and Keith were already in the family room picking to an old bluegrass tune. "Don't stop." I put my briefcase on the floor as Tom rose to give me a hug.

"Sorry I wasn't here when you came. I wasn't expecting you until tomorrow and had to go to a funeral this morning. Sam and I went to Topeka yesterday and the KBI gave me some follow-up work to do. Anyone want a cup of coffee?"

"No," Tom said.

"Hell, no," hollered Keith.

I laughed and retreated to the kitchen. I carried my cup back to the music room. "Now, please keep playing."

"We're experimenting," Tom said. "It's not exactly a bona fide jam."

"Since Josie is coming, I wanted him to be prepared." Keith strummed a few chords.

"Nothing will prepare you for my sister, Tom."

"Haven't I already met her? Or was that you? I can't remember." He grinned.

"Just don't challenge her to a duel."

"I've already clued him in. Told him about her unfortunate contest with Old Man Snyder."

"She was set up," I said.

"Was not," Keith protested. "Swear to God I had no hand in that. No one knows when or where that old man will show up. Or what moves him exactly."

I sank into my favorite chair and watched as father and son forgot I was there.

"So how did the funeral go?" Keith asked when they took a break. "Learn anything new?"

"Not really."

Tom looked puzzled.

"The funeral was a work duty," I explained. "Agent Dimon sent me on kind of a surveillance mission."

If Keith thought my answer was abrupt, a clear deviation from my usual detailed accounts, he didn't say so.

After an hour, I got up and started toward the stairs. "I'm going to turn in." I smiled apologetically at Tom. "I'm on duty for Sam tomorrow morning, but thank goodness I'll be off in the afternoon when everyone is coming in. I'll duck into the historical society just long enough to write my column, then come home and fuss over the family."

Tom stood. It gave me a strange feeling. Was I supposed to tell my own stepson that formality wasn't necessary in his own house? That I was sort of his mother? Should I airily wave my hand that it was perfectly fine for him to sit down now?

I walked on up saddened that in spite of eight years of marriage there was still this underlying tension when I was around Keith's children. Especially when they came as a group. I turned on the Jacuzzi and took a long bath but it didn't do much to ease the queasy feeling in the pit of my stomach. I knew Dimon would love to get rid of Sam. Me too, for that matter.

In fact, all of Western Kansas and our whole patchwork of law enforcement.

Josie called just as I propped myself up on pillows and started on an academic book I was expected to review for *Kansas History Magazine*.

"Hi, Lottie. I'm making a list and checking it twice."

"No need. We're all good little boys and girls out here."

"Seriously. Is there anything you want me to bring from the city?"

"We're fine. Bettina organized everything which means all the preparations are flawless."

"Still have Zola?"

"Oh you bet. In fact, Keith has latched on to her, too, to help with the cattle."

"Great. I assume she's as good around the barn as she is in the house."

"Absolutely." I couldn't think of anything else to say. Normally I would have told her instantly about Agent Dimon targeting Sam. She would have shared my outrage.

"What's wrong, Lottie?"

"Nothing. Everything is fine."

"Your pants are on fire."

"Are not." I smiled. Nothing escaped my twin. We had nearly telepathic communication from time to time.

"Nothing," I insisted. "Really. I'm just tired. Sam and I had to go to Topeka and back in the same day. Then I had to attend a funeral this morning that gave me the willies."

She listened silently and wouldn't give me a break.

"Well, I need to get some sleep."

She said nothing.

"Kiss the pooch for me until I can deliver it in person."

"Good night, Lottie." Her voice was gentle but I was in for a weekend of skilled inquisition.

I was still awake when Keith came to bed. I

nearly told him about Dimon's animosity toward Sam, then decided it could wait. I didn't want to spoil his weekend. Keith adored the old man. If I wasn't aware of the sacredness of male bonding before, I was after Sam deputized Keith. They hoisted the flag together, fished together, and indulged in off-color jokes that I wasn't privy to, rightly suspicious that my latent streak of feminism could be riled up.

In the beginning, I thought their closeness was because Keith felt sorry for Sam because he had no family. Then I'd watched their relationship develop into something different that sometimes made me feel like an outsider with my nose pressed against the window. Sadly, I realized I wasn't and never could truly be one of the boys.

But I had Josie, and if there was ever a shut-out relationship! It went beyond twin-bonding.

Chapter Seven

There were hollows under Sam's sagging eyes when I breezed into the sheriff's office the next morning.

"You don't look like you got much sleep."

"I let Dimon get under my skin. Had trouble dropping off."

"Busy otherwise?"

"Nope. Deader than a doornail," he said. "That passes for good news around here, I guess."

"Anything I need to know?"

"Nope. It's all there in the log. Betty is dispatching."

"Great." But great was not the first word that came to mind when I dealt with Betty Central. She was a stocky, small woman whom I had secretly nicknamed Miss Piggy. Bossy, and a relentless gossip, she was nevertheless absolutely reliable and a tireless worker.

"The phones are switched to her house."

"Okay. For once I don't have to do run back

and forth between offices. I sent my report on the funeral to Dimon yesterday afternoon. Here's your copy."

I handed him the paper. "We'll talk about this some more after this weekend."

He glanced at the sparse information. "I hope to hell that wasn't all you noticed."

After he left, I brooded about Dimon's hostility toward Sam and looked around the bare bones room. The equipment in the sheriff's office should have been junked five years before.

Everything in the historical society is state of the art. I had paid for every single electronic device: the computers, printers, phones, scanners, microfilm readers, flash drives—you name it. I could not bear working with substandard technology. It was my kingdom and I issued decrees at will. But the sheriff's office was Sam's domain and he preferred legal pads and number two pencils. He had grown used to me ducking out when I needed to use modern equipment.

I swiped back a strand of hair that had escaped from my French braid. I walked to the front window, and stared at the barren street, the sun-faded store front opposite. I could see the handwriting on the wall. Sam was going to be forced out if Dimon could implement regional organization.

But not if we solved this case all by ourselves.

Without the help of the KBI. Then Dimon would not be able to claim our methods were ineffective. I would do everything the bureau asked. But I knew for a fact what he would ask me to do would add up to zilch when it came to finding out who murdered Victor Diaz.

The old man coming to relieve me was strictly a place-holder. Keith wanted to be with Tom, and I wanted to be home cooking for the Fourth of July horde. We couldn't ask Sam to be here again this afternoon.

Putting together a few reserve deputies had been Keith's idea. After he read all the rules and regulations for these unpaid volunteers who merely received a hearty thanks for their hard work, Keith thought of three old men he knew who were ex-military and would provide a willing presence at the office if Betty answered the phones out of her house.

Truth was, it looked better to have someone here instead of trying to explain to the community that either Sam or Keith or I was always on call and the phones were switched over when necessary. I waited impatiently for Marvin Cole to show up.

Marvin was eager to help out. Like the others, he had to pass an extensive background check and understood that he would only be filling in on rare occasions, but he had jumped at the chance to do something useful.

He arrived at one on the dot. I appreciated this homely low-keyed man who didn't swell up with self importance while acting as a reserve deputy. Marvin had a flat nose and a deeply pocked face with over sized lips. A friendly frog of a man glad for the chance to jump off the lily pad for a day.

"Nothing going on," I said. "So, I guess you can just go on transcribing."

Transcribing old handwritten sheriff's reports was not necessary. I'm used to deciphering old records through my historical work, but Marvin was affronted by the suggestion that it was just fine for him to sit idly while on duty. Doing something as frivolous as reading a novel was out of the question.

Betty Central would come in at five and work until two in the morning, then switch the phones to our house.

My kitchen smelled heavenly. The odor of chocolate chip cookies wafted through the door.

"Keith here?" I reached for a cookie.

"No, he and Tom are out looking over the cattle." Zola continued rolling pie crusts and didn't look up. Soon cherry would join the French silk, pecan, and peach pies she had already lined up on the island. A German chocolate cake stood next to a tray of assorted cookies.

I dashed upstairs and changed, determined to put murder out of my mind long enough to enjoy the weekend.

Jimmy and Bettina were the first to arrive with their two little boys. Jimmy Silverthorne was half Cherokee and his coloring showed in their sons, Joshua and Kent. When the boys entered the room, they hurled themselves at me like two little linebackers. Although Kent, who had just started preschool, lacked the heft of his kindergartener brother, he made up for it in enthusiasm. The boys bore an uncanny resemblance to Josie and me although their maternal grandmother had been Keith's late wife, Regina. Josie and I are both dark with black hair and have the same dark brown eyes. Thankfully, I was simply "Grandma Lottie" to these two and had been here since their birth.

"Hi, Mom," Bettina hugged me and then hollered "don't ruin your supper!" as they darted to the cookies.

"We won't," they chorused in unison.

"Little liars," Jimmy said cheerfully.

"Keith and Tom will be back in a little while."

Jimmy nodded, walked back out to their Suburban, and started unloading coolers of beer and pop and cold cuts for sandwiches.

The first time Josie came to this event she had commented on the collection of Tahos, Suburbans,

Explorers, and overpowered Ram pickups our family seemed to favor. "What a tribute to the staying power of the Arab nations," she'd said with a raised eyebrow. But the second time she came, her powerful low-bottomed Mercedes had gotten mired in the mud and she never made cracks about our SUVs and our gas consumption again.

Tom and Keith came back from the pasture and the boys flew out the door like little rockets and launched themselves at their grandfather.

Bettina was right on their heels. She hugged her brother like she hadn't seen him more than twice in her lifetime.

By the time Elizabeth arrived, the place was in utter turmoil. A carload of Tom's friends drove up and began hauling food and coolers from the trunk of the car. Later in the year we would have similar doings and guns and dogs would be added to the mix, but this time it was just a musical menagerie.

Toward sundown, I looked out my kitchen window and began checking the clock. Josie was late. I had expected her about five o'clock. Last fall, her big Mercedes had earned Elizabeth's scorn as Keith's oldest daughter hated any kind of ostentatious spending.

A big black behemoth sailed up the lane and we all gasped. It was Josie in a brand new Mercedes

SUV. Tosca perched in the passenger seat like Cleopatra sailing down the Nile in her barge.

Josie parked and we all flocked around the new SUV.

Keith pulled the cargo doors open and lifted out Tosca's portable kennel while I opened the passenger seat door and unstrapped her doggie safety seat. Tosca dutifully submitted to my ecstatic hugs, then as soon as she was released, she bounded toward Keith.

Josie smiled broadly and watched Tosca's reception by various family members. Once Tosca had acknowledged everyone present, she went to the fringe of our cedar windbreak and barked haughtily at all the rabbits to announce that the Mistress of the Universe was back and they had better be on their toes.

This time Tosca had red, white, and blue ribbons tied in a single top knot with a tiny American flag sticking up front. I glanced at Keith and my lips lifted in a helpless half-smile. He disapproved of the flag being used for decorative purposes under any circumstances. His attitude was a legacy from the Vietnam War when this revered symbol showed up on the butts of people's jeans and was denigrated in every conceivable manner.

I'd learned early in our marriage not to decorate cakes or buy T-shirts sporting the flag. Keith flew the Stars and Stripes every day of the world, holiday or not, and lowered it at sundown according to proper flag etiquette in the service manual. He donated time to the local Veterans organization and could be counted on to don his uniform and assist at military funerals. So I could hardly expect him to be thrilled when a frivolous Shih-Tzu showed up wearing the colors.

He looked at me across the yard with a wry smile. With no comment, he carefully set Tosca down. By now, this dog had earned the status of hero. At a ridiculous ceremony in Gateway City just this spring, she'd been awarded a little chest medal for bravery and was designated the one and only member of the Carlton County Canine Corp.

It had gone to Tosca's head and naturally was Betty Central's idea to begin with. One afternoon when Josie was out here, Betty had asked me, Sam, Keith, Josie, and Tosca to come to the sheriff's office. I'd bought a surprise present for Sam's birthday, the only occasion I could think of that we would keep such a huge secret. Instead, Betty had ordered a cake and the little medal struck for Tosca who took the whole ritual very, very seriously. True, she had been right in the middle of a life-threatening situation, but she was a tiny little dog. She had trotted forward like she was receiving the Congressional Medal of Honor.

Truth was, Keith and I did not want to think about the circumstances surrounding this medal ever again. Not ever.

Today, she wore that medal in addition to the flag.

Keith's eyes had sparked at that ceremony and if Betty had even a lick of common sense she would have noticed his instant outrage over any hint of stolen valor. He did not want the service trivialized in any manner. But the medal was not a replica of any legitimate medal, so he had let it pass.

But now his jaw tightened and he stroked Tosca, then carefully extracted the flag from her topknot. The medal and the ribbons stayed. My smile quivered and I carefully handed the flag to Josie whose own smile faded.

"We do not use the flag as a decoration in this household." Keith looked her in the eyes. "Not ever. Not on clothes or as an accessory."

I would explain all this to Josie later. Keith's children and grandchildren stood there with solemn looks on their faces.

Tosca eyed Keith with her huge brown eyes and slunk over to Josie with her tail between her legs like she had been stripped of her medal, too.

"Christ." Keith went to the little dog that whimpered and burrowed deeper into Josie's arms. She would not give him a break. But neither would

Keith relent and give her back the little miniature flag for her topknot.

Josie is a highly regarded psychologist and college professor who has endured much—both physically and professionally—since she became a consultant for Carlton County. But I knew slights from Keith's family were about the last straw and she took any criticism of Tosca hard.

The whole flag issue was escalating into the third World War.

"Let's go look over your new car," I said.

"SUV," she corrected. We walked to her vehicle, arm in arm, with Josie cradling her dog.

Keith caught up with us.

"Some car," he said with a tone of false heartiness.

The family flocked around. I was always on edge when Josie was around Keith's children. Elizabeth glared with disapproval at the car. Her arms were crossed.

Josie saw too much, knew too much about people. I could count on her behaving herself, having good manners, but I knew immediately when she retreated to a professional distance. My heart sank when I saw the switch after she glanced at Elizabeth. Josie would be cold. Removed. All weekend.

"Rides, later," she said. "Briefly, this has a really big engine and a..."

"And a $110,000-plus price tag," quipped one of Tom's friends.

Josie said nothing and her smile froze.

"That's four times what most of my clients earn in a year." Elizabeth didn't bother to disguise her disgust.

Josie switched to resident bitch. I didn't know which stance would be worse: bitch or professional. "Possibly. But you haven't looked inside yet. There are lots of goodies that add to the total. He's way under."

Oh God, I thought. *She's doing it on purpose.* I could feel her baiting Elizabeth, flaunting this high-priced vehicle, picking up on this daughter's scorn.

"Nice to see you have brand loyalty. I hope you got a good trade-in price for your sedan."

"Oh, but I kept it," Josie said sweetly. "It's easier to park and drive around town. In fact, I might trade it in, too, for a new one this fall."

"Ah, Jesus," I thought. There was no hope for any of this. Then inexplicably, I relaxed. This whole weekend was spiraling out of control and it was not my fault and therefore not my responsibility to rescue it.

Tom's friends had no mixed emotions. They scrutinized the instrument panel, admired the leather seats, the high dollar speakers and audio systems, and enthusiastically commented on all the safety features. Tom shot Josie a sympathetic look and winked.

"Time to eat," I said and we all trooped inside. After digging into the informal buffet, we went into the room where we normally gathered to play music. Tuning was more complicated by the time we worked Tom's friends into the process.

I passed on playing my guitar and settled into a comfortable chair to listen while I sipped a glass of good Scotch. For a minute, Josie's first visit to meet Keith's family crossed my mind.

One that had ended in murder.

Tom led things off. One by one, his friends joined in as surely as if they had practiced for months. They had to all have played together before.

"So what's the deal, gentlemen? Do you all Skype each other and practice the same songs every week?"

Tom laughed. "No, nothing that complicated. We played together in high school and through the years we just naturally found ourselves listening to the same people."

"He's a damn liar," said Paul Stone, a tall dark-skinned man who played the upright bass. "He emailed all of us and told us he was coming home and that we'd better get ready."

"Well, that too," Tom grinned. "We all play every chance we get."

"That's obvious," I said. So far, Josie had just sat on the sidelines. I wanted these men to know how talented she was. "Josie, aren't you going to join in?"

"Thought you would never ask." She rose, carried Tosca over to me, and took her violin from the case. She checked her tuning against Keith's and carefully coordinated her instrument to the group. It was jammer's choice and moved in a circle, with each musician in turn calling for a number, usually the one he played best. Josie quickly earned their respect as she was able to pick up on every melody. She was just getting started.

When it came around to her she was well into the mood. Fun, cooperative. I expected her to ask for the "Orange Blossom Special"—a classic crowd-pleasing fiddle tune.

"Let's do 'Limerock'."

Tom choked on his home brew.

"I've been practicing." She looked at Keith, who grinned and threw up his hands.

Just last spring Old Man Snyder had won the music contest with this difficult tune and both she and Keith had become obsessed with mastering it.

"Well, all *right*," one of the men said with some amusement. "Let's *do* it."

She was fabulous. Breathtaking. Not only with her musicality, but also her showmanship. She was a beautiful woman and only when she played music did she let her guard down.

"Well, damn honey," Lyle Aller said softly after they finished. "We need to have a little chat. Do you need a roadie? Got an agent?"

"Forget it, Lyle," I said. "She's got a day job."

"Figures," he moaned. "Well, do you know 'Olympic Reel'?"

"No, but maybe I can fake it."

"Ya think?" He hummed a couple of lines and she listened intently following his strumming and the rhythm. The men immediately launched into the song and in a short time she could play under and over the melody.

Then I saw Elizabeth's face. Dark, hostile. I followed her gaze as it switched from my beautiful vibrant sister to the lead guitarist.

Simply plain vanilla jealousy. That was all. Elizabeth couldn't take her eyes off Lyle. Well, well, well.

She jumped to her feet and headed for the piano. "Let's all sing along," she called over her shoulder.

Elizabeth is a fine pianist in any genre, but she's really exceptional when she plays honky-tonk. To my dismay she launched into a road house country classic "Wild Side of Life." There's only so much showing off you can do with countrywestern.

Bluegrass can involve complex instrumentation, whereas its lower-keyed cousin concentrated on ballads. That fixed Josie, of course. Fixed her little red wagon.

I headed for the Scotch and decided to drink a lot.

Although Sam was on duty, Keith and I have an informal agreement that one of us abstains from drinking in case we need to back Sam up. This was a new rule. One we had adopted after Josie and I ended up in jail in another sheriff's county. Nothing about the misadventure was alcohol related, but it wouldn't have helped our case if Sheriff Deal had ordered blood alcohol tests.

The new rule wasn't working well. It meant Keith and I couldn't go out for dinner and enjoy a meal and a drink unless there was a reserve deputy available. Tonight was my husband's turn to make like a teetotaler.

Like a soldier with pending stress trauma, I eyed the phone, willed it to stay silent, and went back to the living room. I was coaxed into singing my throaty rendition of Kitty Wells' reply to "Wild Side of Life." Tom and company were well oiled. Bettina had long since disappeared upstairs with the boys.

Elizabeth thumped along with her effortless riffs on the piano and giving me a broad wink, Josie got into the spirit of the event, picked up her bow, and managed to insert a soft accompaniment. By the time I reached the third verse she had it figured out and came in with her lovely contralto, echoing the end of the line with just enough hesitation on "you gave up the only one who ever loved you" to change the tone from high camp to appreciation for country classics. In a heartbeat she switched from the superb musicality of bluegrass to an awareness of the human condition and the universal sorrow of life and love and death.

Even though drinking songs and cheating songs are the heartbeat of country western, especially roadhouse country, Josie and I were avid opera lovers.

I knew she really understood now. Understood all of a sudden that the pathos of opera and countrywestern were the same. Lost love, lost chances, unbearable tragedy.

Even Elizabeth settled down into a rare congeniality. We all picked up on one song after another and played until two o'clock. By that time I lost my anxiety over the telephone.

Lulled into a false sense of security by the dog that didn't bark.

Chapter Eight

Angie and her newest husband arrived the next morning. She was two years younger than Tom, wasp-thin, with translucent skin that showed every vein. Childless, she was drawn to Bettina's boys. No one ever said much about her first two marriages except Keith who had dismissed Angie's men as "no-count bastards." He said she had been involved in two abusive relationships.

In some ways, I was more comfortable around Elizabeth who exploded, raged, wept, and bore down on all of us like a violent storm system. I knew to watch my back around Elizabeth. No need to guard against anything with Bettina, who was wonderfully sane. She was warm, courteous and thoughtful, with a rare sense of what was important. Josie insisted she was the only one of Keith's daughters who wasn't crazy.

I don't know Angie like I do Elizabeth and Bettina. This stepdaughter carefully said all the right things like someone visiting a stranger. She swallowed my coffee and declared it was just right, which had to be a lie. She helped with every household task and swore she didn't mind. "It's fun, really. I'm just glad to be around my family."

Today, Angie was inexplicably jumpy and didn't act like a woman glad to be around anyone. Now as we put together a late brunch, I followed her gaze to Keith's portrait of the Sacred Heart of Jesus. Dry palm leaves protruded from the top. He put them there after every Palm Sunday service and took them back to the church a couple of days before the beginning of Lent the following year so the priest could burn them for use in the Ash Wednesday service. I don't like this picture and had once suggested to Keith that we replace it with a reproduction of Odilon Redon's concept of *The Sacred Heart.*

Fat chance. It was the last time I intruded on his religious practices.

Angie didn't like it either. She gazed at the *Sacred Heart* with hostility. She caught me studying her, gave an embarrassed shrug, and turned back to slicing the little membranes in grapefruit halves. She put a maraschino cherry atop each one then grouped them on a bright lime Fiesta plate next to a pitcher of orange juice.

Angie's husband bounded down the stairs.

Steve Bender was in charge of sales for an insurance company and was as outgoing as Angie was stiff. Once when I visited them, I was tempted to count the rows of motivational books, CDs, and videos on closing sales, winning people over, and pepping oneself up long enough to make it through the day.

Steve made it a point to use people's names at least twice in every conversation and could not tolerate any form of negativity.

Obviously happy to begin the day with a knock 'em dead breakfast, Keith said grace. Angie obediently bowed her head although she is not a Catholic. All of Keith's children were raised in the church and Keith never discussed why religion hadn't taken with this one daughter.

Awkwardly, I fumbled for something to talk about. "I hear the Denver housing market is going through a downturn."

"No," Steve said immediately. "That's defeatist thinking."

"Well. It makes sense to me to call a spade a spade and alter strategy," I took care to keep my tone light. "We all have to back off sometimes. Deals sour. Bad days do happen."

"I won't allow my friends or relations to have bad days." He flashed his white, white teeth.

Keith said nothing.

Dumbfounded by Steve's arrogance, I glanced

at Angie who averted her eyes and didn't disguise a bitter half-smile before she rose. "Coffee anyone?" she asked brightly.

Angie had had two miscarriages. Must be fun being married to a relentlessly positive thinker.

I suspected Angie had traded one kind of abuse for another.

There was a blessed interruption when Bettina and Jim clattered down the stairs. They helped the boys choose food from the buffet, then joined us at the kitchen table. Elizabeth was close behind, but took her plate out to the patio table and sat across from Tom. Sunshine spilled into the room. Keith smiled at Tosca's yips coming from the backyard. I took an extra helping of eggs, and began to talk about the weather. The forecast predicted the temperature would rise to a frightening level by late afternoon.

"Do you think Marvin and Sam will be able to handle everything, Keith? I'm worried about people who don't know any better staying out in the sun too long."

"They should be okay, but maybe we should take extra coolers of ice just in case. And sheets," he added, turning to Steve to keep him included in the conversation. "If someone has a heatstroke, we wrap them in ice cold sheets until the EMTs get there."

"We attract what we prepare for," Steve said. "It's the law of the universe. You're preparing for trouble."

Not trusting myself to speak, I rose and joined the assortment of family on the patio.

Tom and Zola were headed toward the barn. Joshua and Kent were trying to set up the wickets for the croquet set. Jimmy laughed at their vain attempts to insert the wire loops into the rock hard summer soil. "Wait until I finish my coffee," he called. "Then I'll help."

"We can do it," they yelled in one voice. Tosca was on serious rabbit control and barely glanced at me. Keith came outside to join us. We wouldn't be going to the fair until time for the parade.

Only Angie and Steve were inside. I could hear their low unhappy voices, but couldn't make out what they were arguing about. A short time later, Angie came outside.

"Anyone up for a rain dance?" she said brightly.

"Not in this heat."

"I've never seen it this dry, Dad. Are your crops holding up?"

"What crops? They're history. It's too late for rain."

"It's like God has decided to pass us over for a year."

Josie came around the corner of the house and joined us. "It's not like we're entitled to rain. Consider it a blessing."

"Some people just simply seem to feel more entitled than others," Elizabeth said. We all knew who she meant. Josie's eyes narrowed.

"So who owns the rain?" I piped up to stop this nonsense before it took on a life of its own.

"Wrong song, Lottie," Keith said. "The title is "Who'll Stop the Rain?" It's early Credence Clearwater Revival."

"That's not right, either. It's "Have You Ever Seen the Rain?"

"Whatever." Relieved, I saw that Elizabeth was revving up to deliver one of her lawyerly lectures instead of baiting Josie.

"As to Lottie's question, 'who owns the rain?' water rights are really quite complicated out here. And it depends on which state you are living in. There's a huge fight between Kansas and Colorado over water rights. Since 1902, Kansas has claimed that Colorado is taking too much water out of the Arkansas River."

"That doesn't account for the rain," Josie clearly didn't want to miss the chance to start a fight.

"That depends, too, on which state you are living in. In Oregon the state owns the rain."

That got our attention.

"If you dig a pond on your property without permission, the state owns the water. It wasn't legal to use a rain barrel in Colorado until 2009."

"We're lucky to live in Kansas because we can use the rain God gives us without a permit from the government. To water chickens, which no one has nowadays. Or to water a two acre garden. If we have any rain to use, that is."

Blessedly there was a howl of disappointment from Joshua who accidentally hit one of the croquet balls into the windbreak. I wasn't up to "friendly" banter.

Bettina and Jimmy went to comfort him and I went inside to tidy up the kitchen.

I was on edge. I thought it was due to family dynamics, but before we left for the parade, I couldn't resist the urge to radio Sam. "You doing okay? Keith and I are bringing extra sheets and coolers if you need them."

"We're just fine. Marvin and the other reserve deputies are all we need."

"Okay. But call if anything comes up."

By the time we drove to town the temperature was

heading up, but at least no rain would spoil the crepe paper stuffed into the wire foundations of floats. The weather station predicted that we would hit one hundred three by late afternoon.

Joshua shouted, "Here they come. Real horses."

Keith's eyes were moist as he observed the little boys respectfully standing at attention with their hands over their hearts when an honor guard led off with the Stars and Stripes. "The Star Spangled Banner" blasted from a boom box.

Then we were all drawn into the giggling wonderment of small boys. Balloons drifted off into the heat-wavering haze of the cloudless sky. The Carlton County high school band had sensibly decided not to wear their wool uniforms and strutted down Main Street dressed in white T-shirts and black knee-length shorts.

The boys dashed out into the street and grabbed candy flung by service organizations.

"They'll be sick by evening," Bettina sighed.

"Probably."

But they weren't. Seemingly impervious to the heat, after the parade, we went to the fairgrounds and they ran us all to death.

The boys made a beeline for the merry-go-round. "Can we ride our special horse, Grandma? Can we? Can we?"

I glanced at my husband's carefully neutral

face. Our carnival was owned by the community. "Our horse" had been painted by Regina. It was turquoise with exquisite roses trailing down its sides.

The ruined metal horses had been salvaged from a bankrupt carnival and hauled back to Gateway City. Their bodies had been straightened, patched, and welded, then sandblasted at a local car body shop. Professional sanding and base paint was supplied by another business. Then local artists finished them up. There was Princess Di, Desert Storm, The Arabian Knight, Dolly Parton—others vying for the honor of being the most spectacular horse.

Regina's was the only unicorn.

Her daughters watched Kent and Zack go round and round. Bettina wiped away a tear as she watched her sons perched on her mother's creation. The boys shrieked and waved as they passed by. If they wanted off, they couldn't be heard over the calliope and the crush of people strolling around.

When they finished, Jimmy and Keith volunteered to go on other rides with the boys, while we women looked over the booths and handwork. The top 4-H booth was easy to pick out. Josie and I watched with bewilderment as my stepdaughters commented on all the food displays of canned and baked goods. I couldn't tell why one jar of canned

pears was superior to another, but I had the sense
to keep my mouth shut.

Then Zola went off to the livestock barn and
Josie and Tom said they were going to get snow
cones.

I went outside the exhibit hall and checked
in with Sam.

"How's it going?"

"Okay. Until Dimon called that is. He wants
us to call a meeting of all the local sheriffs for next
Wednesday."

"But why? Their counties wouldn't be involved
in solving the Diaz murder."

"Didn't say why. Just wanted us to call a meeting." He hung up.

Tom and Josie came back laughing.

"We've just had a couple encounters of the
third kind."

"Not me. Just Josie."

"I suppose someone thought you were me."

"Yes. But I'll start with the one who didn't
think I was you. Hint, hint. An old, old man."

"Old Man Snyder, of course."

"He knew me right off. Said 'how do, Miss
Josie,' then tipped his hat."

"And the other one?"

"I didn't like the sound of it," Tom said. "I was

standing right next to her. But I thought she knew him, so I didn't want to barge in."

"Oh, you're making too much of it," Josie scolded. "Really, you are. But the message clearly was intended for you, Lottie. A man came up to me and told me I should mind my own business and he was warning me for my own good to stay away from the Diaz family."

"You look shocked," Tom said. He turned to Josie. "See I told you she wouldn't take that lightly."

"What did he look like?"

"He was tall. About Dad's height and had blue eyes and sideburns. Curly hair. At first I thought he was sort of pleasant. There was a long line at the snow cone booth. He was right behind us. He made small talk about the weather, of course, like everyone does out here. Then he delivered his little warning as casually as he had talked about the rain."

"I'll have to report this to Sam."

"See I told you she wouldn't take that lightly."

"Do you remember what he was wearing?"

"Jeans. And a western shirt. Blue and tan."

"Could be anyone out here."

"Tom made me come and tell you this," She smiled up at him. "For my own good. Now, we're off to track down the boys. We bought some coupons so they can ride the merry-go-round again."

"Okay. I'll see if the girls are through dissecting all the 4-H entries. We'll catch up with you later."

I watched them snake through the crowds, then sat down on the nearest cast iron bench. Who? I wondered. Someone in the Diaz family? Zola had told me to leave them alone. Dimon insisted that Sam and I were over our heads. Now a rank stranger at a county fair had warned me to stay away from the Diaz family. That made warning number three even if it was delivered to my sister by mistake.

But all of the warnings were given for different reasons.

The burnt-sugar odor of cotton candy blended with wet dust under a leaky vendor's camper. It was hard to think blanketed under strange smells, this mob of people. I was probably making three mountains out of one little mole hill.

Zola was just giving friendly advice. It wasn't a real warning. Dimon didn't want me near the Diaz family because he was afraid Sam and I would botch his investigation.

Only this last one from a blue-eyed stranger had the feel of the real deal to me. It was "for my own good."

Or was it a stranger? If the warning had been delivered to me instead of Josie, would I have known who it was?

Chapter Nine

Wednesday evening I walked into the crowded gathering in the commissioner's room. Keith and Sam were already there and the room was filled with law enforcement personnel from around the region.

Agent Dimon had driven out especially to conduct the meeting. There were four men from Topeka present besides himself and my favorite agent, Nancy Brooks, and Jim Gilderhaus, our regional agent.

I glanced at Keith, who was sitting with arms crossed, eyebrows raised. Sam stood to one side at the front of the room. Since the meeting was in Carlton County, he felt like he should be an unofficial host and "introduce the bastard" he'd said earlier.

When everyone quieted, he walked over to a podium. "Guess you wonder why we're all here tonight. Matter of fact, I'm kinda wondering that myself. But we're about to find out. This here is

Frank Dimon who wants to have a few words with us. He's from the KBI and so are all the other strangers sitting around tonight. Frank, I'll turn this over to you."

"Gentlemen," Dimon began, "I don't need to tell you that the death rate in this area is beginning to attract attention."

I wished he hadn't worn a suit.

"The number of murders per capita is extraordinary."

I had to keep myself from leaping to my feet to contradict him. Crime statistics for sparse populations could distort reality.

"The state KBI has concluded that we have to work out law enforcement arrangements for Western Kansas that will consolidate resources and employ the strategic use of manpower." A fly buzzed around Dimon's head. The window air-conditioning unit kicked on and his papers scattered. He bent to retrieve them. By himself. Not a soul offered to help. Keith and I included.

"Now then," he said awkwardly, after aligning his material again, "of course we have to square this legally. There are processes we need to follow to put this in place, but for now, our temporary arrangement will allow a great deal of latitude to determine what will actually work."

We waited. Something was coming down, and I suspected we wouldn't like it.

Dimon switched on a projector and walked to the screen centered on the north wall. "Here's what we have devised. I might add that a presentation this sophisticated was not whipped up as a result of the incidents occurring this past week."

The first screen of his slide show came into view. "As you can see, we've been working on these ideas for several months."

I gaped at the words, with a perky voiceover reading them to us in case none of us had the ability. "Northwest Kansas Regional Law Enforcement: A Triumph in Effectiveness and Responsibility."

A fully equipped sheriff appeared on the screen and earnestly informed us that small counties were poorly equipped to cope with challenges in changing populations. By the time the fifth slide appeared, showing men around a conference table discussing problems, I was aghast.

It concluded with an architect showing a finished sketch of a regional jail and a criminalist lab to process information.

By that time, I was seething. Dimon finished to thunderous silence. "We are quite proud of this. Our system is being considered as a prototype for instituting a regional law-enforcement center in sparsely populated regions all over the country. Are there any questions?"

I glanced at Nancy who sat with a lowered head pinching the bridge of her nose. She didn't look up.

"Yes, I have a question." I reached for a glass of water and took a sip before I continued. "Who was that first man? The sheriff in the first slide? I didn't recognize him as a Western Kansas law enforcement officer."

"Well, no. Actually, he was a professional actor. Naturally, we want to have the most effective video possible."

"And all the others? They, too, were actors?"

"Yes."

"All the discussions were fake? You didn't film a real meeting?"

"No," he said, his voice crisp.

"I have a question." Everyone looks at Keith when he speaks. He carries natural authority. Not only because of his size and the timbre of his voice, but by his inherent wisdom. "Did you consult with any single person who actually lives out here?"

"No, we didn't."

His stark admission didn't surprise me. I had come to appreciate Dimon's honesty and dedication—if not his humorless ways.

A deputy from Copeland County spoke up. "Why the hell not?"

"Frankly, we wanted people who were more objective and detached to devise the best possible plan that is realistically obtainable in today's economy. We intended and still intend to discuss it with the general population later and make any necessary adjustments it might take to get it up and running."

"Good luck with that," I mumbled. It would be impolite, self-defeating, stupid actually, to laugh out loud.

Last spring, the construction and dedication of Saint Helena's, our tiny little Episcopal church shared by four counties, had nearly revived the old range wars. Half of the counties in Kansas had had county-seat fights, many of them ending in bloodshed. In the early 1920s Goodland had hired a rainmaker and then sued the neighboring town of Colby when it rained there instead of the expected area.

And this man actually expected the people in any given county to give up their sheriff? Their jail? For a regional system?

"Any discussion?" Dimon asked.

"I thought we were coming here today for a briefing about the murder in our feedyard," Keith said. "The murder, remember?"

Dimon's lips thinned. "No questions? No discussion about the regional center? All right. I understand that. I understand you, too, Keith. We have a murder to solve. Maybe connected to something bigger than just local. I know that's why you came here. But hear this," he pointed to the last slide again. "This regional center is coming. It's going to happen and there's nothing you can do to stop it."

Maybe. Other things, other developments had come whether we liked it or not. School consolidation, county consolidation, medical facility consolidation. Consolidation had been as unstoppable as the railroads pushing across the plains. Iron pushing through thousands of acres of sod. Iron pushing the buffalo ahead of it. Iron pushing Indians away, away.

Consolidation as relentless and unstoppable as the wind farms dotting the prairies with their sleek towering structures dwarfing the aging old wooden structures. Corporate giants racing across the plains. The prairie was helpless to stop the onslaught.

I looked at Keith sitting there, faking impassivity, and smiled. I knew what that look meant even if Dimon didn't.

"The murder," Keith said. "Carlton County called in the KBI to figure out who murdered

Victor Diaz. Have you made any progress yet? Do you think there is a problem that reaches beyond Carlton County?"

Dimon frowned. He wasn't through with his lecture yet. He gazed steadily at Keith. His mouth lipped into a little gesture that passed as a smile for him. Then laying one finger aside his lips, the others cradling his chin, he studied my husband as though he were a scientist peering at a new species.

"Actually, we don't have any evidence to support that. But, yes, we think so. The murder was too simply too suspicious to dismiss it all as happenstance."

"Drugs?"

I recognized the speaker as the undersheriff of Copeland County. He was supposed to be the interim sheriff after the death of Sheriff Irwin Deal whose death had been viewed as a blessing by most of the county.

"There's no evidence of drug activity here."

"They wouldn't dare in Sam's county," someone said from the back of the room. There was a murmur of appreciation. Sam brushed the brim of his hat and smiled.

"I do admit Sheriff Abbot has been quite efficient at handling problems in the past, whenever they came up. But times are changing. Methods have to change with the times." There were enough nuances in Dimon's voice to script a Shakespearian plot.

I had told Keith about the proxy marriage debacle. He stared at Dimon. If he had had any doubts before that the agent intended to get rid of Sam, he didn't now.

"Do you mean to tell me that we come over here tonight to have you tell us you hope you will agree to getting rid of our jobs?"

Oh boy. I swiveled to look at the speaker. Justin Harold is a tall, slim man whose big sun-burned ears jutting from the side of his head make him look like a giant mouse. He was part-time law enforcement as were most of the men in the room. Part-time and overworked.

Harold was the sole support of his aging mother and desperate to keep up his land pay-ments. A fair man, he employed several Mexicans every year to help with the wheat harvest. Years ago, his uncle had married a Mexican woman, but nationality wouldn't have mattered to Justin's family. The question was—could they work? Ability to work was the biggest issue. Probably the most prized trait in Western Kansas.

"And you're telling us that you think the murder of a fine man should take second place to bringing in some Hollywood sheriffs to take the place of men who know what they are doing? We give people jobs out here. Real work."

"Gentlemen, it's not like we aren't doing anything at all about the Diaz murder. It's just that, right now, we're coming out here too often. This has involved a special task force, which we don't usually form unless there's organized crime involved. Like illegal drugs. Illegal immigration. Border crossing. That sort of thing."

"Well now ain't that a shame?" Harold said softly. "We're not bad enough."

Condemnation of the government was so thick you could feel judgment flap into the room like an attacking falcon. A massive force of condemnation. I could feel it, taste it. Dimon had aroused the whacky Kansas sense of unity against outsiders. The zeal for justice.

We were the state that had the strongest network of underground railroad organizations that helped runaway slaves make it to Canada before the Civil War. We were the state that later attracted African American immigrants and offered them free land through the Homestead Act. We were the state that just purely admired women like Carry Nation who smashed saloons with an axe. We didn't hold with people who drank. Unless it was us.

I stared at Dimon with wonderment. He had achieved a miracle. United the room against him in just a few sentences. He knew that. He was no dummy. That didn't mean they all agreed with one another, of course. The simply didn't like him.

Justin put his hands on his hips and addressed the room. "This man has already said there's no drug gangs here in this county. He's not interested in a little murder unless drug lords are involved. And there's no border to cross into Kansas. He just wants to take away our jobs."

"Ah Christ, Justin, ain't no drug lords out here anyway. That's in Eye-rack and Afghanistan. A few gangs back in Eastern Kansas, maybe."

"Point is, we do a pretty good job of solving our own problems out here."

"Like, hell." I didn't recognize the speaker. "The KBI wouldn't have been called in if we didn't need extra help."

"So you think maybe we should form a little committee to help this little operation along? A welcome wagon maybe, with homemade cookies and free tickets to the movie when Topeka sends out men hellbent on telling us what to do?"

"It's time to vote," Harold said. "Who is in favor of Dimon's bullshit?"

"Starting a regional crime center is not subject to a vote." Dimon finally lost his temper. He managed to keep his voice under control, but his face flushed. "This is a legislative decision. It's not up to you."

All hell broke loose. I knew how these "come let us reason together" meetings could go, but Dimon didn't. He clearly could not think of how to regain control.

Keith rose, glanced at the agent with something akin to pity and strode to the front of the room. He glanced at me, and with a tiny movement of his head made a silent apology to Sam for taking the place that he probably should have assumed. But Sam gave a slight shrug and there was an amused glint in his eye over the hole Dimon had dug himself into.

I sat with my arms crossed. It was certainly not my place to ride herd over this makeshift mob.

"Stop it, right now," Keith said. "This is a bunch of crap. In case any of you have forgotten, a man was murdered right here in this county. An ugly death."

Dimon looked like a drowning man who had just been thrown a life saver.

"Now, Agent Dimon, do you have anything more you would like us to know? Something you want to ask us?"

Dimon nodded at Keith who then walked back to his seat.

"Gentlemen, although I appreciate your sense

of justice and willingness to stand by your neigh-boring counties, the fact remains there's been a serious crime here. And none of you have the skill or resources to solve it." The room fell silent.

I glanced at Sam. One of the shrewdest men I knew. Too smart to start a public brawl. But I knew that look. It was the same one on his face when he was studying how to break a prisoner. Dimon would regret slamming this man's skill.

Dimon braced his hands on the podium. "And I'll guarantee you that someone is making money out of it somehow, because they for damn sure didn't do it for love. It's hard to imagine that there is any power to be gained by being king of the feedyard. I'm going to delay further discussion about the regional crime lab until you've had time to consider the advantages. I apologize if this has been too much, too fast. It's a lot to take in."

Deeper and deeper. We were too dumb to think very fast. Too dumb to understand when we did think.

"Instead, I want you all to ask around in your own communities and let us know if you can learn anything about the murder of Victor Diaz."

"And that's it?" Keith asked. "That's all you are going to do? Have us ask around?"

"It's all we can do, Keith. We've processed all of the forensic evidence with zero results."

"So we are on our own?"

"That's about the size of it. Now, unless some-one has more questions, I don't have anything else to add. Basically, just keep your eyes open and let us know at once if there is anything we should know. Do not try to confront anyone suspicious. We'll be out here is a flash if anything comes up."

We rose and silently headed for the door.

"Miss Albright, would you stay a minute longer."

Certainly." I looked at Keith and shrugged.

When everyone had left, Dimon shut the door. He still looked shaken.

"Lottie, we want more information from the records at the feedyard. In the meantime, go back to collecting family stories and concentrate on the Mexican families in this area until you hear from me. Will that work?"

"Yes. In fact, I was already planning to appeal to immigrant groups that settled here in colonies. The French, the Bohemians."

"Terrific. Now it won't look like we're paying special attention to the Mexican community. Start building profiles of the families here in this county. Since Maria Diaz helps bring families into the United States I want to make sure there is no con-nection between her activities and her husband's death.

"Okay. That shouldn't be too hard."

We said goodbye. I felt as though I had won a great victory. It was the first time he had called me "Lottie" instead of "Miss Albright."

Chapter Ten

Back at the historical society the following Monday, I appealed to immigrant groups through my monthly column. Then I laid out an ad asking for stories from residents whose ancestors had settled in Carlton County.

> *Tell us your grandparents' stories.*
> *Were your ancestors discriminated against because of their ethnicity? Who were their friends? Their enemies? If your heritage is Volga German, Bohemian, African American, French, or Mexican, share your family story with the Carlton County Historical Society.*

When I was satisfied with the wording, I carried it down to the paper and asked the editor, Ken McElroy, to send the bill to the historical society.

"Any new information you can give me about the killing?"

Ken couldn't stand not knowing everyone's business, although I supposed a local murder was fair game for someone who fancied himself an investigative reporter. Pale, slight, with a harmless appearance, Ken had just enough hair to keep from being referred to as "balding." His light blue guileless eyes fooled people into thinking he could be trusted with every little secret.

"Nope. I'm afraid not." I reconsidered. Perhaps, it would be better to give him a tidbit. Something to take the edge off his curiosity. "And the KBI…"

"Rumor has it that the KBI has tucked its tail between its legs and skedaddled back to Topeka?"

He had cleverly framed it as a question, wanting me to confirm the coffee shop gossip. *Hell, why not?* I hoped he didn't read too much into my bitter smile.

"Right now, I'm afraid that is more or less the case. But I'm sure they are keeping a close eye on people out here." There. I was becoming really good at telling just enough of the truth to appease my conscience without giving too much away.

If I got any better at it, I would run for the state legislature.

"Yes, I can imagine they are," Ken said with a little snort. A pencil rolled off the desk and he bent down to retrieve it. This was not my first rodeo. I knew he had switched on a tape recorder on his way back up. He leaned back and settled his hands across his little paunch, clearly settling in for a nice visit. Hoping I would inadvertently say something worthy of a quote in tomorrow's paper.

"Goodbye, I've got to go now," I quickly turned and walked to the door, then paused. "If something does come up—news, a change, a lead, anything at all, I will make sure you are the first to know."

He gave another little snort, recognizing my ploy to cut off any discussion, and rose with a knowing smile. "Thanks, Lottie; 'preciate it. You know we'll treat you right. No automatic bad-mouthing of the sheriff's department. No matter what they do."

"I know that, Ken."

Monday morning brought the first response to my column. A Bohemian woman came over from the neighboring town of Hanover.

Jane Jordan carried a whole box of artifacts and souvenirs. She had brushed her neat brown hair straight back from her forehead and tamed the carefully permed curls with a nearly invisible net. "I was worried that you wouldn't be open during the lunch hour, so I decided to bring this stuff over bright and early."

"That's fine." I groaned inwardly. We couldn't

collect artifacts because we lacked the storage area. But I never passed up a chance to look through their boxes just in case there was something of historical value. Although most items would be given back to the donor before we had to record it as a contribution, I didn't have the guts to tell them it was garage sale stuff. I left that task to Margaret, who seemed to enjoy it.

"You can't keep them," Jane said. "I just thought it would save time if you went through the box before we get together. I imagine you're busy too." She wore navy double-knit pants of the kind of fabric that lasted at least ten years. Her coordinated white-and-navy print blouse had a soft self-tie bow at the neck. I suspected she had never done anything unconventional in her entire life.

"Perfect! That will give me a chance to prepare some questions if any of the items are out of the ordinary."

"I work at the abstract office. All-around clerical and some research work, but not too much. In fact, sometimes I feel like a robotic copying machine operator. I would love to do what you do. Look into stuff, I mean. Oh, not as an undersheriff, goodness me." She looked at her feet as though shocked by her own boldness. "I mean hunt up documents here in the historical society." She covered her mouth and her fingers drummed her lips to hide her nervous half-smile. "I don't mean to imply that I could...that I have the training, you understand." She rose.

"We could easily use you here if you would like to volunteer."

She sank back down on the chair and looked like she had been granted entré into Heaven. "I would be so grateful. So very grateful if I could."

She blinked and dabbed at her eyes with an old fashioned-handkerchief with a blue crocheted edging. "They are cutting my days to four. There's not much going on in real estate nowadays. I won't be busy enough."

"That's beginning to be a common story."

"I don't expect to be paid, you understand. I would just like to make a contribution."

"I'll give your name to Margaret Atkinson right away. She's in charge of volunteers and I know she will be grateful for the help."

"Oh, here's my number." She handed me a business card from the local title search company. She rose again, then nodded toward the box. "There's some really old letters from my great-great-great grandmother when the family was still in Moravia."

"I don't read Czech."

"Neither do I. They have all been translated." She glanced at her watch. "We open at nine, so

I'd better be getting along." She got as far as the doorway this time. "It's a great family," she said. "You won't find many secrets hidden there. We were good members of any community we settled in. Quick to buy land, quick to pay for it."

She turned back with the wistful look of someone who wanted to tell me more. Family secrets maybe, despite her insistence that there were none.

"My great-great-grandfather and his seven sons came over in 1886. They all spread out. He was an Eagle, I don't know the Czech name for it. It was an organization of the highest order. A blending of physical and mental attainment. Sort of a fraternity, I think. I know he was very, very proud."

"And church? Were these religious people?"

"Not my family. We believed God helps those who help themselves and after a time, I guess God just got downsized."

God downsized! Well, there was a new perspective. She waved goodbye and hurried down the hall. But I knew we had a real find. The ideal volunteer. She had worked in the abstract office since she left high school and obviously relished locating old documents. Everything about her said she didn't mind being bossed around. Margaret would be in hog heaven.

Relieved that I was expected to return these possessions instead of having to find a place for them, I carried the box over to a sorting table in back of the room. Her airy dismissal of God rang a bell. I went to my collection of college dissertations and located a manuscript on the reasons for the immigration of the Czech people from Europe to the United States. There was a whole chapter on religious persecution.

About half the Bohemians were Free Thinkers and hated Rome. The other half were devout Catholics.

The Free Thinkers had survived the pogroms and Crusades of Europe and were eager to come to the United States where they would be free not to believe.

I tapped my fingers on my desk, walked out into the hall, then went downstairs and stared out the heavy glass double doors. How did that work for them, I wondered, moving into a heavily Catholic county? Did they run into the same bias here? Or did the neighbors leave them alone? Restless, I turned and headed back up the stairs, eager to start on the mysterious box and see what I needed to copy before I returned it.

I barely made it back to the office when Inez Wilson, the county health nurse, flapped into my doorway like a hopped up crow. "You won't believe this. You won't."

"Okay. What?" I was in no mood for her guessing games.

"She just came through the front door. She has. Swear to God she has. Priscilla said they asked where your office is. They are coming to see you."

I waited.

"Doña Francesca Diaz. The old woman herself. Don't know how old, but she's lived in Roswell County forever and most folks have never seen her. She lives out at that compound. There used to be a passel of kids and grandkids. But not anymore. They say she still goes to their first house every day to do God only knows what. Her great-granddaughter looks after her. Folks say their grandparents used to go to her for cures and stuff."

"I look forward to meeting her."

"Now don't go making the mistake of thinking that Francesca Diaz is like a…a…a well, you know, someone who knows about healing." Inez leaned forward as though she had read my thoughts. "Heard tell she's a witch and knows all kinds of stuff good Christian people have no business knowing."

Her pager went off. "Oops. Gotta go."

I hastily put back the dissertation and gave the room a quick shot of Febreze® to zap any lingering odor of glue. I wished the room looked more professional. Although I doubted she could tell me anything about her great-grandson's murder, it would be my first time to talk with a woman who knew about the medicinal uses of plants and herbs. I had once heard a professor from Nebraska say that one-third of the medicine used today was present on the prairie in another form, and there was always someone who knew how to put it to use. Certainly Indian women did.

If Francesca Diaz was actually a healer, a *curandera*, it was a once-in-a-lifetime opportunity.

Overwhelmed with sadness at the thought of this woman losing Victor in such a grisly manner, I didn't know what I could say.

She lived in Roswell County, a tiny maverick slice of land that seemed to exist apart from any other governing body. Keith had once told me the geometric shape was classified by mathematicians as a kite quadlateral. The county was occupied exclusively by the Diaz family and had been attached to our own Carlton County for judicial purposes when Northwest Kansas was first settled.

Francesca Diaz was the great-grandmother of a man who had been well known in this county. Yet, curiously her birthdays came and went without any write-ups about celebrations. One would think, even if the majority of the family was scattered across Kansas there would be big parties for special events. Or family reunions. Some kind of a blowout.

Instead she was never mentioned at all.

Chapter Eleven

Moments later, two women appeared in my open doorway. I rose. The famed Francesca Diaz, this tiny old woman, might have stepped out of an ancient painting. Her head was covered with a black lace-edged scarf. She wore a black slightly gathered cotton skirt and a black blouse. No jewelry. Her mahogany face looked like it had been glued together from strips of sun-dried beef.

It takes superb effort to hold oneself that straight. I had never seen such regal bearing in the aged. It spoke of an aristocratic childhood with bevies of aunts and tutors instructing her in carriage and manners.

"Mrs. Diaz..." At the sudden spark in her eyes, I knew I had fumbled. Used the wrong term of address. Should it have been Senora? Doña? Or should I have acted as though I didn't know who she was? There was no going back. "Please come in. Words cannot express my sorrow for your loss."

Both of the women's eyes were red from weeping. "I am so terribly, terribly sorry." Every word out of my mouth sounded inept.

"We are honored to have you visit the historical society." Embarrassed anew by the mismatched utilitarian files and cabinets in my office, I helped the old woman settle into a folding chair and went to the storage closet and got another one for the younger woman.

"I'm Lottie Albright and I apologize for not having more comfortable places to sit." I gestured helplessly at the crazy array of pipes networking the ceiling, the unattractive proportions of the room. It wasn't called "the vault" for nothing.

"I am Cecilia Diaz," said the young woman. I glanced at her modest dirndl skirt, her high-necked blouse, her dark guileless eyes, and doubted that anyone had ever uttered a word of profanity in her presence. Or that she would understand it if someone did. Surely, no one had ever violated her dove-like gentle innocence. She then spoke to the old woman in rapid fire Spanish, who in turn gave a dismissive wave of her hand. "And this is my great-grandmother, Doña Francesca Bianco Loisel Montoya Diaz."

I regretted that I had studied French and ignored Spanish in college. All that registered was the honorific term "Doña" which was used to indicate high birth. In years past, "Doña" indicated a member of the nobility. I would ask Cecilia to write down the stream of names later.

An image came out of nowhere: *The Little House on the Prairie.* A wisp of memory that dissipated like smoke.

Francesca's eyes flared, and Cecilia laughed gently, reached and fondly patted one of her hands. "Yes, and Diaz, Grandmother. You are also Diaz." Cecilia faced me again.

The old woman's eyes never left my face. I gazed at her hideous hands—knuckles gnarled, with bones jutting at twisted angles, one part of a finger missing. Ruined hands, no longer capable of handwork and pleasant diversions. Embarrassed, I quickly looked away.

"I want you to find out who murdered my great-grandson." Her words were clear and totally unexpected. I would have guessed that if she spoke at all, it would be with the harsh rasp of the elderly. But even more surprising was her unaccented English.

"You are surprised. Surprised that I speak English. We are American. My family has always lived here."

I blushed. "Please forgive me for assuming that when you spoke in Spanish…"

"I want you to find out who murdered my

great-grandson. My Victor. Her brother. Just a year older than Cecilia, he was. They played together like twins." Tears streamed down her weathered cheeks. Cecilia reached into her pocketbook and took out a lace-edged handkerchief and dabbed at her great-grandmother's eyes. The faint scent of lavender mingled with the room's usual aroma of glues and old books.

"Certainly we will all try, Mrs. Diaz. In fact the whole KBI is now…"

"I would like you to be the one."

"The KBI has resources," I stammered. "They are much more skilled than I and they have equipment that our county…"

She cut me off again. "You please. Just you."

"That will not be possible, Mrs. Diaz. They are already involved."

"No," Francesca said slowly. "Only you will I help." The rapid Spanish exchange between her and Cecilia began again.

Embarrassed by her great-grandmother's switch to a language that obviously excluded me, Cecilia stopped her. "Please, Grandmother. If you must, tell Miss Albright what you have to say and then we will leave."

"No more discussion." The old woman looked at me sharply. "I want you to find Victor's murderer. I have information that I will only give to you. My great-granddaughter here does not want outsiders probing around in our family's business. We do not want hordes of newspeople inventing facts. But we cannot simply go on living apart as we always have done. Not when there has been another murder."

Another murder. She had said "another murder."

She teared up again. Cecilia reached over to dab at Francesca's eyes.

"I trust you. That is why I will only talk with you."

"But we've never met!"

"We get the Carlton County newspaper. We discuss your column every week. A year ago, I checked your educational credentials, your publications. You are patient. You are respectful. You would be not be tempted to pass on everything I tell you just to show off. In fact, I have considered getting in touch with you for a long time for another reason. To see if you might be interested in some information about my family. The bare facts. Nothing more than a simple genealogy. Now there has been another killing. Now, because you are an undersheriff, I will simply give you enough family information to help bring my great-grandson's murderers to justice. Then I wish to be left alone to grieve the loss of my precious Victor."

Cecilia flushed. "Nothing you say or tell

about our past will help Miss Albright figure out who killed my brother. We're better off living apart as we have always done. I can't understand why you would reverse a lifetime of silence and suddenly expect help from this lady, who is, after all, connected to the government." She turned to me. "Please do not take what I have said personally."

I nodded. Graciously, I hoped. But in fact I found it quite unnerving to be discussed in third-person as though I were off in another room. I didn't know if their doing so was a family or cultural trait. For that matter, they did not hesitate to make explanatory comments about each directly to me. Right now, they carried on their private conversation in English.

"Cecilia, I have ways of deciding that you are not privy to, ways of knowing about people. It breaks my heart that I can never pass them on to you. The chain will be broken."

"And if in order to help, you have to risk having your ways misunderstood by an outsider? Even if explaining some of your 'ways' leads to avenging Victor, after these evil men are dealt with and people tire of the latest hunt, the blood sport, what then? Will they turn on you? Will there be another witch hunt?"

"I do not care. Victor's killers must be brought to justice."

My breath stopped. Killers, not killer. Why?

The sorrow wedged between the two women was heartbreaking.

Cecilia bit her lip and raised her eyes to me as though pleading for understanding. "I do not wish to be disrespectful by not exposing myself to great-grandmother's ways. She knows this." She patted the old woman's hand. "I am Catholic. I keep the morning office and attend Mass weekly and I…"

She was obviously distressed, as she grappled for a gentle explanation that would not imply undue criticism of her *abuela*.

Francesca glanced at her with loving humor and shrugged. "She does not approve of me, you see. My devout Catholic great-granddaughter."

Mrs. Diaz had just confirmed the rumor that she knew ways forbidden to Christians. Through Keith, I knew enough about the church to know Cecilia meant it would be sacrilegious to acquire this old woman's special knowledge. She did not want to be initiated into rituals that would encroach on her own religion and violate the first commandment. She would risk putting other gods before her God. This innocent gentle girl/woman was terrified of what her great-grandmother would have her learn. I understood immediately.

Unbidden, Old Man Snyder, the well-witcher, crossed my mind.

"How I acquired some of my knowledge has no bearing on any of this. I came to you because I know you are a just woman and I trust you not to mishandle information. I simply want you to find out who killed my…" Francesca Diaz teared up again and used a word I did not understand.

"She means 'beloved great-grandson.'" Cecilia put her arm around Francesca's shoulder, then knelt before her and gently dabbed at the old woman's eyes with the handkerchief. She tended to her own eyes before she sat back down.

"I know things," the old woman said. "Things that will help you do the job God has chosen you to do."

I strained to hear.

"Language will not be a barrier," said Cecilia. "When you hear our little exchanges, we are not trying to say things we don't want you to hear. She converses in Spanish only with me because she feels she can express herself more precisely. We do not use the Tex-Mex blend that passes for Spanish here. She adheres to Old Spanish."

"Classical Castilian?"

"Cecilia was the only one who bothered to learn my language."

"Great-grandmother is being too harsh, really. She is giving me undue praise."

Cecilia lowered her black eyelashes. With a

sweet blush, she delicately apologized for Francesca's favoritism toward her. "We all have certain places within our family and I cannot remember when I did not know that I was to care for great-grandmother."

Francesca nodded. "It was expected."

"We all loved her and cared for her, of course, but I was to be the main one. It is not the others' fault. In time, most of the family moved away. Please do not interpret her comment as criticism of those who did not learn Castilian. It is not a useful language. Others simply chose to enrich their lives at universities or have contributed to our financial well-being."

Intrigued by this beautiful woman's curiously formal language, the careful arrangement of words—the use of complete sentences—I felt as though I had stepped back into the 1800s. I blessed my mother's insistence that Josie and I attend a finishing school, although we had behaved like little hellions bent on sabotaging every lesson. Rather than joining group sports as our parents had wished, Josie took fencing lessons and I became a crack shot.

I straightened in my chair, and my legs eased into a ladylike arrangement. I nodded and beamed at them both. Cecilia was obviously the favored one. She occupied the place of honor. In our American tradition, she would be regarded as little more than an indentured servant. We had no comparable role. I knew just enough about historic Spanish culture to know that Cecilia was held in high esteem, indeed. Her days would be spent in service and scholarship. I did not detect an iota of resentment toward a life that another might have found stifling.

Nevertheless, the Catholic Church would prohibit her from becoming the recipient of her great-grandmother's ancient wisdom which probably had overtones of paganism. This had to be a grievous situation for them both.

"Would you care for tea?" I was falling into ways that had cost my parents a pretty penny, and I normally had little use for. We have a lovely formal tea set here at the historical society and drag it out for fundraising events.

With any other women, this would have sounded ridiculous. Tea, indeed. As for visiting royalty. Then I glanced at Francesca's hands again. I blushed to the roots of my hair. There was no way in hell those hands could manage to hold a cup and saucer.

Cecilia quickly turned to her great-grandmother, whose eyes brightened and she nodded.

Flustered, I rose and walked back and took the set from the cupboard. I went to the small sink in the revamped closet off the main room. I filled a pitcher with water, nuked it in the microwave, measured tea into the antique diffuser, poured hot water into the lovely old pot, and reentered the room. Cecilia received the first cup, dropped in a lump of sugar, and handed the saucer to Francesca, who received it with some arrangement of talons and bones I would not have thought possible. She even managed to grasp the handle, although it was achieved with a sideways twist of her index finger and thumb.

This morning, this visit, was easily stacking up to be one of the strangest during my years at the historical society. My office had been visited by murderers, out-and-out lunatics, and men and women who bore such tragedy it broke my heart. But Francesca Diaz and Cecilia Diaz just might top them all.

I wished they were from Carlton County instead of Roswell, so I could include their story in our county history books. But a separate booklet or permission to do an academic article about the Spanish on the plains would have been ideal. Now Francesca Diaz had clearly changed her mind about drawing attention to her family. This remarkable old woman said she could provide insight into a possible motivation behind her great-grandson's murder. I would have to settle for that.

No, "possible" motivation was my weasely word. She said she knew why, period.

"I will need some basic information about your family, of course, for background."

She hesitated, and then nodded.

I considered the number of gawkers in the courthouse, the people who would appear in my office the moment they left, eager to hear details about their visit. "Perhaps under the circumstances, it would be easier if I came to your house, Mrs. Diaz. And people will ask fewer questions if they believe I am there to work on a history project."

"Yes, I would prefer to have you come to my home. There are also things you might like to see on our property. You are very kind. Thank you so very much."

"My pleasure."

"I want you to be the one," Francesca said suddenly.

"There are…issues." A sob caught in Cecilia's throat. Her breast heaved with a sudden intake of breath and her voice trembled. "She believes you are the ideal one to avenge Victor because you…"

"Because you are not afraid of evil people," Francesca said slowly, fixing me with her dark glittering eyes.

Jarred, I stared as they rose. Francesca's age showed in the slow steadying of her feet as she pushed upright, before she once again assumed her rigid posture. But I saw how well she moved, how easily she came up with words. There was no way she was as old as people thought. *Or was she?*

We made an appointment for the following week, murmured our goodbyes and I walked them to the elevator, all the while wondering if there were enough scattered family members still alive to pose for a five-generation picture. Would it even be possible? My heart leapt, momentarily shoving aside speculation that this woman might have information about a murder investigation.

Years ago, when people's life spans were shorter, three-generation pictures were highly prized. Then the gold standard became four generations. Even today, five generations of the same bloodline—great-great-grandparents—were extremely rare.

Cecilia held the door, then helped Francesca step inside without letting go of the ruined hand too warped to grasp the safety rails mounted on the side.

"Again, thank you," she said before they descended. "And after you find the killers, perhaps someone should know about my family's bloodline before I die. Before it's too late. Perhaps you should do that for me, too. Just that. A genealogy and nothing more."

Cecilia gave a slight warning shake of her head and touched Francesca's elbow.

Could she be coaxed? It would require all my negotiating skills.

"It's happening again." She looked at me sadly. The elevator descended.

Suddenly chilled, I did not understand. Not at all.

What was happening again?

Chapter Twelve

Keith and Zola were coming in from the barn. Still unnerved by the visit from Cecilia and Francesca Diaz, I looked forward to their argumentative banter and began rubbing seasoning salt into steaks. Perhaps they could dispel my bitchy mood, which began after I called Dimon to tell him about Francesca's visit to the historical society.

He had immediately bawled me out for not demanding information right then and there "if she really, actually had some. Chance are she is overwhelmed with grief," he said, "and has started to attach some kind of ominous portent to every word her grandson said."

"Great-grandson."

"Whatever. But I've had a lot of experience with this kind of situation. You say she hasn't left the farm for years, so she wouldn't be in a position to know much."

I seethed. "It was my duty to inform you."

"And I appreciate that. But I think you understand why I think you and Sam should leave the analysis to experts."

"I'm in an ideal position to investigate. She sought me out. I'll be going out there anyway to ask her some questions about her family from a historical standpoint."

"Do *not* discuss this murder with her! Leave interrogation to us. I don't want you accidentally muddying the waters or tipping someone off. I won't send agents out there as in my professional judgment that would be a waste of time. However, I can't tell you what to do in your other job, of course, and if you do go there and if anything of interest comes up during your conversations about, what? Family history? Whatever it is you are working on, do let us know. Go right ahead and collect your little stories."

We chatted about the weather, and then hung up.

Dumb bastard. He didn't want our little dogpatch of a county involved in solving this crime. He would have a hard time promoting a regional center if Sam and I figured out who killed Victor on our own. There would be no point in switching to a new expensive system.

Perhaps someone from the KBI would have plunged right into the hard questions when Francesca came into the office, instead of trusting a slower approach. But I knew it would all come in good time. I had informed Dimon like a good subordinate and it wasn't my fault if he didn't know a clue from a club.

Keith and Zola were spatting as they came through the back door.

"Weatherman says it will rain tomorrow. Give us a little more time."

"Better be safe than sorry," Keith said. "And make arrangements now before there isn't a bale left in five counties."

"You two at it again?"

"No," they both said together.

I studied their faces. "What?"

"Pasture is drying up," Keith said. "We need to throw in the towel and start buying alfalfa hay. Before it dawns on everyone else that we're shit out of luck. 'It ain't gonna rain no, more, no more.'" He whistled the next line.

Zola rolled her eyes.

"And my helper here, my right-hand man," he smiled at Zola, "thinks we should give it more time. Hay is at a premium right now unless we get the cheap stuff."

"That's my point, Keith. It's at a premium. One good rain and the price will drop overnight." Zola caught her heel in the boot jack by the front door, pulled off the boot, switched feet and neatly lined the shoes up side by side, then slipped into house moccasins. "Or other farmers will give up and ship their cattle out and there will be plenty of hay for sale."

They went to wash up. I had asked Zola to stay for supper after extracting a promise that she wouldn't do a thing to help. Just let me take over for once.

The phone rang.

"Hi, Sis."

I heard a man's voice in the background. Josie laughed. "Tom says it's 'Hi, Mom,' not 'Hi, Sis.'"

After the family weekend, Tom had gone to Kansas City on a brief contract job to verify the geographical feasibility of a commercial develop-ment site.

"Why is he in Manhattan?"

"He's not. We're both in Denver staying with Jimmy and Bettina. He wanted to spend some time with them, and I had to give a lecture at Colorado University, so we decided to drive out together."

My throat went dry.

"It was cheaper for us to drive than to fly sepa-rately." Josie's bright voice was just right.

I knew. I just knew.

So when had Josie ever been concerned about cheap?

Dealing with our family dynamics was sheer

hell most of the time. This would send all the relationships into an abyss. I closed my eyes, nevertheless knowing that in some odd way they would be a natural together. He was only one year younger than Josie, they both loved music. But he was my stepson and she was my twin, and she had practically sworn off men after her divorce from her first husband. And Elizabeth. My God, Elizabeth with her adoration of her brother and her flagrant dislike of my twin. There would be no reconciling Elizabeth to this.

"Anyway, the reason I called is to see if you want me to stop by for any reason on our way back to Manhattan. Or have my days as a consultant come to an end?"

"All of our days as a law enforcement anything have come to an end if Frank Dimon has anything to do with it. No, we don't need anything. Except rain. Can we expect Tom back here or will he be staying with Jim and Bettina?"

"Actually, he will be driving me home. He has a chance to consult with a construction firm in Kansas City. They want an independent analysis of the soil composition at the location for a proposed building. He wants to talk with them some more."

Josie had always thought the drive across Kansas was hell. Now she was including the long road through Eastern Colorado like it was nothing. Just a lark.

"Okay. Goodbye, then."

Did Tosca like Tom? I couldn't remember.

Two days later, I had made my first trip to the collection of houses and land that was better known as the Diaz Compound than Roswell County. Dust rolled from my wheels. Dry land corn had long given up, curled its leaves inward and formed brittle lines down the betraying fields. The sky should have been bright blue, not a tannish haze.

Never having seen it, I had been amused at the term "compound" that made the Diazes sound like an orphaned Mafia family. Then after I looked up the vast acreage owned by one entity—with very little of it under cultivation—I understood some of the hostility.

All that land, lying fallow. It didn't seem right. A number of young men would kill to get a toehold into farming.

On the other hand, a lot of people hope no one new ever starts farming unbroken land. They think the farmers here now should leave and turn the land back over to the buffalo. A proposal by a Princeton public planning professor to turn the Great Plains into a nature preserve—a Buffalo

Commons—had earned the scorn of everyone I knew. Keith went ballistic when anyone brought this up. He didn't care that some areas had fewer than two people per square mile or that Kansas had lost one-third of its population since 1920. He didn't care that Kansas had over six thousand ghost towns. No crazy bureaucrat was going to shove him off land his ancestors had homesteaded.

At some point, the Diazes had become a family corporation. Using Victor's death as an excuse, I had checked the family's finances and learned they scrupulously paid their taxes and avoided credit card debt. There was very little money coming in. They lived scrimpy lives. No one ever bought anything or went anywhere.

The holdings were not easily accessible from the main road, and I had never driven out here. I turned off the main highway and started down the five-mile dirt road bordered by their property on either side. As I drew closer, I could see that most of the houses, barns, and outbuildings were a crazy mixture of stucco and limestone brick. Construction appeared to have been done sporadically as the need arose and was a curious blend of southwest architecture, dumpy sod-house shapes, and old wooden two-stories. There was even a modular home plopped down on an area apart from the rest.

Massive cottonwoods took my breath away.

I had never seen trees of that size in Kansas. Their silver-backed leaves rippled in the wind, like an undulating piece of cloth. Gusty sheets of greenery fluttered high overhead. Heaven plopped down in the middle of nowhere. One of the trees looked to be nearly one hundred feet tall with an enormous spread at the top.

To the back, I could see the old wreck of the house that had achieved the status of myth in our county. Representing classic 1700s New Orleans architecture with iron balconies, the ruined exterior, the weathered boards, the bare windows, did not look capable of having endured the extremes of our Kansas weather. The whole insane conglomeration of dwellings was shaded by the graceful cottonwood trees, defiantly shielding them from the brassy sun.

Against all odds, lush green grass grew in sections of carefully sectioned primly-edged lawns and a riot of colorful flowerbeds looked like they had been transplanted from a greenhouse. Any gardener would have said this display was impossible any year in Kansas, let alone this summer, when even buffalo grass was fighting for its life. There wasn't a water hose in sight, which I could not understand. Did they carry water in buckets?

Why would this family spend staggering work-hours maintaining lawns and gardens while ignoring thousands of acres ripe for growing wheat?

And living so frugally! Keith would argue that land was meant to be worked. He loved the image of Kansas as Breadbasket of the World. Food, not foolishness.

But it was all so incredibly lovely! A sudden gust sent the cottonwood leaves silver side up. Rippled mica sparkled across patches of blue. My soul quieted. Would all of this be sold and dismantled when Francesca died?

I swung around the circular drive that seemed to connect a number of the dwellings spoking out from its center. To the south was a lovely stucco-sided house with a tile roof. It had a roof-high tower with grilled windows that surrounded a front porch entrance. A swinging gate was built into an arched side entry that accessed a gracefully curved extension. Batten shutters decorated French windows. The house was not large, but perfectly proportioned.

In the middle of the ring of houses was a circular silo-like structure about twenty feet in diameter. I judged it to be about thirty-five to forty foot high. It resembled a modern grain bin, but was made of brick. It was covered by a conical shingled roof. There were very narrow rectangular windows spaced regularly around the top. Windows like those used in old castles to defend against attack.

I parked and stared at towering cottonwoods that seemed to be constantly in motion. Cecilia came out of the house to greet me. "You're prompt. Great-grandmother will like that. She knows you are here, so if you like, I can to show you around before we go inside."

I gazed hopefully at the old New Orleans style house at the back, then caught the flicker of dismay on her face, and switched my focus to another structure. "I was admiring that little house." I waved toward the little Spanish bungalow. "It's interesting."

"Isn't it?" She laughed gently, as though in agreement with my tactful choice of words. "In its time, it was one of the best Sears had to offer."

"That's a Sears house? I didn't know they made any with Spanish architecture."

"It cost two thousand dollars. My great-great-grandfather built it."

"Amazing!" From 1908 to 1940, well-to-do settlers could order these kit houses from Sears and complete the construction. The kits included everything from the meticulously pre-cut lumber down to the last coat of varnish. Over one hundred thousand of these ready-to-assemble houses were built. They were a godsend on the plains where lumber was scarce.

"A distant cousin, George Perez, lives there now with his family. They have four children."

I wanted to see the interior and hoped that as time went on and I became better acquainted, I

would be invited in. "Your lawns, lands, are unbe-
lievable. I can't even imagine the work it must take
to keep this up."

"We all help. Even so, it's a full-time job."

"The water. Where do you get that much
water?"

"Our well." She smiled at my blank look. "The
silo. I'm sure you noticed it when you drove in."

"Of course."

"The family calls it the well house. Let me show
it to you before we go on inside." She led me to the
opposite side of the structure and pushed through
a narrow door. "Our ancestors were small people."

"I guess." I'm slim, but I had to duck. A tall
man couldn't walk through standing upright. Once
I had pushed through, I gasped at the heavenly odor
of water. Life-giving water.

Inside the exterior circle was another circle,
another brick-walled structure over which rose
two upright notched wooden beams supporting a
large log laced with pulley systems. One of them
supported a large wooden bucket.

"You carry water to all these lawns, these plants?"

"Heavens, no. I'm not even sure we could do
that if we formed a full-time bucket brigade."

"How then? I didn't see a single garden hose.
Surely there isn't a sprinkling system."

"No. It's all done by underground pipes. A

network of pipes." She cut off more questions. "Perhaps we should join Great-grandmother."

We left the well house and walked to an iron gate in a high stucco wall and lifted the latch. Inside was a sprawling stucco ranch house that appeared to have so many wings that I suspected they surrounded a courtyard. More flowers again and lush lawns. She saw my look and laughed. "George, is an excellent gardener and my great-grandmother is a stern taskmaster. In fact, he could be a professional landscaper. Not that his talents aren't fully used out here. In the evening, his wife and children and I help him. He and I love this place so very much."

The swaying rustling cottonwoods, the lush yard, the splotches of bright flowers cast a spell. I wanted to lie beneath the largest tree and sleep.

Cecilia opened the massive exterior door and waved me past a foyer into a living room. I'm not an authority on antiques, but I knew enough to place several of the heavy walnut tables and chairs in the eighteenth century. Other pieces had a rough-hewn look with damaged tops. They looked to have been cobbled together by an inexperienced workman who simply wanted to provide places to sit. There were other chairs with rigid leather backs that surely were Spanish Colonial. Fabrics were sunny combinations of yellow and marigold.

Pushed against a wall was a leather sectional

that might have come straight from a discount furniture store. It had reclining levers on the side nearest me and faced a fifty-inch flat screen TV.

The interior of the house matched the curious period grouping of houses outside. Only the grounds showed unified order. Yet, the huge room was scrupulously tidy and the furniture grouped in such a way that there was a pleasing symmetry with each area a microcosm of different eras. Someone in this family had a surprising flair for design and was adept at integrating seemingly impossible elements. I suspected it was Cecilia.

Doña Francesca Diaz was perched on a high-backed chair. In front of her was a low table and an exquisite tea set—obviously top quality sterling—and plates of sandwiches and cookies.

"Mrs. Diaz, I'm in awe of your lovely grounds, your flowers. It's beautiful."

Francesca nodded. "It is one of my gifts." She waved toward the chair opposite. "Please join me."

I sat down.

"It has been a long time since someone has come to tea."

Chapter Thirteen

Weighty silver spoons matched the tea set. Cecilia poured. We nibbled on cookies and fell back on Kansans' favorite topic of conversation—the weather. Then Cecelia collected our cups and saucers and quickly whisked away the tray. She disappeared through swinging doors, but returned immediately.

"I am so sorry you are not here under happier circumstances than to discuss my great-grandson's murder. When I read excerpts of stories in your column, I wished I had written about my family. Not for your books, but so my descendants would know." Francesca glanced at Cecilia. "If I am ever blessed with descendants."

The young woman's lips trembled.

Francesca glanced at her hands. "When I still *could* write."

"But you could record your thoughts."

"I'm not good with technology," Cecilia said.

"And my cousin would be very uncomfortable asking great-grandmother questions."

"But there's someone here, surely. All these houses. Surely they are not empty."

"Yes, empty," Cecilia said.

"There used to be a lot of family here," Francesca said heavily. "Now there is only myself and Cecilia and George's family. He and Teresa have four children."

I was dumbfounded.

"There is nothing for anyone to do here." Cecilia said. "No way to make a living. George became a welder so he could stay."

Francesca glanced at her sharply.

All this acreage and none of it being broken for crops? This land would be incredibly fertile. Of course there wouldn't be a way to support a family on a farm that wasn't raising crops. Of course everyone would have to leave. So that's why the Diaz family had scattered across Kansas.

"Well, on to the reason for our visit here today." I moved quickly from this loaded topic. "You said you have information that might have some bearing on Victor's murder. I would be grateful to know anything you have to tell us."

"His death has everything to do with my family's history. My life. My work. It is not a simple thing."

"Would you like me to record some of this? Even though you are not from Carlton County, I would love to hear what you have to say."

In fact, if what she said had a direct bearing on Victor's death, I really should get it on tape.

The smart thing to do would be to send this statement, however long, back to Frank Dimon. But he had ordered me not to do the smart thing. In fact, he had ordered me not to ask this woman any questions at all about her great-grandson. Leave that to the "experts." The big boys. I was to proceed with collecting my "little stories."

So I would collect her little story.

I held up my hand to stop either of them from speaking and retrieved my cassette tape recorder from my briefcase. I use this older technology for formal interviews to accommodate visitors to our historical society who don't have access to digital methods. Needing formal permission, I showed it to Cecilia, then Doña Francesca. Following a rapid exchange of Spanish with her great-granddaughter, Francesca told me to proceed.

I pressed the record button and quickly stated my name and date, and that I was taping at the Diaz home with the consent of both Francesca and Cecilia Diaz. "Would you state your name please, Mrs. Diaz?"

She nodded and proudly said her name: "Doña Francesca Bianco Loisel Montoya."

"And Diaz," Cecilia prompted.

Francesca shrugged. "Diaz."

Cecilia smiled. "It is not Spanish custom to tack on the husband's surname. The proper way is still the lady's first two given names, then the father's surname, then the mother's surname."

"My great-granddaughter insists that I add Diaz."

"It's not important." I smiled as the *Little House on the Prairie* came to mind again. I doubt Laura Ingalls Wilder had a Spanish adobe in mind.

"Would you like to start with topics of special interest to you, or would you prefer a chronological approach?"

The old woman sized me up as though evaluating my integrity. Perhaps she sensed I would much rather interrogate her as an officer of the law than interview her as a historian.

"I would like to start at the beginning," she said slowly. "When my people first came here." Then she turned expectantly to Cecilia and they quickly exchanged words in Castilian.

"Great-grandmother would also like to talk about her gifts." Cecilia looked down at the hands, spread her fingers as though studying them, and directed her words toward her lap. "She believes you will understand how her gifts are commingled with the family's history when she tells her story."

It was eerie hearing Cecilia explaining this old woman's words and thoughts in the annoying third-person style she had used at the historical society. And Francesca, in turn, continued to interpret her great-granddaughter to me in the same detached manner.

Francesca peered at me intently while Cecelia went on.

"I need you to understand that I cannot listen to this. I do not want to hear any of it. We have not always been treated well. Our family. People used to come to Great-grandmother because she is a healer. Very well-known, in fact." She rose and kissed Francesca on the cheek. "I trust you will treat her well." She left the room.

Francesca sighed. "Cecilia's problem goes deeper than a refusal to master technology. She was truthful when she said she did not want to hear any of this. I have no one who will listen to me. Only Victor honored my memories."

She shuddered. It was almost a sob. There was something painful—very painful—between these two women.

"Cecilia has always belonged to the church. But she will never join a convent until I die, this dutiful, beautiful child. This lovely flower of God.

Caring for me is her offering, her sacrifice. When I die, she will become the Bride of Christ."

I said nothing, touched by this astute insight.

"By now, you've probably heard all the rumors."

"That you know some…alternative medicine methods. Yes, I've heard."

"What a delicate way of putting it. Yes, that's true. And I'm sure you've heard what they call me. Names. Very cruel names."

Ashamed of my fellow man, I could barely stand to look her in the eye. I nodded.

"Let us start at the beginning then," She repeated her name. This time I felt a little prickling—a dim memory—like the lost words of a song. Something I had read about, heard about.

"My family owned vast acreage. It was a gift. Through marriage, our land was joined with other holdings. Then we bought more land. Our fine home still stands behind all the others. I suppose you noticed it when you came in. My workroom is there. It is where I am the happiest. It is where I do my compounding. It is my joy."

"Your compounding. You have no family member who would like to learn these skills? No one you can teach?"

"No one."

Sad that this special woman could not pass

her knowledge along to a beloved apprentice, my mind raced. At least I could get her information down on paper. "We'll talk about your work later. For now, just tell me a little bit about your family before your father's time. When did they come to America?"

"We have always been here."

Disappointed, I realized I would have to do a lot of research to fill in the blanks. No one has "always been here." I had hoped she could supply accurate information about customs through talking about her family's tradition. I had heard she was over one hundred, but she was obviously far younger. I guessed she was in her early eighties. But just to be on the safe side, I used one hundred as a starting point. That would put her birth date at 1913. Possibly her father would be around thirty when he came here. That would be about right for acquiring homestead land.

I would find someone familiar with Spanish and check what Cecilia had told me about the order of Spanish names, then verify the names of Francesca's father and mother. Instead of going back to the family's arrival in Kansas perhaps I would have better luck with asking about her marriage and children.

"Your sons? Daughters? Where are Victor and Cecilia's parents? Have you other grandchildren?"

"They are all gone. Only Cecilia and George and his family are still on the land. Victor lived here. He grew up here. After he was married, that woman made him leave. That foolish, evil woman."

"I'm so sorry."

"My son died in Korea, and his wife died of a broken heart. My only daughter died accidentally. I doubt if most of my grandchildren and great-grandchildren have ever heard of me. So I have no one who wishes to learn. Cecilia won't listen to me. George is not intelligent enough to care about what I could give him. He simply tolerates me because he thinks that is the right thing to do. So."

"I'll listen." And I decided, just like that. My half-formed plan jelled. I would talk her into it.

"Mrs. Diaz."

"I would like you to call me Francesca."

I nodded my appreciation of this movement into a more personal relationship. "I would like you to think something over. Please tell me about your work. I want to get everything down on paper."

"You would not be the right person."

"I would respect your information. If you don't let me do this, your knowledge will die with you."

"You don't have time to be my apprentice."

"I know that. I would simply approach this from an objective standpoint. Much of what we know about Apache history is because a terrific historian, Eve Ball, talked the great war chief Victorio into telling her about his people. She argued that if he did not, his side of things would be written by military historians. It would be a lie. You will die surrounded by lies. Please don't let that happen."

"We could not prevent the lies."

I tried a different approach. This woman dying without passing along her wealth of information about healing would be a tragic loss. "Perhaps not. But if someone like me, who cares, doesn't get it down—no one will."

"No one," she said thoughtfully.

"I'm asking to record everything you know about plants and herbs and healing methods that are no longer used. It will be of incalculable value to botanists in addition to historians. From a medical standpoint alone, you might have information that is unique."

"I know far more about medicine than is known today."

She didn't sound haughty. Simply matter of fact.

"I will have to think about this." She smoothed the folds of her skirt. "You could not stand back and be merely objective. You would have to participate in certain rituals and ingest some herbs in order to fully understand their benefits."

"I would be very willing."

"Perhaps," her eyes softened, "but it would put your soul in danger."

I suppressed a smile. "I do not share Cecilia's religiosity. I would not be hampered by her prohibitions."

"Ah, but that's the point. Her beliefs would protect her. And your half-formed ones make you very vulnerable. Cecilia should be the one," she whispered. "But her soul belongs to another."

"I'll be just fine."

"Actually, you are quite religious, Lottie Albright. You are confusing religion and piety. As I said, I read the *Gateway Gazette*. Did you not spend a great deal of time and energy organizing Saint Helena? A church of your own denomination? Episcopal, I believe?

"Yes, but…"

"And did you not write a rather spirited and sophisticated defense of Father Talesbury's right to house little boys from Africa?"

"Yes, but…"

"You act. Cecelia prays. I'm simply warning you that you are innocent about the forces we will be tapping."

I looked at the floor. Rituals, I could handle, but strange herbs sounded a little dicey.

"Your problem is not religion. Your soul will

be released. Your problem is you don't want to lose control."

Unnerved, I looked away from her intense amused gaze. Josie said the same thing. Often.

"We have not discussed Victor's death, what did you want to tell me?"

She blinked at my abrupt change of subject. "He was going to file a lawsuit. On behalf of the family. Against the United States government. We have been cheated out of a great deal of land. That's the gist of all you really need to know."

"Are you talking about more land than is here in Roswell County?"

"Much more."

Cecilia entered the room. "Please, excuse me. I don't want Great-grandmother to get too tired."

Francesca Diaz looked fresh, unfazed. I was the one who needed a break.

"Certainly. I'll be going then." I rose. "Do think about letting me get your wonderful medical knowledge down on paper." I handed Francesca my card.

"I will take my rest," Francesca said. "Before Teresa brings the children over to see me."

"George's wife teaches school. Their children are in after-care until she finishes grading her papers." Cecilia explained.

Francesca said goodbye, then walked down a long corridor.

"I would love to show you the courtyard before you leave," Cecelia said. "Besides, there are other things you should know." She led me to a door, which opened onto a lovely rectangle of roses and day lilies. There were beautiful jewel-colored annuals: purple petunias, alyssum, and scarlet zinnias edged with white baby's breath. Stone benches faced a beautiful fountain in the middle of a gazing pool. We sat on the benches.

"About Victor. About my brother."

"We don't have to talk about this right now, Cecilia. I know this has been very difficult for you. To be honest, the KBI would prefer that I leave most of the work to them."

"I would rather tell you some things right now than some stranger in Topeka later."

I waited.

"He was the best of us all. A brilliant student. Great-grandmother had such hopes for him. He was going on to law school. Then he met that woman."

What was wrong with "that woman?" By all accounts, Maria Diaz was a wonderful person.

"Francesca was furious. Just furious. She wanted Victor to marry his own kind of people."

She caught the look on my face. "Of pure

Spanish lineage, not Mexican. That was one of the reasons."

I sat very still, not wanting to stop this curious flow of information. Spaniards didn't like Mexicans?

"Then Maria shattered Francesca's dream of this family producing a fine lawyer. Her dream that she would achieve justice in her own lifetime. Finally."

What kind of justice was she waiting for? What was motivating this old woman? "Francesca did mention that Victor was going to file a lawsuit."

"Ah, the infamous family lawsuit," she said bitterly. "Oh, to have the money this family has spent on that lawsuit. Our elusive hidden heritage."

She pinched a dead blossom off a rose bush. "The family has always lived here. Victor should have been right here with us. Not doing manual labor at a feedyard. He should have had the prestige that comes with being a lawyer. He should not have been working in heat and dust." Her tears dried by some internal heat. She could not keep the bitterness from her voice.

"We are all supposed to live here. We *must*—to be included in Great-grandmother's inheritance. But, that is not why I stay. I love it here. I love *her* so. But previous generations could not make her understand that if we did not farm this land they could not sustain a decent lifestyle. This should be a place of joy teeming with life and children.

A pretty yellow butterfly landed on one of the zinnias. It had been a long time since I had seen a butterfly in this part of Kansas which teemed with pesticides. They were safe here in this green Heaven.

"When Great-grandmother dies, I will devote my life to God. There is a convent in Atchison."

Francesca was right. This gentle woman would choose to continue a solitary life.

"Maria would only stay here for one year. She felt imprisoned. She and Great-grandmother didn't get along." She paused and looked ashamed. A look I knew all too well. The impulse to confide vying with guilt over talking about family matters. "Over the years, some of the family wanted to sell part of the land. We needed the money to keep from going into debt, and so we would be provided for."

"Did Victor want to sell some of the land?"

"Yes, at first. Enough to make us comfortable. Only a section. But Great-grandmother wouldn't budge. So Maria talked Victor into going back to school and getting a degree in mathematics with a minor in Ag Economics."

"So he had two degrees?"

"Yes, English and math. But no law degree. And then Maria wanted to buy that pitiful little house just to get away from here. Have you seen it?"

"Yes, I went there after Victor died."

"Can you imagine anyone wanting to live there instead of here? It broke Great-grandmother's heart."

I said nothing.

"So whenever Victor visited Great-grandmother, he was alone. Maria had the good sense to stay home."

I heard a car.

"George is coming home from work. In a couple of hours Teresa and the children will be here."

I rose. "It's time to call it a day anyway."

She hesitated. "Perhaps that is best. George is a welder and has a good job, so it's not that he can't stand to be around people. But he will regard you as an intruder. Thank God Great-grandmother has him. He would never ever part with a single acre of our property. But you need to know—he's very protective of Francesca. He won't appreciate your asking questions. In fact, he doesn't like strangers coming here at all."

I said goodbye and went out to my car. George had already parked and was coming to look me over. He brushed the brim of his hat, keeping things courteous. He was tired. Dirty. He wore grimy gloves. He gave me a hard look. "No need for us to shake hands. I don't think you would enjoy touching me anyway."

He looked like a man who just wanted to be left alone in his Eden after a hard day's work. Alone to revel in his green, green grass and his flowers. I understood.

"I'm Lottie Albright. I'm visiting Mrs. Diaz. Recording some of her memories."

"George Perez," he said, "and I know who you are."

His eyes were blue. I was expecting black. His hair was brown and curly. I was expecting coal. He was slim and had sideburns and wore a western shirt.

He stepped back, and I left.

There was no doubt in my mind that I had just met the man who had delivered the warning to Josie at the fair.

Chapter Fourteen

Dimon called the next morning and asked Sam and me to make "a quick trip to Topeka," so he could outline some work he had in mind for us. We were on a conference call and I knew from the silence on Sam's end that he expected me to come up with a civilized refusal.

There is no such thing as "quick trip" across Kansas.

"We can't, Frank. Keith is home working, and either Sam or I have to be on duty here. Sorry."

"I'm not comfortable discussing the murder of Victor Diaz over the phone."

Yeah, well, murder never was very comfortable. I let him break the prolonged silence.

"Can you meet me in Hays? I'll come to our branch office there where we'll have some privacy. I need to talk to both of you in person."

"Okay. I can do that. Margaret is off today, but I know a board member who won't mind coming in."

The branch office room was bare-bones simple, with a single desk for Frank to sit behind. A barrier between us. Smart man.

He put his legal pad on the table and closed the door. He didn't waste time with any small talk. "We want you to inspect all the employee records of the Carlton County Feedyard for the past three years and give us the names, dates, and social security numbers of everyone hired. Please jot down their native country. We also want copies of their W-4s."

"That's a bunch of bullshit," Sam said. "That's a clear violation of privacy laws."

"There's no need to do this, Frank. I got you the duty roster and you shouldn't need anything beyond that."

"You're barking up the wrong tree, anyway," Sam added.

"I saw Francesca Diaz yesterday and she mentioned…"

"I specifically asked you *not* to question that family." Dimon's ear's reddened. "You *know* that."

"But…"

"No buts about it. We are not going off on some wild goose chase. The fastest and most efficient way to solve this case is to look for patterns at that feedyard and then deviations from that pattern. We have trained mathematicians who can do this."

"Looking through employment records isn't legal, Frank. Not without a subpoena for specific records."

"In these troubled times it's necessary to wink at the means and stay focused on the end."

Pius as a frontier preacher, he spoke in sound bites that he might have memorized from a government memo.

"Ah, the post-9/11 card. Homeland security and all that." Sam couldn't quash his hostile tone. Worse, I knew he didn't want to.

"Looking through those records isn't illegal if Dwayne gives you permission to look through them."

"Not true," Sam said. "He can only give permission to look through records that don't involve his employees."

"Sam's right. Plus, Weston's ethics are top notch and he's nobody's fool. Do you honestly believe he would let us scrutinize every last detail about the people who work for him? People who trust him? What reason could we possibly give him?" Did this idiot think I was going to spy on a friend?

"We think he would do it in a heartbeat if it would ward off an OSHA inspection."

Occupational and Safety Health Administration. An inspection by this agency of the Department of Labor was often triggered by complaints from employees. Even companies with pristine practices quavered at the thought. "Dwayne has nothing to hide."

"Exactly. But it will worry him anyway. Tell him you can go to OSHA on your own and persuade them there is no need to waste time and personnel looking into allegations from one disgruntled employee."

"He'll want to know who it was."

"No he won't. He won't even ask. Trust me, he will come up with the name of a disgruntled employee at once. In fact, his own mind will supply a half dozen."

"He'll insist on the name."

"Not if you tell him that going after whistle-blowers is against the law."

"And you honestly believe these records will lead you to Victor Diaz's murderer?"

He cleared his throat. "Perhaps."

"Perhaps isn't good enough."

"We need to approach this in a scientific manner. As to the inspection. I can make it happen, Lottie. I can see to it that OSHA descends on that feedyard like a swarm of locusts. And they will find something. I can make that happen, too."

I touched my fingers to the hollow of my throat to cover the quick leap of my furious heart.

Then he looked down at his hands splayed on the desk as though he were ashamed and would not make eye contact. Where were his orders coming from? Who was pulling his strings?

It didn't matter why this man was being pressured. I wasn't going to go there with him. "I'll do this one thing, Frank, because I don't want Dwayne dragged through an OSHA inspection."

He said nothing. Just cleared his throat.

"I won't do it," Sam said "I'm going out to the car. I want no part of this."

I waited until I was sure he was outside before I let Dimon have it.

"Let's get something straight. Don't think I'm going to sit still and let you diss Sam. And I'm a historian, remember? I don't need this job. After we find this killer, I'm going to find that ivory tower everyone seems to think historians occupy. And then I'm going to quit law enforcement, including being an undersheriff. I hope to hell I never have to talk to you again."

I slammed out of the office. The man was making me into a liar, a half-liar, a sneak, a betrayer of friends, and the kind of person I despised. When I told Keith about this he would raise seven kinds of hell. And of course Josie would blow sky-high too. She guarded her patients' records like they were Holy Writ.

Keith drove in about an hour after I reached the house. He had spent the day at a farm committee meeting. His two border collies bounded out to meet him and I was close on their heels. He reached down and hugged me close. "No place like home," he said and I knew he meant it.

Arm in arm, we walked into the kitchen and I gave him one of his home brews, then flew around to panfry a steak and microwave a potato. I figured he wouldn't stay awake long, and I needed to get some food down him. He looked exhausted, despite his insistence that he was doing just fine.

He ate in silence, accepted a piece of cherry pie, then asked me to sit down. "I need to talk to you about something."

"Now? Can't it wait until morning? You don't look like you can stay awake another minute."

"No, tonight. Let's talk tonight. I've thought about this for the last couple of days and we keep putting it off."

Alarmed by his serious tone, I pulled out a chair.

"Dimon's right, Lottie. We are both being run ragged. So is Sam."

Please don't make me think about that problem right now. I stared at the dregs in my coffee cup, then at the deepening lines in my husband's face. I shuddered. I'm a fixer. Josie says so. Finding Victor's killer wouldn't be the end of it. I wouldn't be able to quit law enforcement until I fixed everything.

"Well, do you think we should deputize more men? Or women? Women, too. We need more women."

"That's a Band-Aid. Dimon was right. We need a district law enforcement organization and every county needs to cooperate with the funding. Vote a mill levy to build a central jail and bring in new equipment and technology. Hell, right now we have to call in the KBI for practically everything."

Obviously it wasn't the right time to tell him I intended to resign. Stricken, I knew I would never do it and leave him and Sam in a mess. I would soldier on until I'd fixed everything. Until we found competent people. Then I would turn in my badge.

But a regional center wasn't the answer. "Keith, it won't fly. I can't think of any county that will give up having its own law enforcement."

"They have to. What we have now isn't working out here."

My mind raced. I didn't want to argue with him when we were both on edge.

He gave me a quick look, then smiled. "You're

going to be the ideal sounding board, honey. You can probably think of every single objection people will raise, and we can work out answers in advance."

"Well, I can think of one great big huge one right now. Someone is bound to point out that it's our county that is having all the trouble. Their own county isn't going to need some fancy fix and a bunch of foreigners poking around in their business."

"I've asked Tom to hang around here for a while. Designing systems is his specialty and I want a complete plan all drawn up with every detail worked out in advance before I approach other counties. Which I plan to do one by one."

"Sam will never go along with this."

"Yes, he will. He's being worn down, too. How's this job affecting your work at the historical society?"

"It's been disastrous. No point in kidding myself. I can't follow up on everything like I used to. I keep running from one job to the next, and I'm way behind on collecting oral histories. I haven't found the time to call a Bohemian woman who came in with some great artifacts. She's trying to work up nerve to talk to me about something, but I won't have time to listen when she does. No time for in-depth research. Unless it has something to do with my duties as an undersheriff."

"Did you learn anything useful on your visit to the compound?"

"Nothing about Victor, except that Maria Diaz was right about Francesca Diaz hating her guts because Victor just worked at the feedyard instead of becoming a lawyer. That was very obvious. She's a descendant of a proud old Spanish family and looks down on Mexicans."

"That won't do our investigation any good. Dimon is looking for information about Mexicans in this region."

"I know. Victor was born here, just as Maria said. And lived in Roswell County all his life until he went to college, and then got married. That little house here in Carlton County is the first he's ever owned."

Keith pushed back from the table and stood. "I need to get to bed while I can still manage to climb the stairs."

"Sit back down. I have something else to tell you."

I dealt it down and dirty: I would be going through private records.

"And you agreed to this?" Wide-awake now he just stared at me. "Goddamn that man for putting you in this situation."

"There's not many good choices here. Sam won't. And God knows you won't either. So I have to. I'm choosing the lesser of two evils to prevent a lot of damage to a good friend." I bit my lip and turned away. "Go to bed. Now. While you still have the energy to crawl under a sheet."

I quickly scraped the plates and carried them to the dishwasher. When everything was tidy, I turned out the lights and slowly headed upstairs.

Keith had left the bathroom light on. I changed into an airy cotton sleep shirt and started brushing my teeth. He stirred.

"Did I wake you up?"

"I'm not asleep. Lottie, Dimon is right about one thing. I hate to give the son-of-a-bitch credit. But he is. If we don't come up with a system on our own, some crazy politician is going to do it for us. Won't that be a deal now?"

I finished in the bathroom, then climbed into the bed beside him. "Why can't we just get by with part-time deputies and reserve deputies?"

"That's what we're doing now. If things keep happening in this county we'll soon be a permanent feature on CNN."

I moved closer and snuggled against his broad back.

"You're trying to change the subject," he growled, turning toward me.

"Yes."

Chapter Fifteen

When I drove to the historical society the next morning, the cornfields on either side of the road didn't look like they would provide enough grain for a Third World-family of three. Everyone believes the Earth can't blow again out here, but Keith says it can and will if we keep on depleting the Ogallala aquifer. Our farm has only one irrigation well and it was drilled when the Fiene family thought the water supply was endless. Corn was a poor choice for dry land, and irrigated crops weren't doing much better. Wheat was much heartier and made more sense. But not this year.

Usually I can take a more objective approach to the land, the crops, the ungodly heat, but this morning I dreaded the day like an old Depression-era wife forced to cope with stifling heat and seven kids in a three-room shack.

Taking my scattered brain firmly in hand, I bludgeoned it into submission and willed myself to straighten up.

Margaret was there when I arrived. Annoyed, I check my watch. Damn, damn, damn. I liked to be there first and get settled in. All coffeed up.

Faking good cheer, I complimented her on the quality of her newly rinsed red hair. I wasn't in the mood to rack my brain for something else more accurate to say.

She beat me to it. "Thank God you're here."

"What?" My heart sank. What could possibly be going wrong this early in the morning?

"I got two phone calls from a George Perez asking for you. He says you plumb wore out Francesca Diaz with your visit. Talking about Victor's death upset her. It was after midnight before they could get her settled down. I don't understand Spanish, but I know when I've been cussed out. Crazy Mexicans. They're all alike."

"Margaret," I snapped. "That's enough. I don't ever want to hear you refer to Mexicans as 'crazy' ever again."

Besides, the Diaz family was extremely proud of their pure Spanish lineage and they didn't like Mexicans much either. They had made that clear. I groped for the correct way to relay nuances of intra-ethnic prejudices, but it was too late.

Her lips quivered. She drew her skinny body as tall as she possibly could. "You won't have to worry about hearing anything from me again. Not that you ever listen anyway. I know when I'm not wanted or appreciated. You can just do without my help, Lottie."

She left, slamming the door behind her.

I gasped. She always had to be handled with kid gloves, but this morning I hadn't taken the time. I fumed. *Now what?* The news would soon spread like wildfire that I was on some sort of rampage. That I was too uppity to work with anyone normal. That I was a power-hungry bitch.

A formal letter of apology to Margaret, the kind that took hours to compose would probably do the most good, but I simply could not, would not.

First things first. I reached for the phone and switched on the speaker, then decided to record the call. Just in case.

The woman who answered the phone was not Cecilia.

"This is Lottie Albright. Margaret said George called here at the historical society this morning. He was asking for me."

"Yes, I'm his wife. Teresa. He wanted you to know he did not appreciate your upsetting Francesca."

"That was not my intention. Believe me, I am so terribly, terribly sorry. I'll write her a formal apology and if there's any other thing that might help, I'll be glad to do it."

"If you have any brains at all, and I don't think you do, although I understand you have a doctorate in history, I suggest you leave our family alone."

My eyes stung with tears, then didn't, because the tears trickled down my cheeks. "She'll get the apology anyway," I whispered. "Really, I would like to convey to your family how…"

She slammed down the phone. I stared blankly at the dead receiver I held in my hand. Way to go. Not even ten o'clock and I'd managed to tick off everyone I'd come in contact with. I went downstairs to use the bathroom and rinsed off my face, then went to the main floor and pushed through the heavy glass doors.

The buffalo grass courtyard was bone dry. I stepped off the sidewalk a little ways and pushed at a tuft with my toe. Little poofs of dust turned my loafer a dull gray. Gateway City had moved to a water-rationing plan, but it wasn't enough to keep lawns and gardens alive. Farmers were shipping cattle they didn't want to sell because they had to haul water. The drought was doing everyone in.

I went back inside, trudged back upstairs and wistfully eyed a set of stencils. When I was beset with troubles, routine donkey work settled me down, but I was so behind with my real work, that I didn't dare.

I picked up a stack of stories and settled down

to editing. At noon, the thought of food was a blessed relief, even if I wasn't ready to face the questions of the lunch crowd at Maybelline's. I wished we had a drive-in where I could read while I ate and enjoy a little privacy in my air-conditioned car.

But peace was out of the question. Just as I was turning the lock, Jane Jordan trudged up the steps. Groaning inwardly, but determined not to blow an encounter with another human like I had the other two today, I smiled and stepped forward to greet her.

"Hi," she said. "I hope I'm not here at a bad time."

I swallowed. "I'm just unlocking. I took an early lunch." Surely if I didn't go to hell for my whoppers, this teensy little lie wouldn't send me plunging. "Come right on in."

"I can't stay. I have a really short lunch hour. Since they cut my days back to four, we work more hours while we're there. But I wanted to give you our family's story. Since I'm now an official volunteer here, I thought we should make a special effort to contribute. We sort of all wrote it together. And I wanted to give you this, too."

"An official volunteer! That's wonderful." It also sounded just like Margaret's sense of puff-uppery.

"Oh, yes. Some of us have special status with

designated assignments instead of bouncing from task to task."

"And yours is?"

"I return artifacts to members of the community who hoped their…their things might find a place here. Margaret says it's very important to get this done quickly and tactfully before the donor thinks their contribution has been accepted."

The lowest job on the totem pole and I'll bet Margaret didn't even blush when she gave it to Jane.

I turned away to hide my smile.

She followed me inside and handed me the papers, along with a rolled-up poster. I unrolled it and stared at the printing. It was an early recruiting poster for the Ku Klux Klan.

"Thank you so very much," I said carefully. Then added, "This has a great deal of historical significance."

"We were never, never members. No one in our family ever was. But my grandfather, I remember, did not like Catholics."

"You don't have to explain." In fact, this poster was perfectly preserved and came from a time when a lot of the country was violently anti-Catholic. A time when Protestant Americans were convinced that Catholics were slaves to the Pope with arms hidden in their basements and at a signal would rise up and take over the country.

"According to Grandpa, we were accused of things we didn't do." She lowered her eyes and nervously twisted her hands on the handle of her purse. "My grandfather said that poster had been rolled up and stuck in our mailbox. It wasn't his. He may have despised Catholics, but he was not a member of the Klan. He wanted me to throw it away, but I didn't."

There was more to Jane Jordan's story. I could sense it. Much more would come out on another day. She was working up to it.

"We would never ever stop someone from following their own religious beliefs. Freedom to believe—or not—was why the family came to America in the first place."

"Thank you. It's generous of you to bring this in. I'll start on your stories right away."

"I want it out of our house. I don't want my grandfather to know I kept it. But I couldn't bring myself to throw a historical document away."

She checked her watch, then gave me a paper sack. "These are samples of our favorite foods. I see you have a microwave, but kolaches can be hot or cold."

Leave, leave, leave. Salvation. Food. Now I didn't have to risk meeting people I knew at the café.

"I'll run on." She turned at the doorway. "Are you all right? You look a little peaked."

"I'm fine. Just fine. It's been a long week, that's all."

She waved goodbye and I gratefully headed to the microwave. The aroma was heavenly.

Just fine! I was sleep-deprived, starving, and guilt-ridden over having to coerce a friend into showing me his employee records.

I carried the plate to my desk and ate while I read her story. As I had suspected, this family was part of the Czech Free Thinkers movement. They had left Europe to escape the tyranny of the Catholic Church and fled to America where they were free to believe or not to believe. My own great-great-grandfather had been a Skocal, part of a fraternity of elite athletes dedicated to building a sound mind in a sound body.

Jane wrote about the family's great pride in the men's ability to master complicated gymnastics. Proud of becoming Americans, there was no attempt to resist assimilation. The family obeyed the laws and became exemplary citizens. With this came fierce vigilant opposition to any group that tried to control their minds. Their God was reason.

When I'm overly tired, I'm overwhelmed by a sentimental attachment to America's past. And today was one of those times. Tearfully appreciative of the richness of our country's heritage, I envisioned a vast tapestry woven with the many threads of our various ethnic groups.

Hurrying to my notepad, I started jotting down concrete ideas for this sudden vision that had come out of nowhere. Could it be done on a countywide basis? Was it a good idea? Could various groups design a needlework project that would encompass the whole? Probably not. They wouldn't agree on a master designer. Yet it was a fresh idea and lately I'd been worried that I would never again have an original idea. But there would be problems, organizing such a large needlework project.

Not now. I turned off my cell phone then reached for the romance novel one of the volunteers had left behind.

It took my mind off murder and mayhem for perhaps seven minutes.

Chapter Sixteen

Early the next morning, I started on the trip to the feedyard determined to concentrate on the work ahead. I would go through the employee records as quickly as possible, dump the data on Frank Dimon, and then concentrate on finding my replacement as undersheriff.

As I drove, my mind strayed from the pending search to the lethal temperatures across the country. Every TV station reported heat-related deaths on their nightly news broadcast. Norton, a town near us, shattered records with a temperature of one hundred eighteen.

We had gone two winters now without snow. Spring was like July and now there were Death Valley conditions. The patchwork of limp corn-stalks would topple in the first high wind. The shatter-prone leaves rolled inward like ruined parchment scrolls.

The whole country would soon understand

why the price of this commodity mattered. Corn fueled the entire fast-food industry. Everything from hamburgers to soda pop to doughnuts contained corn or corn syrup. Buns, bread, even French fries, tires, and crayons contained corn. Food prices would soon soar. Buyers of Ethanol-powered vehicles were screwed because their fuel prices depended on the production of corn. This year's crop was supposed to be the largest in the nation's history.

God had other plans.

Keith was irritable and morose. He was considering selling his herd of cattle, but everyone else was doing it too, so the prices were down. Even if there had been pasture grass, livestock lacked the energy to eat it.

I was jittery over my husband's uncertainty. He didn't know what to do. Always superbly confident, he didn't know what to do with the land. All the other farmers in Carlton County felt the same way. They were afraid plowing under the failed wheat crop would risk creating dust bowl conditions. Not doing so would cause erosion if it rained. On the other hand, if they did plow, and the rains didn't come, topsoil might end up on the East Coast.

"It can blow here again," Keith had said this morning. "People think it can't, but it can."

Dwayne knew I was coming and that I wanted to talk to him, but he didn't know why. I breezed in as if it were an ordinary visit and waited until he got off the phone.

"Please tell me you're bringing me good news. Closing your investigation, for instance, because you've found Victor's murderer."

"No, starting another investigation, actually. Keeping one from happening might be a better explanation."

He ran his hand through his bright silver hair. A lock fell across his forehead. He waited.

"I'm here to keep OSHA away from this feedyard." My stomach soured. I tried to play like it was a good deed. Dimon *would* make good on this threat.

He did not speak and shot me a hard cold look and examined his clenched hands.

"I won't take long."

"Who? Who would turn me in? And why? What have I done wrong?"

He rose and walked to the large window facing the pens. He turned back. "Nevermind. I've got a pretty good idea who the bastard is. And I'll see to it that he never works for anyone ever again."

It was just as Dimon had predicted, Dwayne's mind had supplied a name.

"Don't do that. Please." Sickened at the thought of causing someone to lose his job, I told him that his suspicions were probably all wrong and even if he were right, he would be in even more trouble by coming down on a whistle-blower.

"That's why I'm doing it on the quiet. We have to check it out, but the KBI doesn't want to draw any more attention to this feedyard right now. I'll give OSHA the information they need, and then get out of your hair."

The lines deepened on his craggy face as if he were maxed out on misery.

"Trust me, Dwayne. I'll be out of here in a heartbeat."

I hadn't planned on dealing with Bart. When he came in and Dwayne told him what I wanted, Bart exploded.

"You want to see all the employee records? Without a subpoena?" He looked at Dwayne. "That's illegal. How many years have I worked here and you have never asked to me to do anything that's against the law. Not once. That's how many."

Then he turned on me. "Do you think we are all fools out here?" His voice shook. I had never known this man to lose his temper. "Do you know how many hours I spend checking people out, seeing to it that we're okay with state and national compliance requirements? I'm half nuts most of the time trying to make sense of rules that are in violation of some other agency's rules." He gestured toward the rows of manuals on a bookshelf. "Want to know how many hours a day it takes to keep on top of this place?"

"Bart, I know you're under a lot of stress right now. We all are. But you're not giving me a chance to explain," I said. "Tell him, Dwayne."

"I don't want to hear any explanations." Bart laced his fingers together and cracked his knuckles. To keep them from curling into fists, I suspected. "You want to know about the one law we do violate? And that one fairly frequently? The one governing the number of hours a driver can be behind the wheel on any given day. What do they expect us to do when we're out of hours due to construction? Pull over to a rest stop and let cattle boil alive in aluminum trailers because some ignorant bastard in Washington has decided we should stop our day right on the dot?"

"Bart..." Dwayne grappled for words. I couldn't think of anything to say either. We were locked in a motionless tableau like we had been playing the child's game of statues. I hardly trusted myself to breathe.

"I can't police this office and the feedyard too,

goddamn it. I can't be here all day and all night. Someone should have been here the night Victor got killed."

"You're too hard on yourself, Bart."

"I'm through, Dwayne. Done here." He headed toward the door.

"Come back, Bart. I can't make it through a single day without you. Get back in here and hear me out."

Bart turned, and with arms crossed, stared at Dwayne.

"Lottie is trying to forestall an OSHA investigation. We figured the fewer who know about this, the better. Think about what you just said. Some of our drivers put in too many hours. You know that. I know that. Hell, we're no different than any other livestock carrier. If we didn't, we'd be in the dead animal transport business."

For once, Bart Hummel's hands did shake. I knew I had misjudged the man. His cool façade could only be maintained if he had total control over systems he created. And he was straight as a string.

"Knew it, knew it, goddamn it. Knew letting those last couple of men hire on would get me in trouble. There was something about them. All their paperwork checked. Valid commercial driver's licenses. No criminal records. But Hugh

Simpson recommended them and they had some distant connection with Maria. Second cousins or something. She was doing a favor for some aunt. But since Hugh is the head cowboy…when he wants someone signed on, I try to make it work."

"Was either of them a Diaz?"

"No. American names, in fact."

"Are they still here?"

"No, I ran them off. I didn't like their attitude."

"Lazy?"

"No. But I put them on the maintenance crew and they were madder than hell. They wanted to be on the cowboy crew. A lot of men wanting to work here want to be cowboys. Even if they don't know one end of a horse from another." He looked at Dwayne. "I would bet my hat those two bastards turned us in for discrimination or something."

"An OSHA inspection would not be due to any neglect on your part." It would come through malicious harassment by the KBI. I hoped my bitterness didn't show on my face.

"Go home, Bart."

The two men looked stunned.

"I mean it. Dwayne, give Bart a day or two off. So he won't be involved. Not at all. In case he ever has to testify under oath."

Neither of them spoke.

"I imagine you know where all your own records are."

Dwayne gave a weak smile and nodded.

"Bart, you're right. What I'm doing isn't right, despite my good intentions. Just go home. Don't come back until the day after tomorrow." I glanced at his work station. "Do you have remote access to this place at your house?"

"Yes."

"Good, I don't want Dwayne to get too far behind."

He picked up his Stetson and gathered some papers from his desk. Even though he hadn't said another word, I knew the crisis had passed.

"And Bart," I called softly. He stopped, but wouldn't turn to face me. "You're a good man."

He was. And if anyone hassled him for any reason, including Dimon, I would see to it that there was hell to pay.

Dwayne and I walked down the hall. He unlocked the file cabinet where they kept all the personnel records. I went to the break room and put my sack lunch in the refrigerator. Then I set to work. I opened my laptop and created a preliminary spreadsheet. The feedyard had all the data on a spreadsheet too, but Dimon had asked for copies of the original W-4s signed personally by each individual applicant.

About twelve-thirty, I took a break and stepped outside. Heat rose in visible waves. The wind was picking up, bringing the odor of ammonia from the massive herds. Feed trucks made their rounds, with contents calculated for each pen. They were equipped with GPS systems controlled by the mainframe computer inside the office which made sure special blends weren't distributed to the wrong pen.

Hugh Simpson rode up and dismounted, then tied his horse to a traditional hitching post that I had wrongly assumed was just for show. Not bothering to tip his hat, he pulled down the bandanna covering his mouth and rushed inside. Minutes later, he and Dwayne came out. Hugh unhitched his horse, mounted and set off. Dwayne headed for a four-wheeler.

"We've got an emergency," he yelled at me over his shoulder. "You can come along if you're up to riding in this heat."

"Okay." I rushed over and jumped in beside him. "What's going on?"

"Cattle too hot in pen forty-eight. They get heatstroke just like people."

"What can you do for them?

"Cool them off, just like you would with a human."

We flew down the lanes between the pens, but

Hugh and four other cowboys were already there placing garden sprinklers in the pen to cool off the stressed cattle.

We hung over the fence and watched.

"This is why I use cowboys and horses. Mounted, the men can see down into the pens. There's usually about eight working full time, riding the pens, checking for sick cattle or critters that are down."

I gazed at the cattle in the pen across from pen forty-eight. Disturbed by the commotion, some of them came up to the fence. They looked fine, taking the heat in stride, but I doubted any of them would look this alert parked in a broiling aluminum trailer forced to stop moving by an overzealous highway patrolman.

Satisfied by the cowboys' progress, Dwayne drove back to the office. "The full western attire is kind of their own touch," he said. "But there's a sound reason for each and every item."

"I figured out that the bandannas are essential face masks."

"Right, and the heavy jeans and chaps protect them when cattle force horses against a fence post."

"As to the boots. Can't imagine sandals would be a sound choice." I smiled at the image of someone trying to work around cow shit wearing flip-flops.

"Nope. They need boots with a decent heel to keep from slipping out of stirrups when they are bending sideways on a horse."

Black sunspots and floaters swarmed before my eyes. Relieved when we drew up to the door, I headed to the bathroom. I splashed cold water on my face. The ride hadn't lasted more than twenty minutes, but I had lacked the guts to tell Dwayne I wasn't sure I could bear it much longer. My face and neck were turkey red. Swept by nausea, I braced my arms on the sink.

Moving carefully, I went to the kitchen and took a bottle of water and extra ice from the refrigerator and returned to the bathroom. I dug some Advil out of my purse and swallowed it to squelch my headache, knowing it certainly wouldn't help my nausea. I wrapped the ice in hand towels and placed a pack on my head. I draped another ice pack across my neck and shoulders, sat on the stool lid, and started sipping water.

If I called 911, I was the one who should be answering the phone.

When I had cooled down and could compose myself, I worked quickly, copying W-4 forms, and matched social security numbers with spreadsheets. My anger toward Dimon built throughout the afternoon. He was interfering with people he knew nothing about.

There were too many records to fax. I would need to deliver it in person. If I finished by noon tomorrow I could get to Topeka before he left the office. *No*, I decided. When he wanted to go home had nothing to do with it. We would have it out if I had to go to his house and break down his god-damned door.

About five-thirty, Dwayne stood in the doorway and watched me work. He glanced at his watch.

"About ready to call it a day?"

"If you'll trust me to lock up, I'll stay for a couple of more hours."

"I don't want you here alone. You stay, I stay."

Whether because he was concerned about my safety or worried about my rummaging around, I couldn't say.

"Okay." I started gathering my things. He had put in a hell of a day and I wasn't going to delay his getting home.

Something in his face told me he really, really didn't want me in the office by myself.

Chapter Seventeen

Keith was in the music room playing an old Eagles song, "Lying Eyes." Puzzled, I went to the doorway and watched quietly for a moment before I turned to start supper. Josie and I were amused by his unconscious selection of songs that signaled his inner state. A couple of nights ago, he had strummed out the old Jimmie Rogers tune, "Hard Time Blues," followed by a plaintive rendition of "Cool Water."

> "All day I've faced a barren waste
> Without the taste of water, cool water…"

He was strangely silent during supper. Worried, I supposed, like everyone else I met on the street. Worried over losing a corn crop, losing his herd, losing his topsoil.

I cleared the table, then went upstairs and showered, climbed into bed and stared at the ceiling. Later, Keith came to bed too, but he didn't immediately fall into his usual untroubled sleep. He gathered some pillows and propped himself up on the headboard.

"Missed you at the feedyard today," he said finally.

"What?" I jolted straight up and turned on my bedside light. The skin around his mouth was white, his lips a dull red, his voice husky.

"What?" My cheeks flamed. Blood throbbed in my ears.

"I said I missed you at the feedyard."

"I was there all day. All day. When were you there?"

"During the time I thought you might be eating lunch."

"I was with Dwayne."

"Hell, I know that. I missed him too. Your Tahoe was there, and his pickup, but he wasn't in his office. The place was as quiet as a tomb. Even Bart wasn't there. I didn't think it would be a good idea to go snooping around the back rooms."

"We were looking at some cattle that had gotten too hot. We used a four-wheeler. You had to have just missed us. Why were you there?"

"My conscience was bothering me. I felt like a real asshole for letting you do the dirty work. Just because Sam and I couldn't bring ourselves to do it. I know you did the right thing. It took me a while to face up to it. You made the right choice, Lottie. I should have been right there by your side."

"Compromise comes easier for me. So I'm the one to do it. But it's a comfort being married to a black-and-white man. I always know where I stand."

Traffic was light on I-70. I had finished my work by noon and arrived at the KBI office before closing. I went through the usual security check, busted into Dimon's office and slammed the door shut. I slapped the information down on his desk.

"Sit down, Lottie, and I'll get you some coffee."

"I don't want your goddamned coffee and I'm going to stand for what I've got to say. You're the one who had better be sitting down."

He said nothing and his face reverted to a trained expressionless mask. Drawing from a page in the KBI handbook, no doubt.

"Scratch me off the list as your go-to person. If you need anything else done, send your agents out."

He still did not speak. Just stared at his aligned pencils.

"I still control your access to information in Northwest Kansas," I reminded him.

He gave me an appraising look, like he was still wrestling with some decision.

"All right." With a reluctant sigh, he placed his hands on the desk. "There is a lot at stake with this new regional system. A lot of money. A lot of jobs involved. I need to close this case fast. By whatever means it takes."

"There's a lot at stake for men living in the counties you want to squash."

"It's going to happen, Lottie. There's no way some old geezer like Sam Abbott has the expertise to find out who killed Victor Diaz. Keith is running back and forth between the sheriff's office and his farm. So that leaves you. A part-time undersheriff and part-time historian. Not a very impressive group of law officers is it? And I suspect you'll cave. What's the good of having a PhD you can't use? You're not going to last much longer."

The bastard! He wanted me to resign.

"So how are you doing, Frank? Made any real progress yet?"

"We will as soon as our mathematician analyzes all the employment records."

"Have you come up with a possible motive?"

"Well, I suppose it's money. It always is. Or in the case of your part of the state, land. Which is the same as money."

"Oh yeah? And why would anyone want it? You know yourself that farming is a crap shoot.

Even the best farmers can't make a go of it some years."

"Some corporation won't look at it that way. Or maybe some foreign investor."

"Frank, I've been trying to tell you. This murder was a personal issue. You won't listen to word I've said about Francesca Diaz's information."

"Oh, that again. Well, our teams thinks the murder might have been a professional hit. And we are looking at some land connection."

"There is a land connection. That's what Francesca told me." I didn't bother to keep the frustration out of my voice. "And as to foreigners trying to acquire land in Kansas, I think you need to do a little homework. It's illegal for them to buy land in this state. Kansas laws are really strict about that."

Dimon flared. "What about all the *family corporations?*" He wiggled his fingers to indicate quotes around the "family corporations."

"The stockholders have got to be blood relation, and one of them must actually live on the land, or work it, or play a major role in the management. There's nine states in the heartland with those kinds of laws."

He wasn't the kind of man to appreciate a lecture. I decided to push a few more buttons. "These laws are in place to protect the nation's food supply from falling into foreign hands, but even if the laws weren't there and corporations had free rein, most years there's no real money to be made off of such a tricky investment. People who farm do it because they love it."

He studied his nails and rose from his chair. A gesture of dismissal. Most of the employees were leaving for the day.

I glanced at my watch. "Well, you have the information you wanted. Good luck."

"Thank you," he said stiffly. "It's been a pleasure working with you. As I'm sure you know, we'll be handling it on this end from now on."

My smile was as stiff as a corpse's as I walked out the door. I had come to bring all the damned copies of employee records and I had come to turn in my badge. Now they would have to carry me out of the sheriff's office feet-first.

The only productive thing to come from the meeting is that he had formally run me off. I was free to investigate on my own.

The race was on. The KBI versus Sam Abbott and local systems. County versus state.

Marvin Cole was holding down the fort at the sheriff's office. Keith had left the house long before I got up.

Determined to settle in to a day of challenging work, I eyed the stories stacked on my desk and picked up the one from Jane Jordan's family.

The phone rang. Cecilia Diaz was on the line. "Great-grandmother is very upset."

"I know that and I'm sorry. I intend to write a formal apology for bringing up Victor's death."

"No, she's upset that Teresa scolded you. She would like you to become her apprentice."

"That's wonderful." I gave my chair a gleeful half-whirl. "At her convenience. And yours, too, of course."

"No she wants to go to the Old House and I refuse. I refuse to go there for the reasons I gave you. The other members of the family refuse because they don't believe in anything. They pay proper respect to her age and appreciate her wisdom, but they basically believe her religion is a bunch of nonsense."

"And you don't?"

"Let's just say I go by the first commandment. Why would we be commanded not to put other gods before our own if other gods aren't there?"

I couldn't think of an answer. In fact, during the baptismal ritual my own church included a call for the members to renounce Satan and all the spiritual forces of wickedness.

"I don't want to know what she does," Cecilia repeated flatly.

"Do you believe Francesca can give me information pertaining to Victor's death?"

"No. How could she? She's an old woman who never leaves the place. In fact, the trip to see you at the historical society is the first time she has left this place in fifteen years."

"Even if she doesn't, this is a wonderful opportunity to learn about herbs and medicinal plants."

"Oh, she wants you to know much more than that. Much, much more."

Chapter Eighteen

My skin was so dry I might as well have been standing in the broiling sun checking for rain clouds every day. Gateway City's main street was deserted. No one wanted to shop. The grass on our golf course looked like the dried moss used for mulch at the greenhouse.

Everyone was conserving water and the yards showed it. Gardens had given up their last sickly plants two months ago. The pervasive gloominess might leave with the first rain, but in the meantime, it seemed all of Northwest Kansas had been sprinkled with cranky dust.

Driving the last mile into the Diaz Compound felt like entering an oasis in a foreign land. There was a mystical quality to the towering cottonwoods, the lush foliage. When I pulled around the circular drive, Cecilia and Francesca stepped out of the doorway.

I parked and helped Francesca into the passenger seat.

"Driving will preserve your strength, Great-grandmother."

Francesca smiled. "My strength is fine. Nevertheless, I appreciate the ride."

Cecilia stopped me before I rounded the car to the driver's side. "She hasn't been to the Old House since Victor died, so this might be difficult for her. Years ago, she went to her workroom every day, then it was just several times a week. Out of respect for Great-grandmother, Teresa cleans and airs out the workroom. Many years ago, my father installed a whole-house fan system on the top floor. It draws out the hot air. Her workroom should be livable, but even so, please don't let her overdo."

"I'm sure we'll be just fine." I hoped my voice was more confident than I felt. A room without air-conditioning didn't sound very appealing.

We drove off.

"Victor sat with me in the Old House every Sunday afternoon," Francesca said.

Old House was a quarter-mile from the main one. Too far to walk in the heat.

"As you know, George's wife called me. I want to apologize. I didn't realize my questions had upset you."

"I was not upset. George and Teresa were upset. They did not want you asking questions."

I listened. *Why did this family dislike outsiders?*

"I have given this a great deal of thought. You are right. Someone needs to know about all the plants. You are the one who is willing to listen. No one else."

She directed me to the back of the house, where we would enter. I parked near the door.

A telescoping steel valance shaded the top of each window. In front was an enormous herb garden. Her wrinkled face lifted for a moment. "I have the largest variety you will find anywhere. George tends it for me. He loves this place."

I could only stare. I had not brought a camera, but I needed to document every variety of plant. The compound was a historical treasure trove. Plants were growing here that were not native to Kansas.

When we stepped inside, the room was cool. My senses were sent reeling from the combined odor of hundreds of hanks, clusters of dried plants, hanging from the ropes strung lengthwise across the ceiling beams. The clean, swept wooden floors belied the dilapidated appearance of the exterior.

"Please raise all of the blinds." Francesca stood in the middle of the room as I went from window to window. The black shades were a twenty-first century touch, as they were the kind that blocked both light and heat. This south extension to the back of the house was not visible from the central driveway. It was exposed to sunshine on three sides, like a massive sunroom.

I glanced at the pulley systems off to the side of each window. There was a variety of shades and curtains that could be lowered. Along one wall were two ovens, and a range with six burners. There was a large double-door refrigerator. In the middle of the room were two high-backed leather chairs with a floor lamp in between. There were no footstools. Surely only a person with Francesca's rigid posture would consider sitting in them. By the lighter areas on the leather, I suspected that many years ago, this room had been well used.

Beneath all the windows stood grayed unfinished wooden worktables, holding a variety of glass flasks and sealed glass containers. There were a number of pestles and mortars. Francesca trembled with anticipation after I raised the blinds.

"I will be able to work again." A windowless wall, broken only by a doorway at one end was lined with leather-bound books—all with Spanish titles. Her face beamed as she looked around. "You will come here every week?"

"Certainly. I arranged for board members to help at the historical society three afternoons a week until we have finished. This is our most important new project."

"Then let us begin." She walked over to a ceiling-high wall of bookcases. "All the names on the labels are in Spanish. I will translate them into English. Then I want you to write down all the plants' names, what they are used for, and the processes for releasing their powers. That will take time."

"Please sit and give me background information before we start. I have my tape recorder with me. I'll pull this chair around so I'm facing you and rearrange this table so it's to one side. I need a place to put my notebook." We sat in the hard-back chairs and I recited my usual preliminary introductory information giving the time, place, and the name of the contributor. I tested her voice on the recording.

She rose and walked over to the first flask. She picked it up and turned it toward me. "I thought about beginning alphabetically, but it was going to be difficult to find the right Spanish words for some of them. Anyway, none of children know Castilian except Cecilia, and she won't come near the place. Now I have decided to begin with the most important plants. I will tell you their English common names, their uses for common healing, then their secret names, and their secret uses."

"Secret names? Secret uses?"

"You've heard of 'Fillet of a fenny snake, In the cauldron boil and bake; Eye of newt and toe of frog'?"

"Of course. That's from Shakespeare's *Macbeth*. The three witches were casting a spell."

"He used the secret names of plants we use all the time. 'Eye of Newt' is common mustard seed, and 'Toe of Frog' is simply a section of the bulb of the bulbous buttercup. Although some traditions think Shakespeare was referring to Jack-in-the-Pulpit, instead of mustard seed."

"Mustard seed. What would mustard seed be used for?"

"Healing or magic?"

I hesitated.

"All the plants have healing properties and magical properties."

I could not turn in an academic article about the magical properties of plants, but I was intrigued.

"You use a combination of magic and healing all the time," she said.

"Actually, I don't."

"Of course you do. For healing, don't you use eucalyptus tea to ward off a cold and coffee beans when you have a headache? As to magic, when does your family plant potatoes?"

"Keith plants on Saint Patrick's Day," I stammered.

"Good. And by the dark of the moon, I hope."

"Well, yes. And our neighbor plants on Good Friday."

"That is not the best time. Plowing on Good Friday causes the ground to bleed, and the zodiac sign has to be just right." Seeing that I was struck dumb, she offered an explanation. "Christ's blood runs out into the rows."

Her laugh was that of a parent indulging a difficult child. She gestured toward the multitude of plants, closed her eyes, and inhaled deeply. "All of these plants will come to life when I make teas or elixirs. Some of them can't be found in the United States and were traded for many years ago. I will tell you all their common and secret names."

"I will try to keep an open mind about the magical properties. As to the healing, I know a little about the mustard seeds you mentioned. They were often made into plasters on the prairie and used to draw down inflammation."

"I recommend it for regulating the heartbeat, too. Those are healing uses. As to the magical, if you bury mustard seed under your doorstep, it will keep evil spirits from your home."

She glanced at me to see if I recoiled. I didn't.

"And Shakespeare's other reference: the toe of the frog—the bulbous buttercup?"

"I've never liked it. The Indians used it for

shingles but since it can also create blisters, that didn't make sense to me."

"And the magic uses?"

"It can drive someone crazy. Stay away from it. Unless you want to curse an enemy."

She was serious. I could see it in her eyes. Watching me now for signs that I would pull back, would not consent to this strange journey.

"You don't have to believe. Just follow the rituals."

Water-witching came to mind. You didn't have to believe to witch. Many who believed passionately could not witch, and others who thought it a bunch of nonsense witched quite easily. I smiled, imagining Keith's reaction when I told him I was learning the magical uses for plants.

There was a black draped object hanging above one of the work tables. She followed my glance. "That's a mirror."

"Why is it covered?"

"Because I didn't want it to trap my Victor's soul."

She saw the look on my face. "Many cultures know this. The ancients. The Victorians."

I threw in a few historical tidbits, so she would know I wasn't turned off by this peculiar discussion. "It's an Appalachian custom too. And I know Jews cover mirrors when they sit shiva."

"The Jews do it for an entirely different reason. It's to keep the focus on the deceased and not indulge in vanity. But many, many cultures know about the magical quality of mirrors. Do you know anything about Feng Shui?"

"Yes." But I was surprised she did.

"You know then that it's very bad to a have a mirror facing your bed."

Fairy tales, Alice stepping through the looking glass. Even Harry Potter. When I thought about it, there were hundreds of references to mirrors and magic.

"Apart from death, it is very difficult to put a soul into a mirror whether for good or for evil. And even harder to retrieve it. Someone must come after it and offer to take its place."

She said this matter-of-factly, like she was talking about a recipe for pumpkin pie.

"Have you ever done this?" My question caught her off guard. Her wrinkles deepened.

"Only for good, so far."

So far. Did she have more sinister plans? I shivered.

When I got home that evening, I ran up to our bedroom and looked at the mirror on the dresser facing our bed. Chagrined at having allowed Francesca's nonsense to infect me, nevertheless, I asked

Keith to help me rearrange the furniture. What could it hurt?

And so it began. Three afternoons a week I drove to out to the Diaz Compound and started tracking the astonishing variety of medicinal plants. I recorded their common names in English and translated names from Spanish when Francesca could come up with the right words. I wrote down their secret names, their magical names, their healing uses, and their magical uses.

Cecilia usually drove off in her old blue Honda during these sessions. She was pleased when I whisked Francesca away to the Old House because she could leave the compound and join a prayer group devoted to the Holy Mother.

After the first week, Francesca taught me some rituals such as sprinkling herbs into the flame of a candle to make spells more powerful. I balked when she asked me to sprinkle herbs around my house for protection because that is Keith's home, too. I knew my Roman Catholic husband would have a fit for the same reason the practices were offensive to Cecilia.

The second week I had to begin memorizing all the plants' names and secret uses. Francesca was a hard taskmaster.

"Snapdragon is the one of the few that will repel a curse. Have you planted any?"

I shook my head. "I didn't bother with flowers this year because the wind was so extreme and it was already too hot for annuals."

"Snapdragons are essential for protection. You need to have a little vase handy and capture its reflection to send a curse back where it came from."

I grinned. I doubted that anyone would formally curse me through some magic ritual, although no doubt more than one family in Carlton County has given me an old-fashioned cussing out.

Her lips curved and she gave slight shrug. She was not without humor. "Just do. Belief will come later."

I eyed a row of flasks set off from the others. "And why are these separated?"

"They can bring about great harm if they are used for that purpose. Intentions that require fire and certain words…" She stopped as though she had gone too far.

My historian's curiosity and tendency toward instant analysis kicked into overdrive. Many, many drugs could not be safely used in combination with others. Or with alcohol. As to the "certain words," we were bombarded with the merits of positive affirmations. There was nothing mysterious about any of this. With incredible naivety, I believed

Francesca and I were talking about the same thing. "I want to know about all your rituals, too. I want to go all the way."

She gazed at me so intently I felt paralyzed. "Yes," she said finally. "Yes, I believe you do. You are progressing very speedily. You will go beyond cataloging plants. I have waited a long, long time for someone who can help with my mortar and pestle. I want help with the herbs that will allow me to *see*. Faces. Especially, faces."

"*See?*"

She held herself very still. "Can you *see*, Lottie Albright? See as in scry?"

"You mean like looking into a crystal ball?"

"Or a mirror, or a basin of water. The natural gift has been withheld from me. But I can do the same thing by mixing certain herbs and performing certain rituals."

"Well, I'm certainly willing to try."

She crossed over to one of the work tables and pick up a hand mirror. "Hold this."

She whispered some words while I peered into the glass. The mirror clouded. The sunlight hitting it at an angle. The sun, and nothing more.

Nothing more than that.

I handed it back and rubbed my eyes. Curiously, there was a glint of triumph as she studied my face. It didn't set well with me.

"Nope. My mind is a blank." She had been right about her first impression of me when she said I didn't want to lose control.

During our breaks, we sat on the torturous chairs and talked about her family. I had a hard time following all of the names. Since she didn't seem to mind the tape recorder, I decided to sort it all later.

"Do you have a written record somewhere of all the names of your ancestors? A family tree, perhaps?"

"Yes, of course. It's at the other house. I'll have it for you the next time you visit."

"I've been doing some research. I believe you would be called a *curandera,* a healer in your culture?"

"Yes, but I was a specialist. A *yerbero.* There are other specialties such as a *consejero*, who is a counselor, and a *sobadoro,* who gives a certain kind of massage."

"Was? You are surrounded by plants that are alien to the plains. Are you not still a specialist?"

"Yes, of course." Her eyes misted with sadness. "I was trained as a *yerbero*. I could have stayed a *yerbero*. I am more now. Much more."

My pulse accelerated. A shaman? Was I going to have the chance to tap into the vast wisdom of shamanism? Centuries of traditions that brought about spiritual and physical healing. But even then, a warning bell sounded somewhere from deep within.

Cataloging the plants was tedious, exacting work. Clearly this would take all summer. So I decided to postpone exploring the topic of shamanism until next year. At the time I was confident the rituals and the chants would not put me in any kind of danger at all.

I brought my own little bags of Earl Grey for our tea and cookies. Occasionally I would accept other concoctions from Francesca to ward off my increasingly frequent headaches, which I attributed to the high sunlight, the odor emanating from the herbs and staying hunched over the worktable as we worked through lists of plants.

"You must learn how to mix now. I can no longer do it."

Surprised, because we hadn't finished all the individual varieties yet, I wondered if she sensed that I was eager to finish this project.

She held up her ruined hands. Tears filled her eyes. "You will have to help."

"Gladly. Whatever you would like me to do."

In gratitude, she laid one of her twisted fists on top of my hands and smiled. It broke my heart.

Chapter Nineteen

Steve and Angie came home for a visit at the end of July. I was surprised. Usually they only came during some big family get-together. They arrived after midnight, and went on upstairs to Angie's old room. When I went down the next morning I glanced out the window over the sink. Keith and Steve were sitting at the table on the patio. Steve was animated, Keith frowned and shook his head and studied his hands.

Steve leaned forward into his convincing mode. Keith bent into a serious rebuttal and lifted his fingers—one, two, three. I smiled. A gesture I knew all too well. Ticking off one, two, three reasons why something won't work.

I had pre-programmed the coffee the night before, and whisked the pot outside to refill their mugs before I fixed breakfast. My cheery "Morning!" was met with nearly simultaneous "Morning" from them both, then awkward silence.

My mama didn't raise no fools. The atmosphere was thicker than my coffee. Bewildered, I made a gracious quick retreat.

In a few minutes, Keith stormed off toward the barn without bothering to come back inside. Steve took off down the lane—I assumed for a walk.

Angie came down the stairs.

"Would you like orange juice?" I tried not to stare. Angie looked like death warmed over. Blue veins visible through her thin white skin. Too-large eyes in her bony skull.

"Yes, please."

I found myself assessing her in the light of what I had learned from Francesca. Automatically, I started cataloguing the herbs that would help her. Ones for healing and supplying missing energy. I yearned to begin with a little pouch of cowslip, nettle, catnip, and adder's fork. Then with a start, I realized I had mentally supplied a couple of the magic names as easily as I had once taught myself to think in French because it was a quicker way of learning the language. Fairy cup and devil's claw for cowslip and nettle. Adder's fork was the "tongue of dog," but I wasn't sure of the secret name for catnip, if there even is one.

In the beginning, I thought all these mysterious names were beyond silly. An affectation. However, Francesca told me the practice had very

ancient beginnings. Herbalists had elite status and
the use of magic names protected untrained people
who might go off tracking down plants willy-nilly
if they knew the common names. Without taking
precautions grave mistakes would be made.

I had immediately thought of "pharming,"
teenage parties with a punch bowl centerpiece
containing a random mixture of their parents'
prescription drugs. Washed down with booze, the
"trail mix" could be deadly. So could ancient plant
mixtures.

Rosemary oil might fix Angie's dry hair. And
definitely chamomile tea for her shot nerves. Lots!

"Pancakes? Or would you rather wait until
Steve gets back? I think he went for a walk."

She stared off into space.

"He and Keith were out on the patio when I
got up. I hope they weren't arguing but neither of
them looked very happy. Do you know what was
going on?"

"Yes, Steve wanted to borrow a great deal of
money. To buy stock options."

Her sharp bark of misplaced laughter set my
teeth on edge.

"For a wonderful investment."

"Oh, Angie. Perhaps another time, he might
have been interested, but we've been so hard hit by
the drought. Everyone out here has."

She shrugged. "I'm sure my husband couldn't believe his father-in-law wouldn't jump at the chance. No doubt he had visualized Daddy being just thrilled with this opportunity."

"He was not thrilled. I can tell you that for sure. I know his body language all too well."

Dumbfounded, I decided to drop the subject until I talked to Keith. "Pancakes?" I repeated.

"Yes. Steve says I must eat."

I went to the grill and poured on some of the batter, glad to have my back turned and concentrate on this task while I tried to think of how to strike up a neutral conversation.

I wanted to ask her if I could help. I slipped the pancakes onto a plate.

When I looked at her again, she was crying. I walked over. "I don't care what Steve says. Don't eat the pancakes if you don't want to."

Tears streamed down her cheeks.

"What's wrong, Angie?"

"Steve wants to have a baby. He wants children." She dug a tissue out of her pocket and blew her nose. "I can't carry a baby. He says it's my fault. It's all in my attitude. If I would just visualize myself pregnant to full-term, I could make it happen. Just imagine a healthy baby boy growing inside; it would happen."

I was speechless.

"I've tried, Lottie. God knows I've tried."

"Keith told me you've had a couple of miscarriages."

She smiled bitterly. "Not a couple. Five. Dad doesn't know about the others. I just didn't tell him. Four of them weren't Steve's," she added. "They were with my first two husbands."

I put my arms around her and we both cried.

"He'll leave me if he…he thinks I'm defective. That's the way he is. Everything in the house has to be just perfect. Everything. And that includes me."

"Has he ever hit you Angie? Abused you in any way?"

She shook her head. "Never. That would not fit his image of himself as the perfect husband."

Just then a movement outside caught my eye. Steve was coming back from his walk. Striding purposefully, in the manner of a man determined to overcome adversity, he stooped to check the pedometer he had strapped on his ankle. From the other side of the yard, Keith's two border collies barked frantically.

I went to the window. Angie rose and stood at my side. A mangy three-legged dog came out of the windbreak and awkwardly loped up to Steve. Old Man Snyder's mongrel. I would know it anywhere.

When it was about six feet from Steve, it stopped and barked. Then turned, trying to get

Steve to follow. When he didn't respond, it moved closer, then held its ground and barked again.

Steve rose, pedometer in hand. "Get out. Get away." He drew back his foot and swung at the dog, missed, then moved closer. He didn't miss the second time. The dog howled and dropped, then managed to struggle to its feet and began barking again.

I flew out the door and swung Steve around just as he was drawing back his foot to kick again.

"What the hell is the matter with you?"

"That dog is sick or diseased." His face flushed. "It displaces positive energy. You shouldn't allow that pitiful bone-pile of a canine to contaminate your property."

Not trusting myself to speak, I scooped up the injured dog and headed for my Tahoe. Keith had driven off to the pasture and there was no point in trying to reach him on his cell phone. It would take too much time to track down my husband. I drove as fast as I could to Old Man Snyder's house to pick him up before I drove his dog over to the new vet.

Justin Crawford had just graduated from Kansas State University. He was lean, redheaded, genuinely sincere, and expensive. Really, really expensive. He wore a white lab coat which folks found strange as hell. Even harder to take in was his notion that being a vet in a rural community meant working with small animals in an air-conditioned clinic.

Keith planned to take the lad aside and further his education when he had time.

When I turned into Old Man Snyder's farm-yard, the dog began to whimper.

"I'm just going to get him, boy, and take him with us. I'll be right back." He started to bark and tried to struggle to his feet. Worried that he would do himself more injury, I picked him up and gently carried him inside the weathered old house.

I found the old man lying on the floor. I gasped and laid the dog on a thread-bare rug before I knelt beside Snyder and checked his pulse. I went to the cast iron pump on the sink and drew a cup of water. I propped him up and held the glass to his parched lips.

"Thank'ee," he said. He drank a couple of sips and then fell back.

"I'll be right back. I'm going to call an ambulance."

"Don't have no insurance." The words came in gasps.

"You won't need any."

The crew came quickly and confirmed that it was heat exhaustion, and soon would have been a heatstroke. "He is badly dehydrated, Lottie," Gene

Romney called over his shoulder as he helped transfer the old man to the stretcher. "He'll need to be in the hospital for a couple of days."

"The county has a fund, but I doubt if he's ever applied for Medicaid. I'll oversee everything that has to do with the paperwork. He sure wouldn't recover from anything here in this house. It's like a sauna."

They left. The dog lifted his head and whimpered at the departing ambulance. "He'll be just fine." He rested his head again. "That's what you were trying to tell us, weren't you, boy? That your master needed help."

I reached down and lifted the old rug, with the dog on top and carried him back out to the Tahoe. "Next we are going to fix you. And we've going to do better than 'the dog' even if I don't know what your name is. You can't remain anonymous. Like a Dog Doe." Doe stuck in my mind before I could choose something more sensible.

I decided to bypass the new vet. I wanted the best for this dog who had saved his master's life. The very best, and that was Keith.

Anger built with every turn of the wheel as I tore back to the farm. I had to get Angie away from that sadistic husband. Tears stung my eyes. I couldn't allow this to go on.

Steve became the unholy focus of all this

last month's frustrations. I welcomed white-hot rage instead of my usual tears. I have always been ashamed of how easily I cry. Then something dark and sinister welled up. Something sicker than rage. I focused on all I had learned from Francesca. There were spells and plants and rituals to break up a marriage. I shut out that *Something* urging me to far go beyond that.

Far beyond merely breaking up a marriage.

There were ways to cause great injury to human beings without laying a hand on them. Without leaving a trace.

Poisoning was for amateurs.

Francesca had just begun teaching me about the secret uses for plants. She had hinted that she knew more. Much, much more.

Doe stunk and his foul odor permeated the car. A dust devil swept across the road and I swerved and slowed in the sudden pelting of sand. My skin tingled. Slammed by the sensation that *Someone* else was present in my Tahoe, I accelerated and sped through the dust.

I glanced in the rearview mirror. It darkened. A shadow shifted.

I skidded, corrected, knew I had over-corrected and was headed for the ditch on the opposite side. Rationality kicked in. I knew the dangers of sudden braking on gravel roads. I eased off the gas pedal, lightly tapped the brakes, and swerved through slow corrections until I stopped.

Arms circling the steering wheel, I rested my head and took deep breaths. *What if another car had been coming?* I could have killed someone.

When I trusted myself to drive safely, I headed out, chilled by the awareness that in the short time I had taken leave of my senses, I believed. Francesca had warned me that I would come to believe.

My right mind acknowledged the validity of the common medical uses of plants and herbs. But I did not believe they could be used to cast magical spells.

Besides, I would never, ever consciously cause physical harm to another human being.

That *Something* pounced, mocked. *You would, and you have.*

In the past year, I had killed a woman and a man.

That's different. It was my job. I had to. It was me or them.

Shaken, I realized I had wanted to use black magic to banish a man I just hated. Just hated.

Doe gave a faint bark. "We're nearly home, boy. Your master is safe, and I'm going to take you to the best vet anywhere."

When I pulled into our drive, Steve's car was

gone. Keith stood in the doorway. I parked and jumped out. I ran over to him.

"Old Man Snyder was on the verge of a heat-stroke. His dog came and got me. He's hurt. Steve kicked him." I dissolved and threw my arms around his neck. I sobbed into his shoulder. "Oh honey, Steve kicked this poor dog."

He patted my hair and then kissed me. "I know. Angie told me." He walked over to the Tahoe, picked up Doe, and carried him to the building where he used to have a small animal hospital. Before his sham retirement, when he theoretically shut down his practice to farm fulltime. When he had naively assumed the new vet would have a modicum of common sense.

"Can I help with anything?"

"No."

He came out a short time later and said the dog had some bruised ribs, but nothing appeared to be broken. "He needs all kinds of shots. I doubt if he's ever had any. I'm going to worm him. And he needs to lie around."

"His name is Dog Doe," I said. Startled, he glanced at me. "Not doe as in Bambi's mother. Dog Doe as in John Doe or Jane Doe."

"Makes sense," he said cautiously.

We walked to the house. "How long ago did

Angie and Steve leave?" At least I wouldn't have to talk to the bastard.

"Angie didn't leave. Just Steve. She's decided to stay."

Chapter Twenty

Francesca sat on the edge of her leather chair, her hands folded in her lap. She sized me up. "Has something happened?"

"No, I'm fine."

More accurate words came to mind, but they were terrifying. *I'm not strong enough to keep the Devil away.* Francesca had warned me that I would be putting my soul in danger if I became her apprentice. She had pointed out that my work to build Saint Helena was hardly the actions of an irreligious person.

I did not want to discuss any of this. "You've become very dear to me, Francesca. I will soon be wrapping up my work here. I will miss our chats."

"You are stopping much too soon, Lottie Albright." She looked at me sharply with a quick flash of anger in her eyes. "Help me up," she said curtly. After she steadied herself, she walked over to the worktable on the south wall.

"Now, I wish to go over here." At the east wall, she pointed to different herbs in five separate jars. "Ladle one half teaspoon of each into a cup. Then heat some water."

I walked over to the stove and turned on the burner under the copper teakettle. When it was steaming hot, I poured it over the leaves.

"I would like to sit again." I helped her, then walked back to the counter and carried the cup over to the little table beside the chair.

"Be careful, it's very hot."

"It's not for me. It's for you."

"I'm not thirsty. Really."

"This tea is not for thirst. You are upset today, and this will calm you. You are stopping too soon, Lottie Albright. Much too soon."

I reached for the tea. "Are you sure you would not like a cup?"

"All right," she said softly. "You choose the leaves. I'm sad and upset. What do you think I should have?"

I laughed softly. "I think you need a little pinch of bay leaves, mixed with balm of Gilead, and carob."

"That is correct."

I went right to the leaves, added them to the cup she liked best and carried it to her. We sipped comfortably. I was relieved that I had been spared an outburst. Wild protests. By now, I was familiar with her sudden flares of temper when I was clumsy, or used the wrong herbs, or if she sensed that I was skeptical about the validity of a ritual.

Calmed by the taste of chamomile and mint, soothed by the dancing motes of sunshine dappling the wood floor, I realized my fears were ridiculous. I had let my fury over a mistreated dog spiral into anxiety over angry feelings that were perfectly normal.

It had all been perfectly normal.

"You're right, of course about my being upset. My stepdaughter, Angie, is staying with us until she has a better life plan. My heart goes out to her. I didn't sleep well last night. And speaking of family, perhaps today would be a good time to focus on yours." I set my briefcase on the table and fumbled around through the papers. I couldn't locate my notebook. My eyes blurred. I couldn't find my cassette tape recorder either.

I had accidentally picked up Keith's mini voice-activated recorder. He would not appreciate that if he wanted to dictate some notes for his practice.

I couldn't remember the first two questions I had wanted to ask, which was just as well, because I lacked the equipment to do justice to her narrative. They were probably not important.

The room was pleasantly warm. The healthful

odor of plants and herbs was a welcome contrast to the brassy stench of motionless air suffocating Carlton County like a grubby blanket. Outside the compound, breathing felt risky, almost dangerous some days. The air in this room was as welcome as oxygen to a drowning man.

"I will tell you more about my family after you help me mix the seeing herbs." Her eyes darkened as she held up her useless hands.

"Of course. Let's start there. You can answer my questions afterward. I'm in no hurry."

I wobbled to my feet. She directed me to the worktable with the isolated flasks. It was so very, very pleasant to do something simple and physical. I took out various leaves and stems and put them all in the marble mortar. I picked up the matching pestle and crushed the leaves again and again until the mixture was fine powder.

She gazed a beautiful red crystal jar. "Put it in that. Then wash your hands very carefully with the soap lying by the sink. Wash them like you are a surgeon preparing for an operation." Her eyes were alive with excitement, her breath artificially steady as though a doctor had told her "breathe in, breathe out" during an examination.

I did as I was told, and placed the jar on the worktable. "Would you like me to label it?" I glanced at her hands. She certainly could never do it herself.

"That will not be necessary," she said with a bitter spark in her eyes. "I'll know."

We sat down again. "You promised to tell me more about your family. I'm sorry, Francesca. I forgot my main tape recorder. This all has to be off-the-record today. "

"Yes. That will be fine."

People often talk more freely when they think it's off-the-record anyway, and I never ever violated this. Francesca relaxed.

Pleasant, so very pleasant to just listen without the hyper-alertness required to direct formal interviews. So very pleasant to listen to this ancient black-clad woman. Even though Francesca dabbled in spells and curses and heaven knew what, today I was more at ease here than in my own household with a miserable husband and a tragic stepdaughter who looked like she would blow away in the first stiff breeze.

I asked personal questions. Intimate questions. Questions I normally would never ask. They were none of my business. Curiously, all of my professional training, my filters drained away. That which prevented me from prying. But it was so pleasant here in the sun, and she answered so freely that I couldn't help myself.

"The lawsuit. A number of people have told me there was a lawsuit that has been going on in your family ever since they were born. Is that true?"

"Oh, yes. And from long before the time when my parents and grandparents and great-grandparents were alive."

"I've been through all the newspapers. I haven't seen it mentioned."

"No. It was from a time when there were no newspapers out here. When Victor decided to become a lawyer, I knew it was time to take it up again. When Victor understood what I had, he became very excited. Until that woman convinced him it was foolish to take up the cause again."

"What cause, Francesca?"

"Our claim to more land. Much more."

"Did Maria know about this?"

Francesca shook her head. "I think she knew land was involved, but Victor told me he didn't want his wife to know everything." Her face twisted with bitterness. "She wouldn't have believed me anyway. Only Victor seemed to grasp the importance."

It didn't make sense. Clearly the Diaz Family did not own vast tracts of land. And she said *own* not *owned*—like it was still hers. I had gone through deeds. The land encompassed in this compound was the extent of their holdings.

"And you believe the lawsuit was a factor in Victor's death?"

"Of course," she said softly. "Of course it was."

My tongue was heavy, wrapped in wool. I glanced at my open briefcase again for my note-book and stared dully at the contents. I could write on the back of one of the papers lying within if I had the energy to find my pen. Had to get all the details down for Sam.

Swiveling my head was hard. I should follow up on something but I couldn't remember what. I should make use of the time anyway. Stupidly, I recalled my usual questions. About health, about school, about marriage. There were others, I knew there were others. I began with health.

"Your hands. I know healthcare was very limited years ago, but when did you first begin to develop arthritis? Was it painful? Could your family afford to take you to the doctor?"

Wrong, wrong, wrong.

I had asked three questions at once, without giving her a chance to answer any of them. I shook my head, trying to click my brains into place.

She trembled and lifted her terrible hands. "This is not arthritis."

"What then? Some other disease?"

"No. This was done to me."

Chilled, I stared at her gaunt face now twisted with rage.

"How could that have happened? Who?"

"Who? People who hated me for the kind of work I do. Hated me without knowing a thing about me. Hated me because I could heal and they didn't understand how I could."

"Oh, Francesca." My stomach lurched.

"They came for me one night. Dragged me and my poor husband out of bed. My beloved Henry. They made him watch. They called me a witch. A child of the devil. A daughter of Satan. The Devil's spawn."

Too stunned to speak, my hands gripped the arms of the chair until my knuckles were white. My teeth clamped like a vise in my jaw.

"They made him watch. They dragged us here to this workroom. My beloved workroom. The same room countless members of their family had come to. For this reason, for that reason. Because they needed my help and their own doctors couldn't help.

Bile scorched my throat.

"They put my hands on my worktable. They picked up a hammer. They put my fingers there and smashed them one by one. Then they cut off one and ground it up with my pestle."

Black spots swirled before my eyes. I swayed in my chair.

"I did not practice the dark arts. Not then. Then I was pure. Like the sun. Never dark. I knew they wanted more than to punish me. Men who mask themselves with religion who insist they are honoring their God always want more."

I did not want to hear. I put my palms over my ears and took deep breaths. Her voice seemed to come from a far place.

"Then they started on the animals. Our poor animals. My husband had horses. Six rare beautiful horses. Andalusian—the horse of kings. They were descendants from Esclavo, the original stallion. They killed them first. Then the dogs."

"Oh, Francesca." My lips quivered. Then I couldn't speak.

"Then they killed my cat. My dear little cat. They said witches always had a cat and that she was my familiar." Tears streamed down her withered cheeks. "They even took her little collar. For a souvenir, one of them said." She closed her eyes. "It had a bell. A dear little bell."

"Francesca." All I could say was her name. Over and over. What words could I possibly come up with? Then finally, "I can't even take in such cruelty. Why? Why would they do such a terrible thing?"

"Oh, I knew why. They may have used our religion as an excuse. His Catholicism and what they perceived as my witchcraft, but they wanted my land. There had always been rumors. They wanted to know where I had hidden the claim to my land. My father's land."

I could feel the color leave my face. The veins on my hands stood out like blue cords.

"My poor husband. They made him watch when they went to work on my hands. They did not need to do anything to him because he never recovered from what they did to me. They hated witches and they hated Catholics. But I knew what they really wanted was to burn my proof of ownership."

"Oh, Francesca."

"I didn't tell them where we had hidden the papers. They couldn't make me tell them."

Faint now, I doubled over.

"They joked, they chanted all the time they were doing this."

I knew I should go to her, but I couldn't move.

"I could not abide such pain. There was no help. No hope anywhere.

"I laid in bed for a month. For a week I could only sip soup and enough water to stay alive and could only speak enough to tell my sister and my children what to bring me for my pain. My unspeakable pain."

"Your children?"

"Are dead. Before, there was one, always one who was willing to learn the old ways. One who could be taught. I was the one from my generation. I told my daughter, the chosen one of her generation how to prepare the medicines, the compounds required to endure the unspeakable pain. She wrapped my hands with a poultice of the healing leaves. Somehow I endured. But my husband did not. It killed him."

Now I understood why this old woman chose to live in isolation.

"Not being able to protect me killed him. He begged me to tell them. But I would not. As I lay there in bed in that room, I changed. Until then I was a shaman; I healed. Afterward, I followed the path of a nagual, a sorcerer, and became the master of that which I had vowed I would never delve into."

The dark. The rearview mirror. It had not been my imagination. She had been teaching me to call the dark.

"I learned the ways of revenge, but I could not *see*. Today you have mixed the herbs that will allow me to see. Their faces. Their names."

I couldn't think.

"The ministers, the priests, they will tell you

that love keeps you alive. But that is not true. Hate is more powerful. And before I die, I will have my revenge."

When I could control my teeth, my stomach, my lips, and start my heart again, I lifted my head. "My God. You poor woman."

"I will be free to die."

"Did Victor know about your hands?"

"No. He did not know. You are the only one now who knows how the hands came about." She thrust them toward me. "None of my grandchildren, great-grandchildren— great-greats now—have ever known. What do they know of grief? All they know of loss comes from video games. And imitations of life. Shadows of the real thing."

I looked at her hands, and then looked away.

"Even Cecilia, my beloved little Cecilia, only wants to think about the pretty side of religion. She wants to cloak herself in Virgin Mary-blue and whisper soft little chants and work among poor people clean enough not to offend her."

Woolly headed, strung between two worlds, I could not will myself to come up to where I belonged—a world of sunshine and light. I knew if I were able to think, I would hone in on validation. Documentation. Some proof that her ruined hands were the result of mob action instead of a rogue disease that had crippled her.

She sensed this. "You don't believe me, do you? You don't believe."

I couldn't answer. It was too horrible. I couldn't take it in.

"Go to the chest under the windows in the west corner. Look in the third drawer down. There is a fine wooden box. It was made by my grandfather. I keep my keys in that drawer. Open the box, then take out the piece of paper. Read the chant silently. I know it by heart. I do not want to think about those words again."

I rose unsteadily. I placed my hand on the back of the chair for a moment until I got my bearings.

"They joked. They left a silly little poem." Her voice broke. "A joke verse. Like a children's chant."

I carefully walked over to the corner. I opened the third drawer and picked up the keys lying on the velvet lining. I opened the lid on the beautifully crafted walnut box nestled within.

There was a piece of rolled paper. I carried it back to the chair where the light was better. I could feel her watching my face. Waiting for my reaction. She got one. I even recognized the verse. It was well-known historically. Very well-known.

> I would rather be a Klansman
> in robe of snowy white,

Than to be a Catholic Priest
in robe as black as night;
For a Klansman is AMERICAN
and AMERICA is his home,
But a priest owes his allegiance
to a Dago Pope in Rome.

Chapter Twenty-one

I heard a soft rustling and eased up in my bed to see Angie quietly closing the door. "I'm awake," I called.

"Keith," she hollered, "Lottie's awake."

In a moment he appeared in the doorway looking solemn. "Finally."

"What time is it?"

"Eleven o'clock."

"You're kidding? I don't believe it. I've never slept this late before in my life."

"I know."

"When did I get home? I don't even remember."

"After eight. I couldn't rouse you on your cell or even the car phone. About the time I was really starting to get worried, you came driving in and went straight up to bed. Without a bite of supper, I might add. Did you eat something while you were there?"

"No. Well, I don't think so. To tell the truth I

don't remember one single thing about my visit to the compound. Not anything."

How was that possible? I eased up against the headboard. "The office. Who is at the sheriff's office?"

"Betty and Marvin are basically it. They will call here if something comes up. Or page me when I'm out in the field. By the way, Tom and Josie are driving out from Manhattan. They will be here late afternoon."

"But why?"

"She called a couple of hours ago and I told her I was worried about you. You know Josie; she wants to see for herself."

"Oh, brother. I don't know if I'm up to an inquisition."

"Lottie, it's not just last night. You've been jittery. On edge. I want you to talk to her."

"As a psychologist?" I rose up on my elbows.

"No, damn it. As your sister. Do you think I haven't noticed you're not up to snuff?"

How could he *not* notice? I had lost weight. There were circles under my eyes. I couldn't blame everything on the heat. "I'll get a physical. I'm overdue."

"Good. That's always the first step. Now, I'm going to make you eat something."

Suddenly disgusted with myself for lying in

bed like a truant teenager, duty kicked in. "Damn it. It's my day at the historical society. How could I have forgotten?"

"Margaret has it covered."

"Margaret? But she quit!"

"Not to worry. I called Margaret and told her you hadn't been feeling well lately and weren't quite yourself." With a flap of his hand, he mimicked Margaret's mannerisms. "She told me you had insulted her. I told her that was not at all like you. You held her in the highest esteem and would she please…"

I started laughing. "Stop, oh please stop. Just give me the bottom line." He looked so handsome, smiling there in the sunlight, one hand braced against the door jam, with a lock of thick brown hair falling down on his forehead. Boyishly delighted by his own orneriness.

"Bottom line, she's back in the office. And I expect you to apologize sweetly." He walked over to the bed and sat beside me. He reached down and kissed me. I grasped his cheeks between my palms and pelted him with more kisses. He grabbed my hands and held them to one side while he eased off the bed.

"Just a minute while I lock the door. Remember, we have a kid around now."

Coffeed, showered, I know I glowed when I walked into the kitchen. Self-consciously I glanced at Angie but she wouldn't have noticed if I were lit up like a Christmas tree. She sat listlessly at the kitchen table staring out the patio door. I poured another cup of coffee and went outside.

No matter how happy Keith and I were in bed, we couldn't stay there forever.

The sun was still hot. The wind still blew. The crops had burned up. And no one believed the Royals would ever win the pennant. Not anymore.

I decided to make a list of everything that was bothering me. I went inside and grabbed my notebook from where it was sitting beside the phone on my kitchen desk. The notebook. For an instant, I remembered wanting it when I was at Francesca's. I had wanted the notebook…and had wanted something else. *What was it?* Bothered by my inability to remember one thing about yesterday's meeting, I wondered if I had been getting a touch of flu. Or something. But that couldn't be true because I felt just fine today. Not even tired.

Back in my lawn chair, I began jotting everything down. Then I intended to isolate the problems I could actually do something about and make a plan.

I started a separate list of things I couldn't affect. The crops and the weather went on it.

My sister.

My stomach lurched. My sister. I still hadn't faced that little problem. Josie was having an affair with my husband's son, and his sisters would blow sky-high when they found out.

Tosca was next on the list. The uppity little dog who had turned on us all. There was no wooing her back either, until she deigned to receive us again. Like she was the queen of England who could pick and choose. I smiled ruefully. Fat chance. Keith would have to live with his sins.

The investigation. I had been kicked out of the loop. No more information flowing to us from the KBI. That was more of a blessing than a problem, but at a county level we weren't any closer to finding that killer than the big boys in the state office.

Angie. The lonely stepdaughter sitting in my kitchen. I could not fix her miserable marriage and I would be out of my mind to try that anyway. I didn't want to fix it. I didn't ever want to see Steve Bender again.

When I finally finished I stared at the enormous column of things that were nagging me. I could not do a single solitary thing about any of them. Even Angie's unhappiness was a problem she had to work through by herself. We could only offer her sanctuary until she got back on her feet.

The big Mercedes SUV roared up the drive late that afternoon. Tom sat in the front seat and Tosca was in the rear, strapped into all her safety paraphernalia.

As I had predicted, the moment after the luggage was inside, and Tosca watered, Josie took me aside and started looking me over. "What's going on, Lottie?"

"I'm not sure. I'm fine, really."

"You don't look fine."

"Yeah. Well. It's been a long hot summer."

"Okay." Her rose and white T-shirt matched the ribbons in Tosca's topknot. Her white knee-length shorts were still spotless after the long grueling drive. Her glance said she was clearly at her professional best.

Instead, I wanted my sister.

"Keith said you haven't been feeling well. Has anything unusual been going on?"

Tears stung my eyes. "Not really. Just general work for the historical society. I've been interviewing an old Spanish woman and recording a number of spells and rituals."

She smiled. "That's nothing that would affect your health."

"I know that." But I didn't. Not deep down inside. "She's also an *yerbero*, an herbalist. I've been recording some of the names of uses of plants."

She froze. "You haven't taken any of these herbs, have you?"

"Yes. Because Francesca wants me to experience the effects."

She lost all her objectivity in a heartbeat. "Please tell me you're not that dumb. Herbs are medications. It's hard telling what you've ingested that is harmful for you. Like all medication, what works for one person can have an inverse reaction on another. Do you remember all the names of the herbs?"

"There were so many. None of them should have been harmful."

"Perhaps. But, Keith needs to know. I'll call that woman and ask."

"She won't answer the phone. You'll have to go through her great-granddaughter." I gave her the number.

"Let me talk to Keith, first. He can listen on the extension and might be able to understand some of the medical details."

I heard only one side of the phone conversation, but it was clear Cecelia didn't understand what they were talking about. Josie asked her to tell Francesca that I was quite ill after yesterday's session. She insisted that Francesca tell her the names of any herbs I had taken.

"New deal, Lottie," Keith said after they hung up. "I know this work is important to you. But herbs are out. Spells and rituals won't hurt a thing."

"Okay." Seen in the light of their logic, it was easy to agree. I would simply take Francesca's interpretations at face value. From a historian's standpoint, it was better technique anyway. Josie was right about the effects of drugs. What cured one person might have an adverse effect on another. My personal reactions were contaminating the data.

That evening Angie walked down to the pond with Josie and Tom. Tosca rested in the special bed she used when she came to Western Kansas. Her sorrowful eyes were full of unspeakable tragedy. Keith glanced at me, smiling at Tosca's little shudder when Josie and Tom went outside together. Tosca had lost her place. She no longer sat in the front seat of the car—literally and figuratively. Her mistress' heart belonged to another.

Keith left the room and came back with a buddy poppy. He had bought several of the crimson crepe blossoms sold by the Veterans of Foreign Wars. He knelt beside Tosca's bed and gently removed her rose and white ribbons. He twisted the wire attached to the poppy around her topknot. The little dog looked up at him and allowed herself to be lifted up and comforted against his broad chest. When he set her back down again, she stayed at his side. The poppy was not the flag—would never be the flag—but it would do.

He went into the music room. I had changed into a soft yellow sundress with an eyelet bodice and a full skirt. I joined him and took my guitar down from the closet where he had built racks and stands for all the instruments. We sing well together and enjoy harmonizing on old countrywestern duets.

He suddenly began a riff of shut-out chords that I could not possibly follow, then softly launched into an ancient Webb Pierce song. One even the most avid music fans rarely heard. Keith has a wonderful voice and held nothing back. What he would not express verbally was always there in his music.

"*I live every day for you. I breathe every breath for you.*"

I shut my heart against the pain of realizing how much he wanted to keep me safe. I knew he was bothered over telling me to stop sampling the herbs. It had been just short of a direct order.

"*And if I'm mean and make you blue. It's my way of loving you.*"

I couldn't look him in the eye. Tears welled up

as I recalled the times I had scared the hell out of him since I became involved in law enforcement. His wounded eyes! It was as though some composer had written this song just for us. Had anticipated just such a time when a man needed to speak these words and a woman needed to listen.

"I can't help these things I do. It's my way of loving you."

He looked at me. Sheepishly. Subtly offering an apology. He was deeply aware of the price I paid indirectly for Regina's suicide. The price I paid for enduring his watchfulness, his excessive protection. His fussing over my happiness. I knew it grew out of old memories and the general wretchedness of the long, hot summer as much as anything.

He sang directly to me, with words he would never be able to frame on his own. The situation was too delicate. But he wanted me to know he was sorry.

I opened my mouth, but couldn't find the words. There was a song. One that was just right, but I couldn't remember what it was. And even if I could remember, I didn't need a song to tell him how I felt. There was a better way. I rose and went over to him and sat on his lap and he pulled me against his chest.

Then words didn't matter anymore.

When my two stepchildren and sister returned from the pond, they trooped into the music room. Angie looked even more miserable than when she had left. Tom and Josie held hands and gave Keith and me nervous looks.

"We think it's time to tell you. I case you don't know this already…" Tom cleared his throat.

"We're dating," Josie said brightly.

We didn't know what kind of a response they expected. Congratulations? It wasn't as though they had announced an engagement. Disapproval? They were adults. They could form relationships with whomever they liked.

The look on Keith's father/brother-in-law face was not that of surprise. The look on my stepmother/sister face was surely that of polite resignation.

Angie left the room.

"Well, now. This calls for drink," Keith said.

I greeted Margaret cheerfully the next morning, asked her to sit down and apologized magnificently, magnanimously, effusively. It was everything a wounded soldier could ask for. She swelled with pride, fluffed her hair and graciously accepted my exaggerated highfalutin explanation that I had "been under a lot of pressure," but "I knew that was no excuse for treating her so rudely, and would she please forgive me?"

And man this damn office, when I have to be gone. Come back, Little Sheba.

"We all have days when we are not ourselves, Lottie. But, it really wasn't like you."

"I am nearly finished at the compound. That will free up more time."

In fact, I intended to finish with Francesca in a couple of weeks. I was still troubled by my inability to remember anything about the last session. It was a clear sign that I needed a vacation. Fat chance of finding time for that. A day-spa perhaps? Something to take my mind off a crime case where every lead fizzled out.

Sometimes when people or a situation are upsetting to me, and I find myself obsessing over the reason why, I find that it's best to simply stay away without trying to understand the *why*. And clearly my relationship with Francesca was falling into that category. Just thinking about the old woman upset me.

"You have a number of calls from people in response to your ad. Two persons with French ancestry, a couple of African Americans, and a Jane Jordan has been trying hard to set up an appointment."

"Jane. Yes, move her to the top of the list."

"Really Lottie, there's no reason to include people who aren't well-known in a county history book. We should stick with our own kind and not go trolling for all these outliers."

I will not get into another fight with this woman. I swear I won't.

I took a deep breath and counted to ten. Then twenty.

"Think of how unusual this will make our book, though," I said cheerfully. Blatant manipulation, but she was falling for it hook, line, and sinker. "In the future people will admire our more cosmopolitan approach to diversity. In fact, you will probably have many, many opportunities for public speaking since you played a big part in this decision to become more inclusive."

I used all the right buzzwords. Ah yes, public speaking! Her face brightened at the thought of giving speeches—the darling of every history organization.

"Yes." She sat up straighter and stretched her neck. "Yes, I can see how we will be setting the standard for excellence."

Worrying that she would change her mind and launch into another ethnic diatribe, I headed her off with a steady stream of chatter until I could head out the door. "Goodness, it looks like another day without a drop of rain. Are you sure you will be all right here? I'm nearly finished at the compound. Then I can move on to some other family."

"I'll be just fine. I was in charge of this place long before you were here, remember?"

I ignored the barb and waved goodbye.

Chapter Twenty-two

When Francesca and I walked into the Old House, the first thing I noticed was a red crystal jar sitting in front of what I silently referred to as "harmful row."

"What a beautiful…" My voice trailed off and I looked at the jar with bewilderment. It had never been there before. Francesca and I were the only ones who ever came into the room outside of Teresa when she came to clean. There was a sharp pain in my forehead. "Where did that come from?"

"You mixed those herbs. For me. The seeing herbs."

"The ones that will allow you to see faces?" I asked, thinking her belief as harmless as a senior citizen grabbing a jar of gingko off the shelf at a vitamin store. "Do you need help taking them? Will they require a tea?"

"Do you not remember anything about your last visit?" She was as still as a statue.

"No, and it scared my poor husband half to death. And my sister."

"I know. They called Cecilia. She told me." There were tears in her eyes. "I never meant to harm you."

I sniffed the earthy aroma of the hanks of plants suspended from the ceiling. Outside, a breeze rippled through the cottonwoods sending them silver side up. A low-hanging branch scraped across the roof. "In fact, they believe that I have stronger-than-normal reactions to medication. They both insist that I stop taking any of these drugs." I shrugged like a teenager who was saying "Mommy won't let me."

"You have become like a daughter to me." Her voice trembled. "I do not want to hurt you. Yes. I can see that you must stop taking the herbs, and simply record my information."

It was that easy to step back.

"But mixing can't hurt me. I'll wear a surgical mask so I won't breathe in any of the substances. The rituals and incantations are still a go. I'm not worried about them."

I was that ignorant.

"Shall I begin by fixing you a cup of the seeing herbs, Francesca?"

"No." Her voice was sad. "There are other

things I must tend to first today. There are a number of things I would like to give you before I die."

"You've never talked about dying before."

"That is because I could not. It wasn't time."

Giving things away. Time to go. This was suicide talk. She caught the concern on my face.

"Do not worry, Lottie Albright. I will not hasten my own death by the poor earthly methods used by people who do not wish to live. I shall simply die. I want to talk of happier things today. I own a number of things that Cecilia and George would not appreciate. I would like to give you my madstone. If I do not, it might be carelessly tossed out some day."

"You have a madstone?" A madstone was priceless.

She beamed at my astonishment. "And mine comes from an albino deer."

"A witch deer?"

Witch deer! How had these words come to mind in a heartbeat? How easily I had slipped into her kind of thinking. How very, very easily. The stone from a brown deer was the lowest ranked. One from a spotted or a white deer was better—but one from an albino was the most powerful of all. Only in this house, this room did I seem to take leave of my senses. My rational mind disappeared. I even thought with her words.

A *"witch deer!"* I would never ever use those words outside of this room. I was thinking in another language, as easily as though I were learning French.

"Yes, a witch deer. A pure white deer with pink eyes. A madstone so powerful it not only cures rabies, it will cure rattlesnake and spider bites."

"Oh, Francesca. I would be honored." So many cultures believed in madstones—the prized hair ball from the stomach of a deer. It was even mentioned in *The Old Farmer's Almanac* and old editions of *Webster's Dictionary.* I knew a museum in Missouri had one.

A madstone could cure rabies.

After being boiled in milk, the stone would stick directly to the wound and draw out the poison. When it fell off, one boiled it in sweet milk again to remove the toxin, and the process was repeated until it wouldn't stick any more. That's when one knew all the poison was out. Charging for its use was forbidden. That negated the power.

There was another hitch. The victim had to come to the person with the stone. The owner could never go to the patient. If a Kansas museum didn't want it, where could I keep it?

I tried to imagine the expression on Margaret's face when someone came to the historical society asking if I would cure them of rabies. Would someone at the Kansas State Historical Society understand if I passed it on to them? Perhaps scientists would like to put it under a microscope.

How could I not accept this gift?

"Thank you. What a treasure." Rabies cures aside, I knew the stone's historical value. Who knew how many other such items she had here?

"Go to the chest again."

I headed for the south corner, then bewildered, I hesitated. How did I automatically know where the chest was located? Why did my hands know the keys would be kept in the third unlocked drawer?

My hands trembled and I waited for the next instruction.

"Second drawer down this time."

Each drawer except the third was locked, but the same key served them all. I opened the second drawer.

"Take it out. It's yours now."

"Oh, Francesca." The smooth stone lying within was grayish-brown in color. The madstone! She was right. It didn't look remarkable. Just a stone to be tossed aside.

"Pick it up. Take it home with you."

"Thank you so very much." I didn't know where to put it. I didn't feel right about tucking it into my jeans pocket.

"There are several squares of leather in the next drawer down."

Unnerved that she had read my mind, I murmured a quick thank you and wrapped the stone in the scrap of leather and put it in my briefcase. I decided to put it on a shelf in Keith's office. If he noticed it at all—and I doubted he would—I would simply tell him it was a gift from an old lady and would cure rabies. The truth, the whole truth, would be regarded as a charming fiction.

"Thank you. I will take good care of this."

I could not look away from her eyes. They were fixed on mine. Her voice dropped to a whisper. "The only thing I ask of you in exchange for the madstone and some of my other treasures is a little more help compounding mixtures. There are only a few more. Ones that will require the use of rituals. A few chants. Nothing more. You will not be required to say any of the words."

I wanted to take a deep breath of pure clean air instead of inhaling the carbon dioxide-laden soup pervading this room. The hanks of plants seemed alive. There were beads of sweat on my forehead, yet I shivered.

Unnerved by her unwavering gaze, I looked away before my brain turned to mush. Looked away and forced myself to settle down and think. I was an academic, therefore theoretically capable of abstract thinking. Reason told me that if I refused to help this lonely tragic old woman I would be acknowledging fear of the powers of darkness. Powers I knew didn't exist.

"Help me," she pleaded softly. "Help me." She looked down helplessly. "These hands."

"Sure," I said cheerfully. *Why not?* "You know I will."

"There are only a few. I've decided not to take the seeing herbs until we are done."

"I'm glad this won't take too much longer. I need to compare your work with that of other ethnic groups."

She smiled. "No other person has my skills."

"I'm sure. But some of the drugs will overlap."

"I have been thinking of many other things since your sister called and told Cecilia you were harmed by our last visit. How is the KBI doing with the investigation of my great-grandson's murder? They have not been here to talk with me."

"As far as I know they have not learned a thing. Sam and I are out of the loop. They have no confidence in our abilities. We have no new information at our county level, either."

"When you first came here, I told you Victor was going to file a lawsuit. I have decided to tell you why. I showed Victor a copy of a map that gave him the courage to take up the torch once again. He understood!"

I wished Sam were hearing all this.

"He was killed because someone wanted the map showing all the land my family owns."

I had been through all the court records, all the databases of recorded deeds. There was simply no record of this family owning any more land than was encompassed by Roswell County.

It was though she could read my thoughts.

"Victor didn't believe at first, either. He was slow to understand. But when I told him our story and showed him a copy of our map, he understood. This map was passed down through my father's people. A treasure map." Her voice was hushed. She was scrutinizing every expression that crossed my face. "A valuable treasure. The most priceless treasure in the world. A treasure without equal."

I groaned inwardly, the thought crossing my mind that this old woman was teasing me. Making it all up.

"So you think someone would have killed Victor because he wouldn't tell them where to find this map?"

"I know so."

I kept myself absolutely still. Simultaneously wanting her to continue and at the same time dreading for her to do so. I wanted to believe, and yet doubted her accuracy.

I was no longer under any obligation to report what she said to the KBI unless as an officer of the court I truly believed it was related to Victor's murder. Dimon would never take her seriously. For damn sure I couldn't tell him a very old woman had given me a madstone and with the gift came obligations. My tradeoff for assuming the gift's burden was obtaining information. Even if I were still working with the KBI, I would never be able to put this in terms he might understand.

I didn't want Dimon to think I was crazy.

"If you are so sure of that, Francesca, why haven't you gone to the people working to solve this case? Why haven't you told me before?"

"I have good reason not to trust the government. I wasn't sure about you either."

"But now you are sure?"

"Now I am sure."

Unbidden, the lost afternoon crossed my mind. "Would you show the map to me, Francesca?"

"Only a copy. The same one I showed to Victor."

After all this time. Finally concrete information about Victor's death. "That would be wonderful."

"Unlock the fifth drawer down."

Eagerly I opened it. Inside was an ancient

parchment. I spread it on the table. The ink had faded and the outlines were blurred. It made no sense to me. The names were all in Spanish. By now I had looked at Francesca's old books enough to recognize ancient Castilian. Puzzled, I looked at her.

There were tears in her eyes. She looked at the map with reverence. "This is just a copy. The real one is hidden."

By my blank look, then the flicker of disappointment over not being shown the real thing, she withdrew in an instant. I looked at her again, dismayed by her retreat.

"Francesca, I'm sure you know that I will have to tell Sam Abbott about the map if I think it has any bearing on finding Victor's killer. And he might choose to pass the information on the KBI."

"No. No. Don't do that. I beg you."

"I didn't mean to upset you. Please calm yourself."

Appalled by the fear on her face, I tried to make it right. "I won't say anything without talking to you first."

"There's no one I can trust. No one. I thought I could trust you. Only Victor understood. He was going to take it to court again. He was smart enough to get it done right."

"Francesca, the last thing I want to do is make you unhappy. Please forgive me."

For a moment she didn't speak. "I trusted you because you are a historian, Lottie Albright. Because you know how to keep secrets. Now you must work very hard to earn my trust again."

"Tell me what I need to do."

"Find me someone who will listen to me. Someone I can trust to help me with the judges, the courts, and the despicable government of these so-called United States of America. A government that has tried to steal my land over and over again."

"I simply don't understand," I said. Her look said no explanations were forthcoming. She was done with me for today.

"It is time to take me back to the main house."

I hoped she would compose herself before I handed her back over to the smiling Cecilia.

On the road home, I tried to make sense of the afternoon. Francesca repeatedly ignored the fact that I was an undersheriff. I was part of the government she despised. She *knew* that! In fact she had come to me in the beginning to beg me to help find her great-grandson's murderer. Surely she knew that at some point other agencies would be involved. I had told her that. It wasn't fair that she would turn on me.

It was twilight and the countryside was supposed to be cooling off. Instead, pastures were still like walking across a bed of cinders. No one went barefoot. Each time I left the Compound, I felt like I was returning to a war zone.

Heartsick over distressing Francesca when she had been kind enough to give me her precious madstone, I tried to think of a way to regain her trust. Where could I find a lawyer with impeccable integrity? Someone who would not get discouraged? Someone whose ethical standards were beyond reproach?

It struck me like a thunderbolt.

Elizabeth!

Keith's young Amazon of a daughter who went careening around Denver leaping tall buildings with a single bound. Championing abused women, slaying their husbands with the jawbone of an ass. Elizabeth was awesome and intelligent and rock-bottom honest.

Francesca didn't say the lawyer had to be pleasant.

Jubilant, I realized Elizabeth was the ideal person to help Angie, too. Elizabeth spent her life helping battered women. She would be the best person to get Angie back on her feet. I felt as if a boulder had bounded off my back.

Keith was out on a call when I got home. His note said Angie had gone with him. I would have total privacy. I stared at the phone trying to pinpoint why this was going to be so extremely hard for me. I picked up the receiver, punched in the numbers and said the words that I hated to admit were true.

"Elizabeth. I need your help."

Chapter Twenty-three

Elizabeth swooped into Western Kansas like a Valkyrie, took one look at Angie, and freaked.

"I want to know how she got into such a sorry state."

It was a statement, not a question. More of an accusation really, that somehow this was my fault.

"Well," I said carefully, knowing I was picking my way through a minefield, "as you know, psychological abuse can be very subtle and can take many forms. I think Steve has been undermining Angie's self-esteem for a very long time."

I did not feel right telling Elizabeth the number of miscarriages her sister had suffered. That was Angie's to tell.

"Thank you for calling me, Lottie." Her words were stiff. Forced.

"You're welcome." I said, knowing her "thank you" came even harder than my "I need help." I grabbed a steaming kettle off the stove, poured the water through a diffuser of Elizabeth's latest herbal tea, and waited for it to steep. "Angie needs someone who deals with this kind of problem professionally. Who better than her sister?"

We sat at the kitchen table and looked through the patio doors. Angie lay motionless in one of the recliners. Her face blended perfectly with the faded white resin.

Elizabeth stared at her limp form. "She's not well," She slammed the palm of her hand on the table. "I don't mean psychologically. I mean physically. She needs to start there first. We've got to get her healthy again." She leaped out of her chair, went to a spot out of Angie's line of sight and scrutinized her sister. "She looks anemic. Like she's lost blood." She whirled around to face me. "Has she had another miscarriage?"

Of course, I thought. *How could I have missed it?* The pallor, the depression, Steve's coldness to his defective wife. The latest miscarriage was recent.

"Nevermind," Elizabeth said. "She wouldn't tell that kind of thing to you."

I held my tongue.

She slid back the patio door and went outside and knelt in front of Angie, then took her hands and began talking to her.

Angie lay stone-still for a moment, then burst into tears. Shamed, she held her hands in front of her face. Elizabeth hauled Angie to her feet and hugged her fiercely. She led her inside the house and guided her up the stairs.

She came back down and marched to the phone. She called Dr. Golbert's office. She brushed aside the gatekeeper's attempts to make an appointment in a couple of weeks and insisted that she be put through to Dr. Golbert himself.

"Elizabeth Fiene here. Angie needs to be seen today if possible. Tomorrow at the latest. Please talk to your secretary and get it arranged."

By the time she hung up the phone, it was.

The next morning Elizabeth practically force-fed Angie eggs and orange juice, leveraged her into the cheery little yellow Volkswagen and sped off to town. They were back at ten o'clock. She ordered Angie upstairs to rest, adding they would begin her graduated exercise routine tomorrow.

Elizabeth's bright blond hair crackled with energy. Dressed in khaki shorts, Birkenstocks, and an intense chartreuse sleeveless top that rivaled the sun's glare, she looked ready to meet any challenge the day might hold. But there was a look in her eyes that said otherwise. Angie's depression had awaked her "suicide's daughter" free-floating anxiety.

"I suppose this godforsaken town's idea of mental health counseling still consists of 'pull yourself together and work a little harder.'" She folded her arms across her chest.

"Actually, yes. There's no professional help available out here. I don't know how much training the Catholic priest has had."

"That's not a good idea anyway. Not for Angie."

"There are other ministers."

"Is there a women's clinic? Support group?"

"Nope. Just AA and Weight Watchers. Craft groups. That sort of thing."

"Okay. Tell me about the other ministers."

I saved Father Talesbury for last. "He's a real piece of work. Hardly the one to comfort or sympathize." I told her all about this rogue priest's project of rescuing child soldiers.

"Him first. I'll go interview him."

My mouth must have dropped open. "But why?"

"To see if he needs help. Angie needs a job. Helping children."

"But she's in no shape to help with kids."

I would have had more luck thwarting a hurricane.

"She'll be in shape in a couple of weeks. Dr. Golbert gave her an iron injection. And some high-powered vitamins to boost her energy. As to the counseling, it will have to wait."

I didn't have to go to the office until afternoon. Outside, the air shimmered off the flagstone path. It simply would not rain. Our windbreak looked like it was headed for autumn, with the cedar needles looking brownish. They fell off at a touch and even if we watered day and night it would be impossible to save all of them. By winter, there would be ugly gaps with snow blowing through.

Elizabeth was never back here on a weekday and I knew she couldn't figure out what to do with herself until Angie came downstairs again. Sighing, she stared out at the hot glare of the mid-morning sun, her hands jammed into the pockets of her shorts.

Too hot to go outside for a walk, in a house kept spotless now thanks to Zola's untiring efforts, no one to fix, no dragons to slay, she practically crawled with restlessness. Suddenly, she turned toward me.

"Lottie, do you know if something is the matter with Tom?"

"No." If my answer was too quick, she didn't pick up on it.

"I suppose you don't know him well enough to notice anything wrong." She looked at me intently. "But he called the other day and said he wanted to talk to me. In person. That's not like him."

I knew, of course, it had to do with my sister.

He wanted to look Elizabeth in eye when he broke the news.

"Why in the hell doesn't it ever rain?"

Her eyes widened at my sudden stupid response. But it served to get the conversation away from Tom.

"Elizabeth, Angie is the main reason I wanted you to come home, but there's something else I wanted to ask you about. When you were growing up, did you ever hear anything about the Diaz Family and a legal case?"

"Oh, sure. Nothing specific. Just that the family had been fighting over land forever."

"Did you ever look into it?"

Instantly alert, her eyes narrowed. "Look into what, exactly?"

"I'm not sure." And I wasn't. Nothing Francesca had told me was secret. Even the fact that Victor intended to sue the government would soon be public knowledge. And the Diazes suing the government was nothing new. I didn't know the location of the real map, and it would be a cold day in hell now before Francesca showed that to me.

For that matter, it might not exist. I didn't intend to press Francesca until I found out if there was a legal basis for a claim. Ascertaining her valid property rights would be very difficult, but Elizabeth had all the right connections.

"Go to your dad's office," I said. "Grab a legal pad. We might as well do this right from the very beginning."

She came back and we set to work. "Doña Francesca claims her family once owned a huge amount of land."

"Used to? Their holdings are enormous now."

"I know that. I've seen a copy of a map, but it meant nothing to me. All the words were in Spanish. She claims to have hidden the real one."

"I thought you were the old documents whizbang."

"Sometimes. What I want to know is—are there old legal records I'm overlooking? I can come to Denver if you'll steer me to the right place. Colorado was once part of Kansas Territory."

Her vivid blue eyes sparked with interest. She was just moments away from applying her incredible concentration to the Diaz entanglements. "Wouldn't that kind of land information be part of the cache of Kansas Territorial records?"

"Maybe. Records before Kansas became a territory were hit and miss. There was some disagreement over the state boundary lines, too."

"So what is it that you want me to find?"

"Not find, I guess, since I don't know what I'm looking for. But if something does turn up indicating the family once owned more real estate, would you please represent Doña Francesca?"

"Sure." She laughed. "Well, not sight unseen."

"I need to be entirely straight with this woman. To be able to tell her that I've found a rock-solid, honest lawyer."

"If I'm going to be her lawyer, I'll have to talk with her in person."

"Okay. She won't agree to have you anyway until you do."

I called Cecilia and talked a blue streak before she agreed to ask Francesca to let another stranger on the property. And that was only after I had praised Elizabeth's abilities to the skies. She called back in a half-hour, and made it quite clear, that my step-daughter would be subject to inspection.

Elizabeth gasped as we turned up the road lead-ing to the Compound. "How can this be possible?"

"Oh, it gets better. You won't believe what lies at the end of this road."

She fell silent for a while. "The waste," she said finally. "The incredible waste. I haven't seen one crop. How much land is here?"

"About five square miles."

"And nothing under cultivation?"

"Not one single acre. Victor Perez and his

family live here, but he and his wife have day jobs. Cecilia Diaz takes care of her great-grandmother and only leaves the place when I'm here to watch over Francesca or when someone from George's family can stay with her."

Elizabeth had surprised me. I expected her to land solidly on the side of the "bring back the buffalo" faction. But no. She was raised a Fiene. Grow wheat and feed the world. Where's the sin in wanting to grow grain, Buster?

"Why would that old woman want more land if she has all this?" she asked.

"I don't know. Having been around her, I believe it's a matter of principle. She says the government is trying to rob her of her inheritance. She says her land is worth a fortune."

"The land right here is worth a fortune."

"I know."

"So how far back have you gone?"

"Just from the time Kansas became a state. Some of the Territorial records are missing. Kansas once had four constitutions, and the Territorial capitol kept switching." I glanced sideways to see if she was offended by my recital of basic information.

"Well, tracking down stuff through her side of the family wouldn't have done you one bit of good, because married women weren't allowed to own property. They were under the Law of Coverture."

"Not here, Elizabeth."

"Yes, they were. Women surrendered all their rights to own property to their husbands."

"Nope. Believe it or not, Kansas was way ahead of the game. The law was passed in 1868. Women could even claim homestead land."

"You forget I'm an expert on women's rights. It's my specialty. I know a lot more about those laws than you do." She smoldered like wet coals. I felt the heat coming from her side of the car.

I took a deep breath. "Contemporary law, maybe. But I know a lot more about historical laws."

And, just like that, we were in a fight. We rode in silence toward the main house.

Francesca and Cecilia had undoubtedly seen us coming up the lane because they were waiting at the end of the walk. Uneasily, I eyed Elizabeth's attire and wished I had asked her to change to something less jarring.

We drove to the Old House while Elizabeth and I feigned congeniality. Once inside, I had my first glimpse of Elizabeth when she was on her best behavior. Francesca walked her around to the various work stations and explained the categories of plants and herbs, while I sat in a chair and watched.

When they had finished the tour, they came

over to the chairs. I stood and relinquished my seat to Elizabeth.

"Go to the refrigerator please, Lottie Albright, and bring Miss Fiene and me a glass of lemonade. The glasses are in the cabinet to the side. Cecilia also brought over some cookies. There are plates on the shelf below the glasses."

If looks could kill, my glance toward Elizabeth would have fried her to a crisp. I got the coffee and lemonade and hovered to one side like an English butler.

Astounded by Elizabeth's ability to say all the right things and rein in her inner snark, I felt like I was at the Mad Hatter's Tea Party with her playing a role.

Elizabeth sipped the lemonade and nibbled at an oatmeal cookie. Neither of the women offered me refreshments. For that matter, Elizabeth now sat in "my" chair and clearly did not intend to give it back. "If you would like to consider having me as your lawyer, Doña Francesca, I imagine you would like me to answer some questions. And I have several I would like to ask you also."

Francesca gave a queenly nod of ascent. Then she turned to me. "I must ask you to leave, Lottie Albright."

I was speechless.

"Yes, please." Elizabeth smiled sweetly. "The

car is air-conditioned," she said to Francesca. "She'll be fine. Just fine. And she always has a book along."

Dumbfounded, I picked up my purse and my briefcase and headed toward the door.

Elizabeth came out with Francesca thirty minutes later and we drove her back to the main house.

"Well," I asked on the way home, "did you learn anything?" Elizabeth was hiding something. I could feel it.

"Lottie! You know better than that. I'm surprised at you. That's all privileged information."

If I hadn't needed to steer, I would have whacked my forehead with both hands to knock out the stupidity.

I had persuaded Elizabeth Fiene—the world's most honest lawyer—to take on Doña Francesca as a client. Now this tiny Spanish woman who might have insight into Victor's murder was committed to a lawyer who had undoubtedly told her "not to discuss anything with anyone."

I couldn't ask Elizabeth about how the map connected to the murder because she had agreed to pursue Francesca's claim. And I could no longer question Francesca, either.

We would see. Murder trumped civil cases.

I drove in cranky silence. Elizabeth whistled.

When we reached the farm, I went into my office and came out with the 1879 edition of

Dassler's *Compiled Laws of Kansas*, slapped it down on the desk, flipped through the pages and hollered for Elizabeth to come take a look.

"See there?" I pointed to the text giving Kansas women the right to own property, sue and be sued, and carry on a trade or business. "See?"

She sniffed.

Both smoldering, we left for separate rooms.

Tom and Josie came through that weekend on the way back from Denver. Elizabeth was white-faced after she and Tom came in from the patio. That evening when we all played together, there could not be any doubt we were looking at lovers. Josie flushed and looked down during ballads she would have thought corny before.

Tom's eyes stayed on her during every song. Charismatic as a movie star, he caressed the lyrics like they were written especially for my sister.

Thin-lipped, Elizabeth plunked through a polite minimum of tunes before she announced that she had a headache and was going up to bed.

Then Josie picked up her violin. Light from the setting sun outlined her body and her fingers flew like fire over the frets. Her skin glowed. She had never looked more beautiful.

Angie developed a tummy ache. Tosca retreated to her bed in the kitchen.

Keith and I endured. When we walked up the stairs we saw them strolling toward the pond, arm in arm. They turned and the setting sun profiled their long, slow kiss.

Chapter Twenty-four

Jane Jordan called and asked if it was okay to come to the historical society that afternoon because it was her day off. I was all too ready to set aside the stories I was editing.

"Monday, I'll start returning stuff for Margaret, and I thought I should start by having you look at my own family's box first."

Jane sat on the edge of the chair and we went over the artifacts one by one. When we came to the Klan poster, she closed her eyes. When she opened them, she had a bleak expression on her face.

"Even though you believe your ancestors weren't Klan members, every family has a black sheep. Someone who functions outside the core family's pattern."

Something was worrying this woman. She tucked a stray hair back under the net and evened the soft bow beneath the collar of her blouse.

"Are you sure there wasn't someone?" Virtually

every state in the union had a Klan chapter in the twenties. Surely Carlton County had one, too.

"No." Her jaw tightened. "No. Never. No one was ever a member. I wanted that evil poster out of my house, but I didn't want to burn it because I took a history course at a community college and the instructor felt very strongly about destroying historical material. I knew this was important."

I could not think of what to say next.

"It's not true. We were never, never involved. My grandfather was shocked that people thought we might be, just because we weren't Christians. We are now. Christians, I mean."

Something about this poster was a sore point with her. Almost as though she took this poster personally. Or perhaps she was simply pained by this reminder of one of the darkest periods in Kansas history.

"My people came to America to have the freedom to believe. To be able to worship any way we wanted. Or in our case, not worship, I guess. We didn't want to be Catholic. That was all. And because we didn't want to, and because the Klan hated Catholics, I guess Catholic-haters and Free-Thinkers all got lumped together somehow."

She quivered like a little Chihuahua. Her eyes never left my face as though checking for any sign of disbelief. Her legs were drawn back under the rung of the chair and she hugged her clipboard to her chest like she was defending herself from a sword thrust. I wanted to take her hand and suggest we continue this another day if it was upsetting her.

"We were not involved!" She untangled herself. "That's all Grandpa would say. 'We were not involved.' And he just said what his father told him. I've always been afraid we had participated in something terrible," she finally blurted, "but I don't know what it was. That's the truth. No one will talk about it."

"That's not unusual. Years ago, very few people ever talked about family scandals. They didn't make the rounds of talk shows to air their dirty linen in public."

"There was no scandal not to talk about." She planted her feet firmly on the floor. She stared at her shoes.

"Are you worried that if your family owned this poster I might think you aren't fit to work here?"

"Yes," she blurted, her eyes tearing up.

"Don't give it a second thought. We have volunteers here whose family histories would shame the devil."

Her eyelids fluttered in relief.

"We'll just keep your Klan poster here temporarily while we try to find who gave it to your family in the first place. We can't store it permanently, not because it's so abhorrent, but because we don't have the room, and because it's so commonplace it has very little historical value."

By the time she left, she had settled down.

I was becoming increasingly curious. Was the woman's family hiding something? Suspecting it wouldn't do me one bit of good to Google "KKK" and "Carlton County," I tried it anyway. With no results.

There was a tremendous resurgence of Klan activity during the sixties when blacks wanted to register to vote and school segregation ended. It emerged again in 1988 when David Duke, the Grand Wizard himself, became a presidential primary candidate.

But nothing about Carlton County and the Klan.

I stuck it out until closing time then decided to see if there was anything brewing at the sheriff's office. If so, Marvin would have called me. When something is really, *really* brewing, he calls Keith.

The land, the grass, and the sky were uniformly gray. There was no wind. I tried to imagine what it would have felt like in a one-room soddy in this kind of heat. One family had nine kids. It was two miles to the creek because all the claims closer had been snapped up at once.

Historians were just now zeroing in on

children's histories. The poor kids! How did they stand the heat? One older woman had told me of the peace and quiet she felt in the afternoon when she and all her children prayed the rosary. All the mysteries. All one hundred fifty decades. How had the kids felt? Was that calming for them, too?

Some kids just roamed around and came back by sundown. They spent many happy hours at the creeks, which were much larger back then. Much, much larger. Not like the dried-up trickles masquerading as streams now.

In one joyful family story, the writer told of going with his brother and sister down to their pond. His mother held up an old cane pole on the grass and told the kids to come home when the shadow fell at a certain place. They stayed there all day long. His story was filled with the wonder of childhood. Days spent outside, fishing, digging for frogs, water fights. Today, the mother would have been arrested for child-endangerment.

Sam's Suburban was not parked in his usual spot, but he was sitting behind his desk, doodling on a yellow legal pad. I glanced at the lines spoking out from a center circle.

Something. Something was on his face.

"What?" I drew up a chair.

"Now, I don't want you getting all excited." He reached for his pipe. "Don't go making too much of this, but I'm pretty sure there were two men involved when Victor was killed."

"You've heard from the KBI? Their forensics team found something?"

"Nope. But I've been looking through the photos of Victor's footprints."

"I've been thinking about that, too. A man with his throat cut can't run very far."

"He could run far enough if it was a botched job, which it was or they wouldn't have had to shoot him. I've been looking at the autopsy information. They didn't get the jugular and the carotid artery. Just mangled his trachea. He was fit. Likely, the bastard grabbed him from behind and thought he could manage by himself. When Victor struggled, he lost his grip. That's when Victor headed toward the shit pit."

"Okay. Makes sense, so where are you coming up with the two?"

"No real evidence. Point is, he ran. He didn't like the odds. Just one, he would have tried to fight him off before the bastard could get to him with a knife. And nothing shows a knock-down, drag-out."

I mulled this over. Even if Dimon and I hadn't gotten into a turf war, I knew I wouldn't have passed along Sam's totally unscientific speculations.

He picked up his legal pad and stood. "I need a lift. Suburban shot craps and I won't get it back until tomorrow."

"How is Angie doing?" he asked on the ride to his house. "Tom told me she was having a hard time."

"A lot better. Elizabeth worked out a strict routine and it's working."

"She still around?"

"No, Elizabeth went back to Denver a week ago. I was afraid Angie wouldn't stick with it when she left, but she did."

"When did Tom and Josie leave?"

"About two days ago."

"For Manhattan?"

I looked at him sharply. So he knew, too. But the old man always, *always* knew everything. Long before he was ready to discuss it with anyone else.

"Yes, for Manhattan."

"Figured."

We pulled up to his front door. "Sam, about your thinking it might be two men. Dimon doesn't want us on this case at all."

"He can't stop us from working in our own county."

"Maybe not. In fact, he's not going to pass one speck of information our way and he sure wouldn't like hearing this idea of yours. He's not much into speculation, so I'm not going to say anything about two men. Or anything Francesca tells me for that matter. He's like talking to a rock."

"Okay. I've never liked the bastard anyway. And if that's the way he wants to play it, we'll not report on a damn thing except the weather." He gave a wicked grin. "What is Francesca Diaz telling you?"

"She believes her grandson died because the murderer wanted to get his hands on a map. I tried to tell Dimon that he should interview Francesca, but he just thinks she's just craving attention."

"Does Mrs. Diaz have the map?"

"She says so, yes."

"I take it you've never seen it."

"No. I've seen a copy, but not the real thing."

"Will she show it to you?"

"That's not going to happen. She says the map is proof of an ancient claim to land and she doesn't trust the government. And now that she has a lawyer, she won't show it to either one of us."

"Wait her out."

"Her new lawyer is my stepdaughter. I can imagine how that would strike Dimon. He already thinks the whole county is inbred and Fiene-filled with devious incompetents."

"Maybe it's a good thing he doesn't believe

a thing Francesca says, or he might get a search warrant."

"A lot of good that would do. She would never tell him a damn thing."

"How hard can it be to coax an old lady to give up information?"

"You'd be surprised." No one had to tell me how Francesca would react to bullying. "What could Dimon do? Torture her?"

There was a long silence.

"He would think of something. He didn't hesitate to scare the hell out of Dwayne Weston with an OSHA inspection."

Keith called on the way to the house. "Josie and Tom are on their way."

"Back so soon? They just left."

Overhead was a hint of blue sky instead of solid brackish tan. I was so happy to be spending an evening with my sister that the dust rolling from behind my tires seemed tolerable for once. I wanted to feel her out about Francesca's abilities. *Ways? What to call whatever it was this old woman did?*

I didn't feel right about asking Josie if she believed in magic when I had just convinced myself that I didn't. I smiled, imagining her scorn. But anyone could tell I still wasn't sleeping well.

My hair was lifeless, my skin was dry. Nevertheless, just having her around would lift my spirits. We could talk about Angie. She obviously needed professional help.

I swerved to miss a rabbit. Across the road a huge circle irrigation system sat idle, as purposeless as a disabled Mars rover. Even irrigated corn looked like it was spitting back water instead of absorbing it. It drooped like a sulky child forced to drink.

My joy over an evening with Josie without the whole family around trumped my worry over Keith's ruined daughter. I started thinking constructively about what I could say to help Tom's sisters cope. The Three Furies.

Soothing phrases came to mind: They would get over it. They had to lose their brother to a woman some time.

I flew into the kitchen and took steaks out of the freezer and selected a bottle of wine and put it in the refrigerator. Keith came home a half-hour later. We looked at each other. I was in his arms in a second.

I hugged him hard. "It's been so long since Josie and I have really talked. She's been distracted and I've missed her."

"After supper I'll take Tom into town for beer and bar talk so you can have some privacy."

Josie's SUV sailed up the drive about five

o'clock. The wine was nicely chilled. The seasoned steaks were ready for the grill.

Tom got out and reached for a small suitcase. He breezed right past me. I stepped onto the front porch and with an exaggerated low bow, swept an arm across my chest to usher Josie inside.

She remained on the steps and held herself stiffly apart. Tosca was not in the car. "I really have to run on."

Keith stood in the open doorway. She gave us both tepid little social hugs. The kind that counts for nothing.

"Can't you at least stay for supper? Dinner."

"No, I really need to start back to Manhattan. I don't want to be too late. Harold says Tosca is really getting tired of my being gone." Harold Sider, a former FBI agent turned college professor, was her colleague at the university. "He's been such a dear to keep her."

She might as well have slammed her fist in my stomach. She didn't want to talk to me. She was avoiding me. It had never happened before. "Of course. The dog. Your little dog. Have a good trip."

"Have a good life," Tom added softly.

Josie froze, then looked at me with a stiff smile and a quick tragic flicker of her eyes. "Well, thank *you*, Lottie, Keith. Even if I can't stay."

She walked briskly down the walk and got in her car.

Sick at heart, I put my steak and her steak back in the refrigerator. I carried Keith's out to the grill. He followed me.

"I don't know what's going on with you two, but if there is anything I can…"

"I don't know either, Keith. Last week everything was just fine between us. Or at least I think it was. She really only had eyes for Tom."

He held himself very still and gave a small cautious nod. "Would you like for me to finish cooking that?"

"Just yours and Tom's. I've lost my appetite. Must be the heat." I winked back tears. I carried my glass of wine, and Josie's glass of wine over to the patio table and sat there intending to drink them both. When Keith finished cooking he carried the steaks inside, then rejoined me at firefly time.

He reached for my hand and kissed my fingertips.

"Love you," I said softly.

"I know."

He went to bed long before I did. I sat in the dark and wondered how I had come to such a sorry state. My sister was acting like we were casual acquaintances. My husband was anxious and overly solicitous. A foolish KBI agent was trying to do Sam

Abbott in. And I was worried that my stepdaughter might blow her brains out.

There were no stars and if there was a moon, I couldn't tell. Grayed wisps of ghost dry clouds lurked in the night sky, thwarting anyone who might enjoy watching the heavens.

There was nothing I could do about any of my problems. As near as I could tell, there was only one person who was thrilled when I showed up: Doña Francesca Bianco Loisel Montoya Diaz.

The next day I finally managed to put in a full morning's work at the historical society without a single personal or professional crisis. I thought about the best way to get a look at the map. The copy was hand-drawn, and obviously made before there were copy machines. Perhaps it wasn't an exact duplicate. I couldn't tell for sure until I saw the real thing. Ironically, just a week ago I had been seeking ways to avoid the Diaz Compound, now I was trying to think of excuses to get back into it.

Then I had a lucky break.

The phone rang. "Great-grandmother would like you to come out," Cecilia said. Her voice conveyed quiet disapproval. Since any contact between Francesca and me seemed to end up in some sort of emotional upheaval, I couldn't say I blamed her. "She says you two have unfinished business."

"We do, indeed." I glanced at the clock. "I'll be there around two. I owe your grandmother some work in exchange for medical information about her plant collection."

Exhilarated, I hung up the phone.

Chapter Twenty-five

My goal was simple and I rehearsed it on the drive over. I wanted to see if that mysterious map existed without trespassing on any confidential relationship Francesca had with Elizabeth. And while there, I intended to help mix some herbs she wanted to combine, but couldn't, because of her useless hands. Then we needed to develop a plan for finishing the project.

And just once, perhaps, I could spend an afternoon without causing turmoil. Surely I was mature enough to conduct myself with honor.

We got off to a good start.

Then Francesca blew all my intentions sky-high.

"I'm happy you and Elizabeth hit it off," I said.

I wasn't fishing. I swear I wasn't. It simply would have seemed unnatural to not mention their alliance at all

"She'll do," the old woman chuckled. "She'll not leave any stone unturned."

Even though I was determined not to pry, I had a whole list of unasked questions. Had she told Elizabeth that she suspected the map was connected to Victor's murder? Had she shown Elizabeth a copy of the map? Did she tell Elizabeth where the real map was located? If there was such a map.

Despite all these questions, I intended to take the high road. I would only ask about things pertaining to the murder.

"Francesca, I'm sure Elizabeth has asked you not to discuss any aspect of your map with anyone. And naturally that would include me. I respect that. But you've already told me you think Victor was murdered by someone who wanted to get ahold of it. Please believe me that Elizabeth's responsibility has to do with defending your claim. My interest and responsibility has to do with finding your great-grandson's murderer."

She gave a dismissive wave of her hand. "As to Elizabeth's instructions, I will talk to whomever I choose, Lottie Albright. No one will tell me who I can and cannot speak with. Elizabeth Fiene will do nicely as my lawyer. She has the passion to take on the government. But I will not have her order me around."

Oh, brother. This was not my doing. My goal of

honoring her professional relationship with Elizabeth was shot all to hell. If Francesca chose to tell me something, I wouldn't be able to stop her. For that matter, I had no way of knowing if Elizabeth knew Francesca thought acquiring the map was the motive behind Victor's murder.

"Today I will tell you where I keep the map. You will understand why it is the reason Victor was murdered."

She sat very still. Her eyes sorrowful. They never left my face. "You've become like a daughter to me. One should trust a daughter. We will go to the well house. Now. Before you help me with the compounds."

I helped her into the car. Even though the distance to the well is short, we still had to contend with the heat.

There should have been a sign over the door to the well house: "Peace to All Who Enter Here." Each time I entered, I wanted to stay. We were met by a soft flutter of pigeons as they left the high beam and escaped through the slits at the top of the casing. It was moist inside and the light coming through the slits was filtered and welcoming. Francesca sat on the two-foot wide brick ledge that abuts and encircles the entire exterior wall like a bench.

"I love it here so," she whispered. "When I was young, I would come here with my children. My dear children. It was always cool. We would nap here on these bricks sometimes. I brought pillows and blankets. I would come with my knitting and tell them stories. We would stay here until evening."

"It's never hot in here."

"No, never." We sat quietly for another ten minutes before she spoke again. "Now, I must show you where the map is kept."

She rose slowly and once upright walked over to the well itself. It had a high covered peaked roof anchored to wooden uprights large enough to have been railroad ties. An oaken bucket hung from a beam that spanned that spanned the diameter. An elaborate pulley system attached to this beam.

The structure was strong enough to hang a man, but because of its size and the elaborate exterior physical structure, it was anything but commonplace.

"We do not use this well anymore," Francesca said sadly. "It's wasted. One of my children added the bucket because he thought it was cute. Cute! As though anything dealing with water has ever been cute."

"I guess I assumed the well was watering your yard and garden."

"No. There's a stream. A large stream beneath the well. Technically, the well has nothing to do with it. The well is an entry point to the stream. It could have been put anywhere along the course of the stream. Years ago the pulley system was needed to lower buckets into the water. The well's depth ends just below the roof of the cave the stream flows through."

"Where does the underground stream start? Where are the headwaters?"

"I'm not sure. At one time the well was out in the open. Then my great-great grandfather built this structure to deter passersby. He didn't want our well to attract cutthroats heading farther west. So he built the enclosure to disguise the well. I'm sure you've noticed it looks like a small granary."

"Or a small silo. When I first saw it, I thought it looked like a silo."

"Now I will show you where I keep the map."

My heart pounded.

"We used to simply draw the box up with the pulley system. After the...incident, my husband said we needed to do a better job of hiding the map. We couldn't take a chance on one of the grandchildren drawing it up accidentally. This apparatus is more complicated than it looks. One of the beams rotates. It's important for you to remember that."

What incident? Why would a rotating beam be important? This was the second time she had hinted that something dark and terrible had affected her family.

"Before I show you everything, I want you to pledge on your sacred honor that you will keep the location of the map secret until such time as you are sure it is the last step to proving ownership."

My sacred honor.

Perhaps I no longer had any left. But I did not take this kind of pledge lightly. "Francesca, all I can promise is that I will guard this secret as a sacred trust and only reveal this location if in my judgment it becomes absolutely necessary."

"It will have to do. Someone must know. I cannot let this secret die with me." Her seamed face fell even further. "People have died to keep this secret."

"You can trust me. You do understand don't you, that it might be necessary to tell my husband?"

"Yes. That is only proper. You will watch and think and decide if Elizabeth's efforts have progressed to the point where it will be necessary to bring forth the map. And your watchful husband who worried about your involvement with me will watch over you like an eagle." She smiled wryly at the image of the watchers watching the watchers.

"You can trust my judgment."

"Yes, I am ready to do that now." She walked over to one of the beams. "Stand next to me."

I did.

Ruefully, she glanced at her own disfigured

hands. "Now spread your fingers and walk your hands back around the rim, pivoting off your pinky to your thumb, one, two, three, four times."

I hoped my hands were the same size as hers used to be.

"There now, look at your little finger. Look straight down the side of the well. You should see a little zinc washer."

"I see it." It was barely visible and blended with the soil.

"Don't disturb it. I don't want any dirt dislodged before we have to bring it up. The ring is attached to a cord—very strong—and when the time is right, wrap the cord around the center of the pulley and then connect it to the rotating beam. There is a gold case at the bottom of the stream. It is very well-sealed and weighted to prevent it from shifting. Inside is the map and deed."

All this, and I still was not going to see the "real" map.

"So there is a deed, too?"

"Yes."

I had not seen a copy of the deed. Just the map.

"And is the copy of the map you showed me an exact replica of the one in the well?"

"Of course."

"And won't Elizabeth need a copy to decide whether or not to go to court?"

She frowned. "She will. That and the deed. But I will only give it to her when I'm convinced she will be able to make some progress."

"Why are you showing this to me instead of to Elizabeth?"

"Because I can't let the secret die with me. I have chosen you. I believe your stepdaughter is a trustworthy person, but she has too much confidence in her own abilities. She needs to prove herself to me first."

"Did you show her the copy?"

"No. Only you. Besides you, only Victor. I told Elizabeth a copy existed and I would let her examine it later on after she conducted her research. I might have put you in danger by taking you into my confidence. Why would I want to risk putting Elizabeth in danger unnecessarily? She will research very thoroughly and I will know in a very short time if she intends to take my case to court."

She saw my face. "Now, don't get in a snit. I think your life is sacred. I wish you no harm. But Elizabeth is a lawyer. She is trained in logical thinking. She would never, never help me mix my herbs. She would dismiss it as superstitious nonsense. I knew at once not to tell her about the magical properties of plants. She was interested in their healing purposes, of course, but nearly everyone is. That same mindset would insist on seeing the copy before she began her research."

Even though I still hadn't seen it, I was now convinced the map existed. I had seen the little zinc washer, the rotating beam. Whether or not a valuable document lay at the bottom of a stream was another story altogether. The problem was, I needed a duplicate of that hand-drawn copy to take to Sam, and I doubted Francesca would let it leave the compound. I would have to bring out a portable scanner, or use a special camera.

"Francesca, I need to ask you something. Have you ever seen this map?"

"No, because it was placed there generations ago. But on my father's honor, it exists."

My heart sank. What if it was a myth? She had never seen it.

"Let's go back to the Old House now and take care of the tasks you want done."

Once there, she went immediately to the workstation on the west wall. It was still well-lighted and pleasant, but in another couple of hours rays from the setting sun would hurt my eyes.

"Light the candles first." Her voice rose. "With each herb you mix, sprinkle a little in the flame of the candle. That enhances the effectiveness of the herbs."

I obediently sprinkled pinches of snapdragon,

yarrow, and maidenhair fern in the candles before I blended the supply of herbs in a mortar.

"Dog's Mouth, Devil's Plaything, and Hair of Venus," Francesca said, supplying their magic names. There were other combinations. I funneled each batch into a jar and labeled the contents with names she dictated in old Castilian, which I had to record one letter at a time. The sun dropped below the top of the window. It was time to quit. Soon George and Teresa and all the children would be returning home.

"Before you leave here today, I will fix you an amulet. You need protection. I know that now. Your problems are caused by other…other things than the herbs. Go get another square of leather."

I went back to the drawer and selected a silky tan patch.

"First, trim it into a perfect circle. Then we will put the protective herbs and stones in the center. Then remove very small stones of malachite, obsidian, and onyx from the labeled jars to your left."

I rubbed the skin between my fingers before I rounded the square. "It's soft."

"It's from your power animal. So is the cord."

"I have a power animal?" I looked at her.

"Yes, we all do. Yours is the owl. You put a very high premium on wisdom. You treasure your mind. Now put protective herbs and stones in the center. Add a lodestone, too."

I tied it with a thin leather cord.

You must wear it at all times."

"Francesca, I can't work as an undersheriff with a medicine bundle dangling from around my neck. It wouldn't look good."

"Tuck it inside your bra," she snapped. "You also need to know about returning hexes and how to bring yourself out of a mirror if your soul is captured."

I was tired. The sun was in my eyes. She was the only one I knew who had any knowledge of hexes and spells. I doubted anyone in Carlton County wanted to send my soul inside a mirror. They might want to send me to hell, but not inside a mirror. I yawned while she recited the combinations of drugs. The snapdragon was the only flower that sounded familiar.

To my credit, I didn't so much as raise a skeptical eyebrow when the process was accompanied by her chants and the tossing of herbs in a candle flame. Her excitement grew with every compound.

She asked me to mix one last batch.

That was the last thing I remembered clearly. I remembered hitting the floor, hearing her screams. I remembered being loaded into my Tahoe.

I remembered Keith hauling me out.

Chapter Twenty-six

The next morning, I think it was morning, I was still very, very sick. I woke up in my own bed. Keith heard me get up and go to the bathroom. He was up the stairs in a flash.

"What happened?" I asked as I made my way back to the bed and collapsed.

"You tell me."

"All I remember is hitting the floor. How did I get home?"

"I got a phone call from a man saying he was related to Doña Francesca Diaz and that he wanted to make sure someone was around, because you had gotten sick and he was bringing you here."

"George Perez, I'm sure."

"I said I would come get you, but he said he was well on the way. He drove up in your Tahoe. He was followed by a young woman in an old Taurus. Riding with her was an old woman who looked like she was auditioning for Batman's grandmother."

"That was Doña Francesca Diaz. And her great-granddaughter, Cecilia."

"Yes, they introduced themselves. Anyway, George and I managed to get you up the stairs and into bed. He wanted to take off immediately, but he didn't have a separate ride so he had to stay until Mrs. Diaz and the other woman were ready to leave. I wanted to take you to the emergency room right away, but Mrs. Diaz was adamant that drugs and injections might be harmful. She assured me that you suffered from heat exhaustion and would be fine in the morning."

I recalled the time in the feedyard when I knew the heat was getting to me. But, heat exhaustion would not knock me out for a whole night and well into the next morning. It had to have been something else.

"She said you had not taken any of the herbs."

"I didn't, Keith. Not even a pinch."

"She told me she was a kind of nurse, a healer, and that she knew as much as anyone at the hospital."

"That is probably true," I mumbled.

"She had a black satchel with her and started ordering the young woman around. She asked me to stay with you while they went through the house. I'm not sure what in the hell all they did. They left a bouquet of snapdragons on the dresser and another bunch downstairs and several little bouquets of herbs in different places. And rocks. I'm finding little pebbles in strange places."

I swallowed.

"Can't see where that would hurt anything, but it's a funny thing for a nurse to do." Keith's face was solemn. He left my side long enough to open the curtains. "Then she went down into the kitchen. Angie helped them find things. She said the young woman looked fit to be tied, but Mrs. Diaz told her how to fix some kind of tea and she did it. They brought a tray back upstairs and made you drink a couple of sips."

"Oh, Keith."

"Then they left."

Tears started down my cheeks. I reached for him and clung for dear life. This was the second time I had ended up in bed after a visit to Francesca.

"Lottie, what in hell is going on? Something is. I know you don't like it when I tell you what to do, but I want you to stay away from that place. Please." He smoothed back my hair and leaned over and kissed my forehead.

"I won't go there unless you are with me."

"Okay. I'll settle for that."

"First, let me tell you what happened yesterday and you'll understand why we might have to make more trips to the compound. I learned something that might have a connection to Victor's murder. "This will take a while." I brought him up to date.

"Whew! An underground spring!"

"Yes, and that mysterious map."

He shot me an appraising look. "If it exists. And if there is something there worth dying for. What if Dimon is right in thinking Mrs. Diaz believes an old family myth that has no basis in fact? What if she is just wanting attention? "

"She's not seeking attention. She's trying to avoid it. After all, she's lived in seclusion for years and years. It took the murder of her great-grandson to draw her outside her home."

"You've got a point there." He stroked a finger along his jaw and mulled it over. "She doesn't sound like someone who craves the limelight."

"Nevertheless, the next time I go there, you can come ,too. My historical research into the medicinal use of plants is finished anyway. Yesterday I helped Francesca mix some herbs that she couldn't manage by herself. As to my sick spell…"

"Spells," he said. "Spells. Twice now something hasn't been right when you come back from that place."

"I've been thinking about that. I don't think it was heat exhaustion. I believe the aroma from the plants, the naturally high carbon dioxide content in that room gets to me, whereas Francesca is immune to them."

"All I ask is that you don't go there alone anymore."

"I won't."

"I hope you don't put too much stock in what that old woman is telling you."

"I don't. I take it all with a grain of salt." *I think.*

He gathered me up and hugged me against his chest. "Sleep," he said. "That's an order."

"Okay."

He closed the door behind him and I sank exhausted against the pillows. Angie came in carrying a breakfast tray containing scrambled eggs, toast, a glass of orange juice, and coffee.

"You're looking so much better, Angie."

"That's more than I can say for you. Dad was worried sick. Mrs. Diaz had to talk hard to keep him from taking you right to the emergency room."

Watching Angie work, I knew Elizabeth had made the right call when she insisted her sister would be the happiest working with children. She was a natural caretaker.

Elizabeth! I had just told Keith I wouldn't go to the Diaz Compound again without him. But what if Elizabeth needed a copy of the map for her purposes? Francesca hadn't shown it to her. I was the only one who knew the location of the real map. However, the copy would certainly be enough for Elizabeth's investigative purposes until she decided to move forward in a court of law.

I poured a cup of coffee and thought about it. No. Unless a clear link to Victor's murder emerged, it was Elizabeth's job, not mine, to persuade Francesca Diaz to give her a copy of the map to make her case. *Good luck with that.*

Did I have a duty to tell the KBI about any evidence I thought had some connection to Victor's murder? No siree. Dimon had made that clear. Not if it was just speculation. In Keith's opinion, Francesca might be attaching too much importance to family myths. I didn't think so, but it was a possibility. I wasn't going to rule it out.

I would take Sam Abbott's "speculations" over Dimon's hard-wired hotshots anytime.

Thus, I argued myself back to sleep.

Elizabeth called two days later. "Bad news, I'm afraid, Lottie. There is no mysterious Diaz claim and brace yourself for even worse news. They don't even own the land they are living on now."

"That's impossible," I stammered. "That can't be true."

"It is. I hired a researcher to go through the

Territorial records, all sixty-one boxes and sixty-five volumes. Six reels of microfilm too."

"From the time Colorado was part of Kansas Territory?"

"Yes, and then I had my researchers look into a special National Archives collection held at Atlanta, Georgia."

Who had paid for all this? Who had this kind of time? I wondered.

"You said it yourself early on. We just didn't understand what Francesca's claims really meant. There was no record of any deeds. No proof of land ownership whatsoever. There were a couple of lawsuits mentioned in various Kansas Territorial newspapers but they were all presented as a joke. Sort of along the lines of 'it's spring again and time for a certain Spanish family to do battle over a land claim.'"

"But you, Zola, everyone seemed to know about these lawsuits."

"I know. But we were kids. Come to think of it, it wouldn't make sense that we knew about any kind of lawsuits at all, but we did."

I was sick. Just sick.

"What are you going to do?" I asked finally.

"Nothing. I'm not going to a file a suit because there's no case here. If I were going to be her attorney, I wouldn't be talking to you. I just wanted you to know that for some reason Francesca might be making a lot of stuff up. I'm going to make a flying trip back to Kansas to tell her in person she has no basis for pursuing litigation. I also promised to take care of another unrelated bit of business."

"Will you stop by?"

"Just long enough to say hello."

We hung up.

This changed everything. Although I had seen a copy of the alleged map, now I suspected it didn't mean anything. As for the reason why Francesca might be making it all up, I suspected that was to con me into helping her mix her herbs. She had started innocently enough, just wanting to me to know this map might be the reason was Victor was killed. Then after I talked her into letting me record the healing uses of all her plants, she sensed I was the ideal apprentice. She had lured me in deeper by hinting that her family had a secret heritage. Something that would change their lives. And I fell for it hook, line, and sinker.

I opened my desk and started sorting thumbtacks into different colors. Josie says I have compulsive tendencies, but I see no sense in putting much stock in the opinion of a smoker.

When I settled down and could think again,

I was less cynical. Francesca didn't fit the profile of a scheming hustler. She was simply a deluded old woman. There was no doubt in my mind that Francesca Diaz *thought* the family owned more property. Ownership would never become an issue unless they tried to sell it and an abstract company started looking into it.

I paced and hoped the phone didn't ring. At the end of the day, I decided I didn't go around challenging the property rights of other people in the county, so why should the Diaz family be an exception? A lot of the families in Northwest Kansas had acquired land where boundaries were fuzzy. Old abstracts had disappeared. Especially during the Territorial period. During the organization of various counties, some of the county clerks had been incompetent—to put it mildly. There had been vicious county-seat fights in over half the counties in Kansas. Old wooden courthouses had burned down. Sometimes county records had been taken at gunpoint.

But if the Diazes ever tried to sell their land, all hell would break loose. In the meantime, the only thing that was actually my business was if anyone in that compound knew anything about a murder. And I was beginning to think that no one did, and that included Doña Francesca Bianco Loisel Montoya Diaz.

Thank God for thinking. For cold logic. Having decided to do absolutely nothing about anything, I swept the thumbtacks off the desk into their little plastic container and locked up for the day.

Cecilia called the next morning and said Francesca wanted to give me some compounds for Angie. She sounded weary, disapproving, tired of taking orders from her great-grandmother. I was sure whatever Francesca thought might help Angie would be safe and effective.

I had told my husband I would never go there alone again.

Keith had just headed out the door. I caught him at the end of the sidewalk. "We need to make a quick trip to the Diaz Compound. If you don't want me to go without you, that means you're going to be at her beck and call too."

I was glad he was going. I wanted his impression of the place.

Keith didn't say a word for several miles. "Just because it has always rained again doesn't mean it will this time." He said finally. He scowled and I laughed. He reached over and pinched my thigh.

When we reached the road that would take us into the compound, he let out a slow whistle.

"I've heard about this place, but I don't believe it. Just *can't* believe it. It's like Brigadoon. A place that has come up out of the mists."

"It's literally out of this world." I remembered how I felt when I saw it the first time.

"Look at those trees. And that pasture. Look at the height of that grass."

He stopped the car for a minute. "This beats anything I've ever seen. Elizabeth tried to tell me about it, but I guess I thought she was exaggerating."

"There's other surprises. Wait until you have a chance to really look things over."

We picked up Francesca and drove her to the workroom. All the while Keith looked like he had stumbled into Oz.

Francesca surprised me by turning on the charm.

"I'm so sorry we had to meet under such strange circumstances the other night, Mr. Fiene. I'm delighted to see Lottie so hearty and hale now. Do you accompany her often?"

He started to say only when he was on official business, but checked himself. "Only when she asks me to come along." He gave me a wicked grin. He drove, Francesca was in the front seat beside him. I sat in the back and was at the ideal angle for him to see me stick out my tongue in the rearview mirror.

"I hope your daughter, Angie, is doing well.

I have some compounds I think might help her. I hope Lottie told you I have some compounds that will help her, too."

We went inside, she showed him her work-room and the Spanish books. By the lively exchange of questions and answers, I knew he was quite impressed with her understanding of medicine.

"Would you like to look around outside while I talk to Lottie about getting some material trans-lated? All the houses are empty except mine and the Spanish bungalow, so feel free to go inside them."

"I would love to. This is quite a place you have here." Keith went off to inspect the property.

Francesca waved toward the wall of books. "They are rare and precious. I need a sensitive scholar to do the translating. Not an amateur who thinks this abominable modern-day Mexican mixture can be substituted for ancient Castilian. I would like you to recommend someone who is worthy of the task."

"The Kansas State Historical Society has a list of linguistic consultants. I'll talk to them tomorrow."

"Now help me mix the compounds for Angie."

We walked over to a worktable and I took pinches of herbs from various jars and funneled them into a little bottle.

"She should be fine now. Mix these in tea

twice a day. Call on me when she wants to become pregnant again."

Startled, I looked at her face. How had she known that Angie had just lost a child? I doubted this extremely private daughter would have volunteered the information to Francesca the night she and Cecilia brought me home.

"It's a very simple compound," she said. "It builds back the blood. And will help her spirits."

Dr. Golbert had said she was slightly anemic. Apparently with just a glance, Francesca thought the same. It would be very interesting to have the two practitioners get together.

"I appreciate it, Francesca. Now, let me find my husband and we'll take you back to the main house."

"One final mixture, please, before you leave. A mixture to accompany the seeing herbs."

I smiled and glanced at the red crystal jar. "You haven't taken them yet, I see."

"No."

"Have you changed your mind?"

"No. I've delayed. It is a grave thing to see and then act on the seeing. Even if one has spent half a lifetime preparing for just such a moment."

I was uneasy. "Well, let's finish the compound right away. My husband will want to go as soon as we're done."

Keith was right outside the door, staring up at the roof where it joined with the exterior wall.

"All through?" He looked at Francesca curiously, then thanked her for taking the time to mix the herbs for Angie.

"I didn't. I can't because of my hands." She held them up. He winced, then his eyes traveled up to her ancient face. "These are medicines I usually keep around for my own family and some of their friends. For years now I've lacked the ability to compound the ordinary mixtures I need to have on hand. The supply is replenished now. Your wife has been very helpful. I've become quite fond of her, you know."

"Well, what do you think of the place?" I asked Keith on the way home.

"You mean other than the incredible waste of good pastureland?"

"Yes."

"I think the whole place is weird as hell, if you want to know the truth. I did quite a bit of poking around. And every single house I had time to check was built with the techniques that would have been used during the time period the houses represent."

"Why? There's a Sears house. So I understand

that. But why emulate old construction methods? It's not like the place is a living museum that attracts tourists."

"The strangest thing of all is the workroom building. What you call the Old House. There were no nails. I mean none. Metal nails have been around since the Bronze Age. These people used wooden pegs. What would be the point of doing that? "

"The main house is furnished with a hodge-podge of period furniture. It all looks like it was actually used at one time."

"I measured that cottonwood. It's actually thirty-five feet around."

"Guestimating?"

"No, for real. There's a tape measure in the console in the Suburban."

"That's surely the largest cottonwood in Kansas."

"And there is something else that is even more peculiar." The evening sun lighted his profile. "You said there were four kids living here. Right?"

"George's kids. But I make it point to leave before George or his wife gets home from work. So I've never seen the kids."

"There were no animals on the place. Not a single one that I could see. Not even a dog."

Chapter Twenty-seven

It was a rare happy morning. I buzzed around the kitchen like a fifties housewife who measured her self-worth by the quantity of food she could produce. Elizabeth had called last night. She and Bettina were coming home. She had devised some goofy plan to have a grown girls' slumber party to cheer up Angie. She twisted her little sister's arm to get her to ditch her kids and husband for the weekend.

Elizabeth was determined to find an instrument for Angie and was bringing a set of drums and a tambourine. She had decided music was good for the soul, and Angie would, by God, become an active participant in her own mental-health rehabilitation.

Then early this morning, Josie had called and said she would be driving back to Western Kansas because she wanted to see Tom. "I need to talk to him in person."

Keith was thrilled that all of his family would be here and his pleasure was contagious. I had made a truce with the heat. I simply stayed inside every day of the week, whether at home or working in the historical society or at the sheriff's office. I played like that was the normal thing to do. The heat, the dust would pass. I was sure it would. The trick was to wait it out.

Margaret called before nine.

"You might as well take another full day off. Jane has been cut back to three days a week at the abstract office, so she wants to put in more time here."

"I'm sorry to see her lose the work, but it's sure our gain."

"She's priceless. Right now, she's out criss-crossing the county returning donations. She loves visiting families. In fact, she's so good at this that I want her reimbursed for her gas."

"Maybe we can wangle full mileage from the county commissioners instead of taking it out of the general budget."

"She's going to the Diaz Compound today. She found a tiny penciled name on the back of the Klan poster she brought in. It's faded. We could hardly make it out. But it was Diaz. I'm sure of it. We both looked at with a magnifying glass." She sniffed. "I'm surprised you didn't see it."

"I'm sorry. That was certainly an oversight."

"No problem. She's going to take it and a little collar out there. It's for a cat, I think. Anyway, it has a Spanish label. It was in with some of the items no one has had time to return. I have no idea where most of it came from. It's from long before we started a formal record system. There's five boxes in all."

There was a sudden stab in my head. I pressed my palm against my forehead. There was something I should remember about Francesca and the Klan. And a cat. There was something about a cat.

"I'm glad you and Jane are getting on so well."

"I don't know what I ever did without her."

Zola came into the kitchen and said she was sorry that she would have to shortchange my cleaning day. "Blame your husband," she said as she hurried out the door. "He's the one who keeps messing things up. After I help Keith for a couple of hours, I'll barely have time to shower and start supper before the girls get here."

"Actually, I'm the one who derailed him. I dragged him over to the Diaz Compound yesterday and that put him behind."

"Whatever. Anyway, feeding livestock takes precedence over dusting furniture."

"Don't I know!"

I waved her outside and went into Keith's

office. He is a tidy man, and it isn't much of a chore to flick around with a feather duster. I got to the shelf with the madstone and smiled. He hadn't even asked why it was sitting there.

Light reflected off Keith's tiny voice recorder on the floor at the edge of the desk. I remembered accidentally putting it inside my briefcase instead of my own cassette player one day when I went to Francesca's. The day that had disappeared from my mind. One of the two days when I had ended up in bed. It must have fallen out of my briefcase when I took out the madstone.

I scrambled down the step stool, picked up the recorder and tackled the difficult toggle menu. It wasn't clear-cut like my cassette player. It would be great if I had recorded some of the missing day. I pushed the menu button, right, then left, then dead center. It started into a playback mode. I listened while I continued dusting.

The step stool was barely high enough for me to reach the top shelves. I listened to small talk, the pleasant sound of teacups set on saucers, the distant hoot of an owl. Then I froze with the feather duster in my hand.

I climbed down off the stool and sat in Keith's chair and listened to the most gut-wrenching narrative I had ever heard. I could hardly take it all in. That hazy afternoon was coming back.

Reconstructing itself like a kaleidoscope that formed bits and pieces into shapes and colors.

It was coming back now. All of it. Her terrible story about the night when the Klan decided to punish Francesca for being a witch and her husband for being a Catholic.

Her hands broken, shattered. Her husband mad with grief. The killing of the animals. Their dear animals. The wonderful Andalusian horses. The horses of kings, Francesca had called them. Their dogs. And her precious cat. Because they thought her little cat was a witch's familiar.

I remembered the incredible child-like poem that seemed to underscore the horror of it all.

Those hands. How could I have forgotten any of it? The warm room, the tea, the carbon dioxide, the heat?

I bent over and clutched my stomach but endured until the end. Endured until I heard Francesca say she would get her revenge. The seeing drugs. Dear God, I had personally mixed the drugs that would allow Francesca to go back in time and see the faces of men who had harmed her.

Revenge. She had dedicated her life to getting revenge. God only knew what she planned to do. What had I mixed the day Keith and I were there together?

And Jane was headed there right now with a Klan poster and a cat's collar.

I scribbled a note to Keith—Trouble. At Compound"—left it on the counter, then tore out of the house. My promise to never go to Francesca's alone just got trashed. He was in the pasture and might as well have been on Mars. I couldn't take the time to track him down. I needed to reach Jane right away.

I glanced in the rearview mirror. A tower of dust rose behind me. My heart was in my throat, my blood pounded in my temples. My hands were gripping the steering wheel so tightly, my knuckles were white.

Francesca wanted revenge. She was determined to get it. She lived for it. She had said that hate was stronger than love. I had no doubt that in Francesca's mind that included punishing the sins of the fathers through the children.

Skidding on a patch of gravel, I over-braked, over-steered, then took my foot off the accelerator. I couldn't help Jane if I were lying in a ditch.

Scenarios swirled through my mind. *What would I find? Would Francesca allow her to get into the workroom?* Only if she didn't know what Jane was bringing, I decided.

Cecilia would probably leave if Jane said she intended to stay for several hours. She seemed more comfortable now about leaving others in charge of Francesca. She was probably getting used to people tromping through the place. Me, Elizabeth, Keith. No visitors for years, and then a veritable stream of people going back and forth.

Fear eased just enough for my brain to kick in. Jane absolutely would have called in advance to make sure Francesca was home, but she wouldn't have mentioned what she was bringing. Yes, I was positive that would be the case. So Cecilia would ask Jane to drive herself and Francesca to the workroom. And then she would leave for the afternoon.

And then? I swallowed tears as I imagined Francesca's reaction to the poster, the little cat's collar. Jane's confusion.

Francesca had vowed to get revenge for her ruined hands. Her desecrated family. The slaughter of their animals.

But what she could do? *She couldn't do anything. Not anything. Not with those hands.*

Unless she kept herself together long enough to persuade Jane to put on the kettle for tea.

She couldn't manage a single thing on her own. Would Francesca get her to drink a lethal combination of herbs? Probably mixed by my own hand. The Bohemian woman would certainly stay for tea just to be polite.

I prayed I would not be too late.

Perhaps Francesca would cause harm by other means. I shuddered, realizing I actually believed Francesca could cast a spell. Believed that she could conjure up a hex. I was infected with her madness.

Jane's little Honda was parked in front of the workshop. I pulled up beside it and slammed on the brakes. I jumped out and rushed inside.

Francesca was lying on the floor. There was broken glass all around. Herbs strewn across one of the worktables. Sparkling in the sunlight was the red crystal jar, still full. She had not taken the seeing herbs or any of the mixture I mixed last.

Jane was nowhere in sight.

I rushed over to the old woman and felt for a pulse. It was faint, but there. The Klan poster and a little collar with a bell was on the floor beside her.

She started to rouse.

"Don't move," I ordered. "Lie still. I'm going to the car and I'll call the hospital. They'll have an ambulance here immediately."

"No. No." She tried to roll to one side so she could push herself up with her elbow. "No. Tea. Protection."

There was a cup on the table and glass of water.

I gave her the water first, then held the cup to her lips. She took a couple of more sips. "Now you."

"An ambulance. I need to get to the satellite phone in my car and call an ambulance. "

"No. Protection first. Both of us. Protection first." Her voice rose.

Her pulse accelerated so rapidly I knew she was on the verge of a stroke. Not wanting to upset her, I finished the cup.

"You have your owl amulet?" Her voice faltered.

"Yes."

"Must try. Must try to protect you. Put your soul in the mirror. Get me a mirror."

"No. The ambulance first."

"No. You."

Her breathing quickened again. Her heart beat faster. I saw a hand mirror on the work table and brought it to her. She quieted. I held the mirror up to my face and she began to chant. I impatiently repeated words I didn't understand.

"Where is Jane?"

She closed her eyes for a second and her breath faltered. Her eyes drifted to the poster and the little collar. "Her family. It was her family. They had the collar. Didn't need to *see*. She brought the evidence with her."

"Francesca, no! I still can't believe it. Where is she?"

Her pulse galloped.

"Jane," she whispered. "Jane Jordan. Danger. Danger." She glanced toward the door that led to the rest of the house.

I rose. My mind raced. I had come here without a gun or any kind of weapon. I didn't dare go to the car and call for help. I could not risk leaving Francesca here alone for even a second if she was trying to tell me Jane Jordan was in the next room.

The quiet little worker bee I had trusted.

I looked around. I didn't know what I would be dealing with. I tiptoed to one of the worktables and grabbed a granite pestle.

My heart pounded. Blood throbbed in my temples. I eased over to the door. I carefully twisted the crystal knob.

Jane Jordan wriggled on the floor.

Her mouth, hands, and feet were bound with duct tape.

Chapter Twenty-eight

I tossed the pestle aside and reached to pull the tape off Jane.

Not smart. I should step back and check the surroundings first. Before I freed Jane. I knew that, but I couldn't focus. I shook my head to try to clear it. My fingers started to grow numb, then they trembled. I waited for my dizziness to subside, but still couldn't manage to grasp the end of the tape.

What had Francesca put in the tea?

Jane squealed. Her eyes widened.

I turned. But I couldn't make my feet work. Couldn't think. My legs were unsteady.

Oh no, oh no, oh no. What had been in Francesca's tea?

I drifted in and out of my mind. First everything was sharper, then blurred and distant. Then there were hands under my armpits and a man's voice. No, two voices, I thought. There were two. And they were dragging, dragging me toward the well house. And Francesca, too.

Behind me she wailed, keened like some primitive animal.

We were shoved into the well house. The walls contracted, expanded, wavered before my eyes. The bricks glowed in ever-changing colors like iridescent crystal.

Francesca's voice sounded from a distance. Like it was coming from the well opening. But when I turned, she was right beside me.

Her eyes glittered. "I'll never tell. Never." She lifted her ruined hands. "See these? Do you think if I were capable of enduring all this I would now tell?"

"No, you see this." He aimed a shotgun toward her stomach. Then he glanced at her hands. Studied her hands. "Or perhaps you need something more. Now tell us where the map is."

"I will die first."

"No you will die after you tell, old witch. After."

"I can choose. I *will* choose. I will die now."

She seemed taller. Straighter. Then she faded in and out. She slipped, wavered before my eyes.

"Sadly, I'm leaving you between, Lottie Albright. In the mirror. But I must go now. And someone else must come after you." Her voice was faint, distant.

"Francesca!"

She sank onto the floor. Her eyes fluttered.

"Leaving you between. God forgive me. You

won't be able to stop it. Mirror." Her voice was thick with pain. Her breaths were shallow. "In the mirror. Here or the other side."

Her mouth stilled.

Then there were hands dragging me toward the ledge of the well. I could not resist. Could not think. I heard an owl hoot. Calling my name.

There were two men. Two men. I had seen them before. At the feedyard? No, at the funeral. They were the two men harassing Maria. The ones who claimed to be distant cousins while she insisted she didn't even have an Aunt Lucia.

Hadn't Sam said there were two men? Suddenly they loosened their grip.

I heard a car. More than a car—a monster—coming up the lane. A roaring coming up the lane.

Josie's Mercedes drove past the open well house door.

Elizabeth and Zola were with her. It didn't make sense. Why were they here? My mind wavered, cleared. My note to Keith. They had probably seen the note I left in the kitchen.

They were driving toward the Old House. Francesca's workroom. They would see my car. Think I was in there, and see all of the broken glass. Jane would thump her feet.

She would do something. Make some kind of noise when they called out.

My stomach lurched. Jane would tell them Francesca and I were in danger. *Please God, don't let those women come here. Don't let them come toward armed men.*

Tears stung my eyes. But my brain sharpened, sorted, tried to decide how to protect them. None of these women would immediately think of going to the well house. None of the three of them had ever been here. No reason to decide to check inside the well house. Jane wouldn't know where the men were taking us.

Josie would know to call for help. Immediately. Her cell phone would be out of range, but she could use the satellite phone in my car. Would she think of that? In time?

My heart thumped in my chest. There was no reason for any of these women to immediately suspect we had been taken to this place. *Don't come. Don't come.* I chanted it silently over and over again, like a mantra.

But Tosca figured it out. Became a bloodhound in the space of a blood speckle.

Sick at heart, I heard the yipping little dog tearing toward us.

The men had been still up until then. But this was a game-changer. One of them stepped into the doorway and fired at Tosca.

He missed.

"Tosca," Josie screamed. "Tosca. Tosca. Stop."

She ran toward Tosca, scooped her up and held her tightly against her chest.

"Go back," I screamed. "Josie, go back."

I turned to the man holding the shotgun and lunged at him. "You bastard. Those women are unarmed. Defenseless." I swayed. My words were slurred. "What do you want from us?" He backhanded me across the jaw. I hit the wall and began sliding toward the floor. I rolled to my feet.

"Josie, Elizabeth, Zola. Stay back." Then my vision stabilized. All my senses sharpened and suddenly I could think again.

Shouldn't have used names. Shouldn't have let them know there were only three women. Unarmed women.

The man with the handgun walked outside and motioned to Josie. "Get inside with her. Now."

Carrying Tosca, Josie stumbled into the well house. Her sobs echoed off the stone walls. She carefully laid the trembling shih tzu on one of the stone benches.

She stood next to me and I reached for her hand, hoping to transmit some of my newfound strength.

"Well now, ain't this something." The man with the shotgun was red-faced with a large stomach and arms like hams. I remembered his face now.

His rudeness toward Maria Diaz at the funeral. His thighs bulged in his jeans. I decided it would be a mistake to think he was slow because he was so big.

The dark-haired man with the handgun edged back for a better look. He looked eager to spring, like a pit bull. Hair-trigger eyes. Excitable. He transferred the gun to his other hand. I looked away, not wanting to give him an excuse to hurt us.

"Yes. Indeedy. This is something. Can't believe our luck. Can you, Leon?" He looked at Josie, then me, then back again. "One for each of us." Their eyes traveled over our bodies. "And just think. One of them probably has some information."

"We're entitled to this information," Leon snickered. "How long do you think it's going to take, Jerry?"

"A while. A good long while. And I believe it requires enhanced interrogation techniques."

"Very enhanced." Leon pulled out a pocket knife. He pulled Josie toward him and ripped her blouse down to her waist. Then he slit the front of her bra. Her breasts glistened in a ray of sunlight coming through the slit at the top of the well house. "Oh my, yes." He looked at me. "Double the enhancement."

"But let's not take any chances on leaving those other two alone. They might be dreaming up all kinds of mischief."

"Only way out is to drive past us, Jerry. No problem."

"No, we'll tend to them now. Right now. Or sort of take care of them. I think they would be happier back here, don't you? With their friends?"

Leon looked around and eyed the ropes hanging from the pulley system. He stepped forward and ran his hands over Josie. "Yes, they will all be happier united with their friends." He pinched one of her nipples. "God, I want to make this woman happy. Right now."

Jerry gave a soft chuckle. "The other women first." He turned to me. "What did you call them? Elizabeth? Zola?"

"Tie them up," he ordered Leon. "Don't want no slip-ups. You'll get your reward. Promise. Two for you and two for me."

They took the rope from the rotating beam and tied our hands above our heads. Then they hoisted it over the beam and swung us over the well. The pain was excruciating.

They went outside. "Oh Zola, Elizabeth, darling. We're coming for you." Their voices receded. I fought against the pain. My breath was coming in tortured gasps. They had guns. There was absolutely nothing Zola and Elizabeth could do to defend themselves. Nothing but hide.

My head bent and all I could see beneath us

was black. Not good to look down. I wouldn't do it again.

Suddenly there was a soft whoosh of air, a movement behind us. Someone was swinging me away from the well. Zola came round in front and lowered me to the ground and untied my hands. She did the same thing to Josie. Her hands were steady, her mouth a straight line. She unfastened the rope from the beam and coiled it so fast she might have been doing it all her life.

Had been doing it all her life, I realized.

"Stay here," she ordered.

We struggled into a sitting position and watched her slip through the door. I didn't see her cross the yard and knew she had slipped around to the front of the well house and was probably moving quietly toward the Old House.

I was the first to get to my feet. I looked at my sister. "Don't try to come after me."

Too eager to get two more women, the men had gotten careless, over-confident. They weren't making any attempt to be quiet. Gravel crunched beneath their feet. "Oh, Elizabeth, Zola. We've got something for you."

Jerry guffawed. I ran behind George's Spanish bungalow and came up to the Old House just as they shoved the door open.

Elizabeth was standing behind it, holding one

of Francesca's granite pestles. She bashed Jerry in back of the head and grabbed the shotgun as he fell.

Leon rushed forward and aimed before Elizabeth could raise the shotgun to her shoulder.

The air parted, zinged, and a rope fell over his shoulders pinning his arms to his side. He was still clutching the handgun, when I rushed through the door and picked up a piece of broken glass.

"Drop it. Now. If you want to keep those fingers."

He did.

Zola walked toward Leon, coiling the rope as she went. When she was ten feet away, she sent it sailing around and around the length of his body and yanked him off his feet. He hit the floor with a thud. She was on his back in a flash and tied his arms in back and then bent his legs backward and secured them to his hands.

"Grand champion calf-roper," she said, shooting arms away from her sides, as though she were being judged in a 4-H event. "Five years in a row." There was nothing modest about her grin. "Grandfather would be proud."

"Where's Jane?"

"We untied her and told her to stay in the room. She's not exactly combat-ready and we didn't want to take a chance on her being used for bait."

I walked to the car and used the satellite phone

to call the house. There was no answer. Keith was probably still in the pasture. Sam didn't answer either. It was supposed to be his day off. In cooler weather he usually went fishing, but I suspected he was holed up in a movie theater today. Betty Central was dispatching. I called and asked her to send an ambulance for Francesca's body. "Then get ahold of the sheriff in Copeland County and tell him to come to the Diaz Compound. He needs to pick up two men and take them to his jail."

Josie and I ran back to the well house. She knelt beside Tosca, who was trembling with terror.

"I'll help load Jane into your car so you can take her to the emergency room. I believe she's okay, but I want her checked out really well. After you take care of her, go find Keith. He's probably in the north pasture. Tom will likely be there, too. We have everything under control here."

"Okay."

"Watch your driving. Remember you're on gravel roads. Elizabeth and Zola will keep watch until the Copeland County sheriff gets here." I hesitated. "One last thing. There's a hand mirror in the Old House. Please put it in my Tahoe. And there is a red crystal jar of herbs next to it on the counter. Please flush them down the sink."

"Are you okay?" She glanced at me as she picked up Tosca.

"I'm fine. Just a little woozy. I'll wait in the well house where it's cool." I waved her on. I managed to walk back and pass through the door. I sank to the ground and cradled Francesca's head in my lap. I felt for a pulse long grown silent and began to weep.

Then the walls of the well house shifted colors again and I swirled down.

Down into total blackness.

Chapter Twenty-nine

I hear Josie whisper, "She's had a nervous breakdown."

I am in my own bed floating on a feather sea. I turn my head to one side, too weary to wipe the tears that stream down my cheeks. *Nervous breakdown is not a professional term*, I think wearily. Josie shouldn't use it.

I fight to retain my thoughts. My thoughts are in the hand mirror at my side. I pick it up one more time. I am still in the mirror. Francesca left me there. But there is no one who will come after me. I've worn a groove scratching it over and over with my wedding ring.

"I think we should take it away," Josie says. "She's obsessed with that damn mirror."

No, no, no. They don't understand…Keith comes into the room and gently removes it. He leans over the bed and softly kisses my forehead and smoothes back my hair. I cannot make them understand that my soul is in the mirror. I cannot stop the trickle of tears and cannot speak.

He gently closes my door. *I'm doomed. There is no way out now. I'm left in the mirror forever. I need Francesca.*

I sleep again. My need for sleep seems to be insatiable. It's too deep. Is this what it feels like to die? From a distance I can hear Keith's guitar. Oh, my darling, my husband. I want to come back. I'm not through with this world yet. I want to stay here. I struggle and struggle. I know the song. I know it.

"You'll call my name and I won't answer. You'll call my name but I'll be gone."

His voice is deep. Tragic.

I won't go. I'm not ready yet. Please I'm not ready. I'm asleep again now. It's too deep, not a natural sleep and I'm being sucked under. I don't want to be pulled under. Under and yet away. Then I hear a violin. It's not Josie's. The style is different. The melody is incredibly sweet. Keith's guitar is fading away. Fading.

From a distance, I see a white horse galloping toward me. It has an iridescent aura. I know when I mount, it will carry me up into a star-strewn sky. Then the stallion stops, neighs, rears on his hind legs and stays frozen like a polished marble statue. It has come for me. We listen to a last perfect note from the violin. The sky is utterly empty. There are no people and it breaks my heart. There is no sound but the violin. Just the deep void. I do not want to go. Grief floods through me as I walk toward the horse.

Then I see a man coming down the road the horse traveled. He looks shabby and disheveled. He does not belong on this beautiful star path. He is an Earth person. He draws closer and I realize it is Old Man Snyder. He has come for me. Exhilaration pulses through me like I've been struck by lightning. Francesca has sent someone.

Then he stops and listens and in a bit, I hear it too. From afar another fiddle, begins. Old Man Snyder doffs his old fedora, looks at me and gives a slight bow. He lifts his bow.

The other fiddle launches into a tune so exotic it might have come from the East, from another culture. And I understand that this entity is challenging Francesca and would like me to stay in the mirror.

Old Man Snyder nods his head and matches the complexity of the minor composition that captures the poignancy of Gypsy violinists. Snyder launches into an insulting, repudiating bluegrass tune with his signature double-bow technique that jolts all my senses. He is of the Earth and proud of it.

I sob at the incredibly sweet strains of the

foreign fiddle, a ballad now. Poignant. Exquisite. All the heartbreak of every lover who has been betrayed, been lost. This is how Keith will feel if I must go.

Oh, I don't want to go, my darling. I do not want to leave this world.

There were a few discordant strands, violent and urgent, and I understand then that some kind of deadly contest has begun. Whirling, first brave, and then frantic. The pace picks up and then it's impossible to take in. Earth and hell blend. Heaven and the white horse are fading away. The instruments become as one.

And I understand now that before God created heaven and Earth, he created music. In the beginning there was music. That is how the world began. With a spherical hum, a vibration that set the worlds spinning.

I can only see Old Man Snyder. I cannot see the Other. But I know who he is. Francesca had told me about him. Tried to warn me. He was there when I fought the urge to hurt Angie's husband. My own Book of Common Prayer warned me. He was there. He is here.

Then there is silence. Not the silence of finality, but the breathless expectation that prefaces the beginning of an aria in a great opera. Or that expectant hush before the conclusion. Old Man

Snyder seems to listen for an instant and then the two fiddles duel once again.

And the Bible says Jesus descended to hell for three days after he was taken from the cross. The necessary hell that put the anguish in music. The discord, the melancholy. The wild despair. Was that why the Father sent you there? To bring back what was missing from a sweetly perfect heaven?

I want life. All of life. My quarrelling step-children and sunshine and drought. My crazy contradictory Kansas. Little children and silly dogs. I want the blend of Earth and heaven and hell.

I am the one who should be meeting this spirit. Old Man Snyder is taking my place. It is not right. The music winds down, fades. He looks at me across some dimension I don't recognize and tips his old fedora.

He walks off with his fiddle tucked under his arm.

When I awoke the next morning, sunshine was streaming into the bedroom. There was no one around. Weakly, I shoved my feet into my slippers and walked to the bathroom. I lowered myself onto the stool with the help of the towel bar, then managed to walk to the sink where I washed my hands and brushed my teeth. I wanted to shower, but I was too unsteady. I reached for my pink summer seersucker robe and walked to the top of stairs.

I could hear voices coming from the kitchen. Keith, Josie, and Zola putting in her two bits. I eyed the steps and decided they would be too risky.

"Hey," I called. "What does it take to get a cup of coffee around here?"

"You've been out of it for five days," Elizabeth said. "We were worried sick. I don't know who has been the most frantic, Dad or your sister. How much do you remember?"

A dream, I wanted to say. I tried to remember fragments of a dream. It was slipping away. What I did remember sounded crazy, even to myself.

A fever dream.

"Francesca? What about Francesca? She's dead, isn't she? I sort of remember some of what happened."

Her face was solemn. "Yes. I'm sorry. I know how much she meant to you."

"That poor woman. That lonely old woman."

"The cause of death is undetermined. The men wanted to throw her down the well, I'm sure, but she died before they could get the job done. The KBI had hoped to pin murder charges on those bastards. Not that they don't have enough attempted murders charges to put them away for life or more."

"Tosca?"

Elizabeth grinned and filled me in. For once she had enough sense not to refer to Tosca as "that worthless little dog."

"She's going to be fine. She's playing the most recent traumatic experience for all it's worth, of course. I understand she and Keith had reconciled before her latest misadventure."

"Oh, yeah. Big time." I told her about the buddy poppy.

"That's my dad."

"And Jane? What about Jane?"

"She's fine. Scared as hell. Seems as though she was returning some articles and when Francesca saw them, she fell down like she had been clubbed. Jane started running toward the house to get to a phone. The two men had been lurking around. They wanted to catch Francesca alone. But they thought Jane had seen them. So they tossed her into the ante room off of Francesca's workroom."

Tears trickled down my cheeks. "She had a hard life. She didn't deserve to have a hard death, too."

Elizabeth looked at me and scowled. "We're not too sure what all you remember, Lottie."

"Still just bits and pieces. What made all you women dash in like the cavalry?

"We found your note you left for Keith.

Believe me, I wouldn't have had the guts to step foot on the place otherwise. Remember when I said I had to make that flying trip back to Kansas to tell Francesca she had no basis for pursuing a lawsuit? She fired me on the spot and told me never to darken her doorway again."

"You said you had other business to tend to also."

"Yes, she had asked me to prepare a will. I took Zola with me that day so she could witness the signature." Elizabeth reached for the bedspread and twisted it a little before she looked me in the eye. "And I'm glad I did. After Francesca threw her little hissy fit, Zola managed to calm her down and came up with another solution. She has an uncle in Meridian who is a lawyer and she contacted him the very next day."

"Who did she leave her estate to? Cecilia or George?"

"I don't know. Zola doesn't either. She wouldn't say if she did. All she did was witness Francesca's signature after her uncle was done. What I took out was just a boilerplate will with the intentions of making all the alterations and additions while I was there." Elizabeth gave the little half-smile I so adored in Keith. "That was before everything blew up."

◇◇◇

Everyone had gone home and now there was just Keith and me and Angie in the house. All the daughters had fussed over me like I was a total invalid, but Elizabeth and Bettina had day-jobs to get back to. I wanted to rebuild my strength but had to force myself to get out of bed. I felt oddly drained of energy. It was still too hot to walk even in the evenings. Zola wouldn't hear of my touching a thing around the house.

I had missed Francesca's funeral. It was private and limited to the family. They couldn't find a church that would allow a service because all the denominations worried about saying words over a pagan. She was buried on the compound in the little fenced cemetery where her husband and children were laid to rest. Even though it was well past her time to die, I would feel the loss.

Reduced to watching old westerns, I sank into my chair and switched on the TV. I bypassed *Gunsmoke* and *Paladin*, and settled on *Little House on the Prairie*. Overly sweet perhaps, but it suited me right now. I couldn't handle much turmoil. The episode ended and rolled through the names which gave proper credit to Laura Ingalls Wilder, who wrote the classic books on which the series was based.

It was like a bolt of lightning striking a tree. Laura Ingalls Wilder. How could I have been so blind? Her father was the famous Kansas senator, John J. Ingalls.

Senator Ingalls had written a long essay about Regis Loisel and the family squabble. Ingalls detested the man and regarded the "filthy hilda-goes" as forerunners of the border ruffians. It was the most lengthy complex lawsuit in Kansas history.

How many times had this show come to mind when I heard Francesca's string of names? Doña Francesca Bianco Loisel Montoya Diaz. Her father was a Loisel. And her mother's family was Montoya.

Francesca was a descendant of the French Canadian fur trader Regis Loisel who had received an enormous land grand from Spain! I had goose bumps despite the heat. Montoya. Montoya was another great land grant family. If the two families had intermarried, it was hard telling how much land was involved.

How many times had I heard her and Cecilia say "We have always lived here"?

Francesca was the heir to the Loisel fortune and had proof of the location of the lost land.

The infamous Loisel land grant was due to a historical dirty trick: the Treaty of Fontainebleau in 1762. When "we" were the British and there was no America. When the French knew they would lose the French and Indian War to the Brits, they gave "Louisiana" to Spain in a secret treaty. Louisiana then covered the entire Mississippi Valley from the Appalachians to the Rockies.

The next year, when the war ended, "we" and France hammered out the Treaty of Paris, which ended the French and Indian War. The Brits got everything east of the Mississippi, and France got everything west of it. Eastern French Colonists who didn't want to live under British rule were given eighteen months to move west where they thought they would be governed by France.

Then, surprise! They were in Spanish territory, not French. The cagey French King Louis wrote a charming note to the governor of the territory asking that he play nice with the settlers there, as he had given a good chunk of the country away to Spain.

All hell broke loose. Treaties flew around like politicians' promises. French settlers tried to throw out the newly appointed Spanish governor. By the time President Thomas Jefferson and Napoleon agreed to the Louisiana Purchase, land-ownership was quite muddled. Maddest of all were the families who had received enormous land grants from the Spanish government due to the Treaty of Fontainebleau.

The Spanish government had given Regis

Loisel a huge tract of land after receiving his petition claiming it was his just reward for doing whatever it took to get along with the Indians and "in the interests of future commerce."

No doubt about it. Loisel had been a real humdinger. He had extended fur trade from the Missouri River to the Rocky Mountains.

Just like that, he received a staggering number of acres. The governor told him not to bother with having it surveyed.

Loisel made a will on his deathbed leaving everything to his wife and two daughters and named his business partners, Jacques Clamorgan and Auguste Chouteau, executors. Clamorgan stole the whole grant from Loisel's heirs by buying the land for ten dollars' worth of deer skins.

With the Louisiana Purchase, land grants made by the French and Spanish were honored, but Clamorgan's claim simply didn't sound right to confused government officials. Loisel's land sold without his family knowing—for a mere ten dollars? Really!

Loisel's heirs and Clamorgan's heirs slugged it out.

This took a half a century. Lawyers came and went. Heirs came and went, but the lawsuit went on forever. Finally in 1858, the land went to Loisel legal heirs, but the claim was to be relocated to "any vacant lands."

Just wherever. And whoever claimed to be an heir. They popped up like jackrabbits. Then the fight became over the location of those "any vacant lands."

As for the Montoya land grants, that would require more research.

Francesca wanted me to know the proof of the location of the "any vacant lands" lay at the bottom of the stream under the well.

I flushed with excitement. I looked at the time and date on the clock. I was the only one who knew the secret the well was hiding. I had the hand span required to rotate thumb to pinky to thumb to locate the buried zinc washer.

County was a clear winner over state.

I picked up the phone to tell Dimon what I had learned and then thought better of it. He would claim the credit. I sat down and quickly composed a story and emailed it to Ken McElroy, editor of the *Gateway Gazette*. I had promised Ken he could publish details about Victor Diaz's murder first. He would be tickled plumb to death to be ahead of the pack with this bombshell of a story. I knew he would honor the "please hold for verification" in the subject line. The story:

"Sheriff Sam Abbott and Undersheriff Lottie

Albright discovered the motive behind the Victor Diaz murder case today. Albright, working closely with the late Francesca Diaz, learned of a mysterious map which Doña Francesca claimed entitled the family to a substantial tract of land.

"The KBI was making no progress whatsoever," Undersheriff Albright said. "Sheriff Abbott had to step in and take over the investigation. He tapped into an information network that agents from Eastern Kansas would not have access to. This paper will provide further details in tomorrow's edition."

Then I called Dimon and asked him to meet with Keith and Sam and me at the compound.

"I can't get away today," he said.

"Oh, for this you can. I'm going to show you why Victor was killed. Bring a search warrant for the entire premises. And bring a cinematographer."

"I'll start right away."

Chapter Thirty

Several KBI agents turned up for the event. A couple of the men stared up at the towering cottonwoods like they had fallen into Disneyland. It was after five and softening into evening. Dimon must have driven like a demon to arrive so quickly. Keith put a protective hand on my shoulder. I gave it a squeeze.

"All here?"

Dimon nodded.

My heart thumped. It was important to be professional, but this was no longer a pleasant place for me. "There's room for us all in the well house. Keith, you and Sam and Dimon need to watch."

"And a translator," Dimon said. "I've brought a translator with me. Someone who can read Old Castilian. Even though no one will be speaking it."

Dimon and Keith had to duck to get through the opening. The translator fit just fine.

My biggest worry now was that the case

containing the map might have leaked and the documents would be soggy and unreadable. I looked at the solemn group of men who circled the well. They gazed with wonder at the interior of the magnificent round structure. A pigeon flew and the man on my right started at the sound. The soft peace emanating from the ancient walls dared us to violate its innermost secrets.

My hands shook. I had better be able to produce. "Gentlemen. It's time to start."

"Hold it just a minute," Dimon said. "Let me make sure everything is working first. I want every bit of this on record."

We waited while he conferred with the man operating the video camera. Dimon had him play back a few frames to check the quality, then nodded.

I felt as though we were documenting an archeological dig. On a par with a tomb of the Pharaohs.

I walked to the foremost beam and stretched my fingers out from its side. Then I rotated off my pinky to the thumb, then the pinky again until I had repeated the process five times.

There was no washer. I felt the blood drain from my face. Then I leaned over the top of the well and looked at the sides. The washer was a couple of inches away. I immediately put my index finger on it so I wouldn't have to search again.

I nodded at Dimon. "It's here."

With the camcorder whirring away, I made an formal announcement that I was in the presence of Keith Fiene, Sam Abbott, Frank Dimon, and two of his agents. I paused and Dimon supplied their names. I gave the time and date. "The purpose of this gathering is to validate the late Francesca Diaz's claim that there is a map at the bottom of the stream beneath the well. We believe it will explain why Victor Diaz was murdered."

That said, I gave the washer a slight tug. There was a strong light cord attached and with a gentle pull it stripped away from the layer of soil concealing it. Down, down, down until it was no longer buried.

Then the cord went limp. There was no tension. I couldn't tell if it was slack because it was free from the side of the well, or slack because there was nothing there.

I turned to Dimon. What if I had dragged all these men out here for nothing? Then I remembered what Francesca had said about putting the cord over the rotating beam. "I'll need some help at this point. I'm not tall enough. We need to get this cord wound around that beam. We might need a ladder."

But one of the men came forward and didn't

mind balancing on the edge of the bricks. He secured the rope with a kind of knot I didn't know existed.

"Okay. Now. Turn the beam, but be careful not to get this tangled up in the pulley system."

"We're not going to risk it," Dimon said. "Jim, go back up again and take the other ropes down and put them to one side."

"Sure you don't want to do it?"

Dimon gave him a sour look.

What if the beam would not rotate? What if there was nothing there?

Keith moved closer and I backed up against him. He wrapped his arms around me as though to hold me upright if things went wrong.

The beam slowly turned. The rope tightened. "Thank God," I murmured. "I was afraid it wasn't attached to anything." The rope suddenly thrummed with tension.

"Stop." Dimon waved away the man rotating the beam. "We've gone to too much trouble to screw things up now. Jim, there's a wet suit and a rope ladder in the truck. You're going into that hole. We're not about to take a chance on that rope breaking. Chances are that whatever is at the bottom is buried in mud and silt. Don't wait too long to put on that oxygen mask. Do it before you really need it. I'm going to tie a little spade on your back. Do *not* risk breaking that rope."

Jim was back in short order and hooked the rope ladder over the brick edge then disappeared into the depths. We followed his progress with a flashlight, but couldn't see much after he reached a certain point. After what seemed like an endless wait, Jim gave the rope a little flick, and the men started to pull up the load.

When it reached the top, Dimon swung it to one side and gently eased it to the ground. It didn't look like much, but it was there. Covered with mud and silt. Dimon pulled up a bucket of water and washed it off. He turned the bucket over and set the box on top, and washed it some more. The guy with the camcorder walked all around it.

Even if it didn't hold a thing of any importance, the box itself had to be worth a great deal of money. It was obviously gold with fine engraving done by an artist. I was happy for George and Cecilia. I was even happier that Francesca was finally vindicated.

No wonder she kept insisting "we have always lived here." As a descendant of one of the original land grant families who had subsequently married a Loisel, her family had indeed "always been here."

Before there *was* an America.

"The seal seems to have held," Dimon said.

"There doesn't appear to be any leaks. I don't know what they used, but this seal is sound." He stood. "Good work, Lottie." He stuck out his hand. "We'll get this back to the boys in Topeka right away."

"No, by God." Sam stepped forward. Keith was right beside him. "We are going to open this box right here in the presence of all these witnesses. Right here. Right now." He took a pocketknife out of his pocket. "Make sure you are getting all of this," he said to the cinematographer.

I held my breath as he edged the knife around the seal. "Lottie, I think you should have the honor of taking the last step."

I knelt and slowly opened the lid. Inside was a leather pouch, also sealed and marked with a Spanish coat of arms. We opened the pouch and inside was the precious map and an accompanying deed. The translator stepped forward and began to decipher the ancient Castilian. She read with little emotion, understanding the words but not their implications.

But I did. My temperature must have dropped two degrees.

In addition to the land, the Loisel family was granted everything below the earth too.

"Don't tell me it's another promise of gold," Dimon groaned. "Do *not* tell me I've wasted our time and resources on a high-class scavenger hunt.

Do *not* tell me we've gone through all this to find a worthless map whose value is based on some sleazy promise. I suppose it's the location of Coronado's Seven Cities of Gold. Or Quivira. Or some other missing treasure."

I could only take it in one slow second after another. I stood, straightened, inhaled slowly, and turned toward the agents. "Dimon, one family, one single family was given the rights to all the Ogallala Aquifer by France, then Spain, then France again, then the United States Government. One family controls all the Ogallala Aquifer. All the water rights in Western Kansas."

Dimon lost all the color from his face. "Water rights. Water rights." He stared at the cinematographer. "Turn that goddamned thing off."

"No. Keep it on," Keith said. "I want every bit of this recorded."

"Sorry," Dimon said. He swiped back his hair. "Sorry. Wasn't thinking. But my God." He waved at the cinematographer. "I want a close of up this map and deed."

He stared at the collection of agents as if he were assessing them. "Lottie, take care of the chain of custody. Do *not* screw this up. I want every step recorded perfectly and these documents transferred to a vault. I want the deputies from the sheriff's department in three counties to escort and witness the placement of the records in the KBI center in Topeka."

"No," I said. "That's just not going to happen. Francesca Diaz died to protect this map and deed and keep them out of the hands of the government." The cinematographer was still recording.

"This is in my jurisdiction," Sam said sharply. "Unless I invite the KBI in. You were supposed to solve Victor's murder. You didn't. Lottie did. Now I want sheriffs from three different counties to escort and witness the placement of that box in storage under armed guard at the Salt Mine Museum in Hutchinson. Where the sun don't shine and bastards like you can't make it disappear."

Keith looked at Sam and couldn't hide his grin. It was the only storage place of its kind in the Western Hemisphere. Some of the most precious artifacts in the world were stored there because the humidity never varied. Hollywood's most precious film footage was deposited there. Salt mines were where the Nazis stored a lot of art confiscated during World War Two. Sixty-seven miles long and six hundred-fifty feet under the prairie, its high security was maintained through shaft access only. Perfect. Just perfect.

Dimon looked at Sam with something akin to respect. But he was as rattled as I've ever seen him.

"With this single piece of paper, someone could tie up all the irrigation in Western Kansas."

"How can a well and one single stream be that important?" asked one of the agents.

"It's not," I said. "The well house itself, the well, and stream don't have much to do with anything. It's the control of water rights granted in that piece of paper that is important."

"Goddamn it all to hell," Dimon said. "Whoever gets this place could charge towns a fortune for access to water. They could hold all the farms hostage. Hard telling how much land is involved, too." His mouth was a straight line. He turned to me. "Do not discuss this with anyone. Until the government has had time to develop a policy statement."

I looked at Keith, suddenly understanding Francesca's antipathy toward the government. It's "policy statement" would be that the United States legally owned the land through the Louisiana Purchase. Not some rogue Spanish family that didn't know when to quit.

I smiled. Tell that to the Sioux Nation trying to win back the Black Hills. That lawsuit had been going on since 1877.

"Too late, Frank, I've already filed the story. The *Gateway Gazette* has been waiting for a note from me to run it." I held up my iPhone and pressed send.

"My God!" The color drained from Dimon's face.

"No wonder Francesca said this was the most precious commodity in the world." Saddened, I thought of the wily old woman that no one took seriously. "I don't understand how those two men knew about this map. Elizabeth and I both did our best to check out Francesca's claims and couldn't find anything that pointed to it."

"I told you in the beginning there was big bucks behind this somehow. Somewhere," Dimon said.

"But Victor would never, never betray his family and give up their inheritance. He would die first."

"Exactly."

"Those two thugs didn't find out through advanced research techniques," Sam said. "Stripped to the bones, who has the most to gain now by locating this map?"

"Victor's wife," Keith said.

Sam nodded. "The usual suspect."

"Maria! Of course. She's Victor's heir now." I was slow to believe what Sam knew to be true immediately. "Maria despised Francesca's witch-craft. She hated Victor's obsession with the family's lawsuit. Which she believed amounted to nothing. But Francesca's quarrel had not been with the family. It was with the government. Through all her work with immigrants, Maria probably knew it was crazy to go up against the government."

"That woman was not involved in Victor's death. No way," Keith said flatly. "Maria was devastated when Dwayne told her Victor was murdered."

"There's always unintended consequences. She's involved somehow. Let's go."

Maria looked at us in bewilderment when she opened the door. "What? Why have you come?"

Dimon pushed on inside and we followed. "I think you have a great deal to tell us. Lottie, read the Miranda warning."

"I'm here legally. I have rights."

"Yes, you do. That's why we are going to read them to you." I did.

Her face was white. "Why would you read me my rights? What are you accusing me of?"

"We believe you had a hand in Victor's death."

Shocked, she lapsed into hysterical sobs. "My Victor is dead. My wonderful husband is dead. And you think I was behind his murder?"

"We believe his killers wanted to know where a map was located."

She sank down on the couch. "Estelle's husband got us into this. This was Estelle's doing. She is so careless. I should know better than to ever trust her with secrets."

"What did Hugh do that got Victor killed?"

"He talked to the wrong people."

"So Hugh knew about the land? The water rights?"

"What water rights?"

We were all watching Maria's face. Clearly, she was unaware of the value of the land. Victor was the only who really understood. "What do you know about the land Francesca said the family owned? Did Victor ever talk about it? Did Hugh know about it?"

"Who doesn't know? Everyone out here has always known about Francesca's obsession with some land claim. I thought it was a passing fancy of a crazy old woman. I've never thought the land existed. Then something changed. One Sunday afternoon Victor came home very excited. He said Francesca had shown him a copy of a map and he believed the family had a valid claim to more land."

"But she didn't tell him where the real map was located."

"No. Of course not. She was simply stringing him along. It was a trick to keep him coming over every Sunday. She wanted total control over him. "

Dimon was piecing everything together as fast as I was. Maria didn't really understand about the importance of the map, and Victor did.

"I told Estelle because I was just fit to be tied. He belonged here with me on Sundays. He worked hard during the week. He should have gone to church with me and then spent a lazy afternoon. Estelle told Hugh. Then Hugh joked about it to some of the men in the feedyard. Called Victor 'Old MapQuest.'"

"And that's when things started going wrong," Dimon said.

"A couple of men showed up one day, and they took the map seriously. Very, very seriously. They asked Victor about it. They had worked at the feedyard about a year ago until Bart ran them off. When they came asking questions, Victor told them it was none of their business. He made them leave and told Hugh to shut up and tend to his job. Victor told me about it after he got home that night. He was mad at Hugh. Said he gossiped like some old woman."

She broke down again. I went to the kitchen and got her a drink of water.

"I didn't meet them until Victor's funeral. They told Hugh one of them had married a second cousin of one of my aunts. But I have never heard of this woman. There were all kinds of people at the funeral that I've never met. Distant Diaz cousins."

"These are men who know how to extract information," Dimon said. "Hugh is lucky they didn't include him in their inquisition."

She dabbed at her swollen eyes with a tissue. "We could have lived well if Francesca would have agreed to selling come of the compound land. But no, she had to keep everything intact. Why? Why? The line would die out in another generation because Cecilia will become a nun and George doesn't have the brains to manage it."

A car pulled up and parked beside my Tahoe. Hugh and Estelle Simpson came through the door.

Hugh looked miserable. Like he was practicing for prison. "God, I never intended for all this to happen. If there is any way my testimony would put those bastards behind bars. Any way at all."

Dimon looked at him coldly. "Oh don't worry, we are going to bring you in for questioning. We'll find a way."

Chapter Thirty-one

Dimon came back to the house with us. Playing the gracious winner, I tried to talk him into spending the night. He declined saying the drive time would do him good as he needed to think about all the ramifications of the map. The evening was still and the air had cooled a little. He was an awkward man and seemed uncomfortable with accepting our hospitality.

"At least don't go on an empty stomach. Let us feed you first."

He turned down a second home brew and sensibly switched to iced tea as we sat on the patio poring over the case.

"I called the office on my way over here. When my agents learned of Hugh Simpson's involvement, they were able to get more information from those men."

"Why would they think they would benefit by getting ahold of that map?"

"I think they planned to kill Victor all along, just not in such a spectacular way and only after he told them where the map was located. I'm positive they would have started pressuring Maria after things died down. Which they never did, of course. Die down, that is." His voice trailed off.

"Neither of them looked like he could think his way out of a paper bag."

"They had a half-baked plan. But it was just for getting the land and their sights were just set on Roswell County. First step was finding out where this map was located. They killed Victor before they got any information and then they zeroed in on Francesca. With Victor and Francesca out of the way, they planned to convince Maria there was a distant cousin relationship. She's the kind to turn toward family. Since she had no children."

"Especially with Hugh and Estelle out of the picture. Do you think they planned to kill them, too?"

"Don't know. The stakes were really high. It wouldn't surprise me."

Shadows were deepening, but no one wanted to move inside. Dimon set his glass on the table and checked his watch. "But Maria wouldn't have any money. All she would have is land."

"No doubt they would want to sell the land

at once," Keith said. "I can't imagine they would want to live out here and farm it."

I grinned. "Who could they sell it to? Without a clear title, no farmer would risk buying it. It's against the law for big corporations to buy Kansas land. Most of the men involved with family corporations out here are pretty savvy. They would know they can't plant irrigated crops because the government won't allow new wells."

"Those damned water rights. My God, what a mess. Well. I'd better get a move on." Dimon stood and shook Keith's hand.

"About that regional center…" Keith said.

Dimon stopped, but he didn't look back. "Yeah. Well, it's still on the drawing board. As things stand now, just keep on as you always have done."

I called Josie the day after Dimon left. I told her about all the strange directions the case had taken. There was a short intake of breath.

"I've missed you," she said. "It's been a while since we've really talked. I'll be out there before sundown tomorrow."

Maybe I was deluded, but it seemed to me like the weather was gentling down. Just a hint of cooler times to come. A hint that the world would straighten out. I had fixed tea. There was a plate of ladylike sandwiches in the refrigerator. Keith was to pick up Sam and go to Maybelline's for supper.

That evening she drove up the lane and parked. Arm in arm we walked over to the patio. We talked and cried together.

Josie stretched out on the recliner with Tosca on her lap. We watched fireflies. I couldn't see her face, but I could hear the sorrow in her voice when we talked about Francesca's death.

"About me and Tom," she said. She cleared her throat.

"I didn't ask. You don't have to explain."

"It's over. Before we had to face any of the problems. I'm the one who broke it off and I think he was glad."

"You would have made the ideal couple."

"No. No. It wouldn't have worked. Remember that song Keith taught me one of the times I was out here? The one about following someone to Texas? Then somewhere else. And another place after that." She hummed a little of it.

"'Elusive Dreams.' That's the name of it."

"That's Tom, Lottie. He's an old-fashioned cowboy. A drifter. Keith doesn't want to admit it and his sisters sure as hell don't want to."

Riled, I spilled some of my tea. "That's *so* not right. He's highly educated and makes a small fortune compared to most of the people around here. You make it sound like he's an indigent bum."

"I didn't say that. I said he was a drifter. You forget I'm a psychologist, Lottie. I know all the signs. He will always be packing up and leaving. Always. And if I wanted any kind of a life with him, I would have to do the same. I'm not willing to live like that. I need more structure." She tickled Tosca's tummy. "And so does my dog."

"I will need some time to think that over. It's hard for me to see Tom that way. I guess I've bought into his sisters' assessment. That he's wonderful and perfect and the ideal man for any woman."

"Some of that is right. He is quite wonderful." Her face was shadowed in the deepening twilight, but I could hear the catch in her voice.

"But it wouldn't work?"

"No, it would never work." Abruptly she changed the subject. "Living out here as you do I don't know where you found the time to make so many friends. A lot of people called or came by to ask about you. Even Old Man Snyder."

My heart squeezed. Another memory. A dream. A dangerous and unbearable dream. "He... he...was all right?"

"Yes. Why would he not be? In fact, he brought you some flowers. Some snapdragons. He said he picked them from his own garden. I put them in a vase in your bedroom."

"Did he stay and visit with you? Did you two fiddle together?"

"No. He simply dropped off the flowers and left."

A burden dropped. One I hadn't know I was carrying. It had been a dream. That's all. He had not taken my place. He was fine. Just fine. And would fiddle again. Thank God. He would take up that battered old fiddle again in heaven or hell or anywhere he had a mind to. And drift in and out of our lives at will.

"Sometimes I envy your life, Josie. You only have to answer to Tosca. Sometimes I feel like I'm riding a carousel and can't get off."

"That's a lifestyle choice, sister dear. And a damned stupid one. I've been waiting for you to cry uncle. You have two jobs. You can only handle one. Make a choice."

Jane Jordan came to our house a couple of nights later. Angie and Josie had gone to Hays to shop and I knew Jane was grateful for a chance to talk with me in private. She carried the rolled up Klan poster in one hand and the cat collar in the other.

"I didn't know. I swear I didn't know. "

"How did you find out?"

"My grandfather told me. He came to the hospital to pick me up after Josie took me to the emergency room. I had the poster and kept it and the collar with me because I didn't want anyone thinking that hateful poster belonged to the Diaz family. We had already caused them enough harm. On the way home when Grandpa saw the poster, I thought he was going to faint dead away."

"He recognized it."

"He did. And then he told me. There was an uncle, years ago. It was like you said, a black sheep. A hateful man. Crazy, they thought. The family didn't want to have anything to do with him. So my people were involved after all."

"So you know about what was done to Francesca?"

"Yes. Grandpa told me. And I can't sleep for thinking about that poor tortured old woman. The shock. The shock of it all when I handed her the collar and unrolled the poster."

"Jane, it's over now."

"I can't get it out of my mind. I just can't."

"Let's put an end to this."

I reached for the poster and started up the grill. I laid the poster on top. I took Jane's hand and together we watched it burn. After she left, I picked up the cat collar and put it on the shelf beside the madstone. I needed this visible reminder of a time when greed and religion had formed a bond with Satan.

Sam and Keith were outside the sheriff's office. They had just hoisted the flag. Tosca was cradled in Keith's arms. She gazed up, her tail held so stiffly I could have sworn she was trying for a salute.

Josie was staying a couple of extra days because we had to formalize our statements about the terrible day at the Diaz Ranch. For the last two nights Old Man Snyder had come over and he showed Josie some of his fingering techniques. But our favorite evening entertainment was watching Doe try to give Tosca three-legged lessons. She admired his abilities tremendously.

Josie looked at me and smiled. The unfurled flag swayed in the breeze. The red and white stripes brightened in the sun's rays. I looked lovingly at the two men who always gave me the feeling that all was right with world.

"Gonna be a scorcher," Josie drawled.

I sprayed coffee and reached for a towel, turned and check to see if she was also "chawing tabaccy." She tried to look innocent.

I had received a call yesterday from Francesca's lawyer saying there was going to be a formal reading of Francesca's will and he wanted all the named heirs present. I immediately thought of all those rare Spanish books. I suspected she had left them to me. Surely she wouldn't take a chance on leaving those books to anyone else.

"A reading of the will is only done in old movies," Josie said. "I thought Elizabeth was Francesca's lawyer and she would never stand for such high drama."

"Nope. She got canned. But you can come too. I asked, and he said you would have to stay in the background and not say anything. He said Francesca wanted it done this way."

She rolled her eyes.

We drew up to the courthouse.

"That's Elizabeth's Volkswagen," Josie said.

"So it is." Bewildered, I pulled up beside it. "What is she doing here?"

"Don't know."

"So what happens to all the Diaz land now?" Josie asked as we walked up the steps.

"Well, under Kansas law the wife inherits the husband's assets unless there is a will stating otherwise. Maria hasn't been guilty of any crime. Other than wanting to leave Kansas."

Josie smiled.

"But I think it's going to be a mess." It was more than a mess. Victor had died before Francesca and without owning much. I suspected there would some surprises in the will. And there was more than one lawyer present, including one sent by Dimon.

Realistically, there was no way in hell the United States government would allow any inheritor to bring all the High Plains to its knees over water rights.

Elizabeth nodded to us when we walked into the room.

"Hi. I didn't expect to see you here."

"I'm Maria's lawyer," my stepdaughter said. "And Cecilia's lawyer is a man who usually represents the Benedictine Convent."

Josie and I exchanged glances. Why did any of these people need lawyers to hear a will read? And why in the world would Elizabeth consent to be Maria's lawyer?

Zola's uncle was plump and colorless with sandy hair and prissy lips. "I'm Albert Conifer. As the administrator for the estate of Francesca Diaz, I summoned you here for the reading of her last will and testament. I am quite pleased that she specified that it be done in just such a manner, because under the term of the former will which was made by her husband, now deceased, through a lawyer, now deceased, everything would have passed to Victor, now deceased."

"Why are other lawyers here? It's not like we need these shysters running up the prices," George Perez interrupted.

Conifer ignored him and pushed on. "There were an unusual series of requests in that will in addition to the bequests that are legally binding. It would be best to see how many of her wishes we can all voluntarily agree to. Before the court has to straighten all this out. If this goes well, I'll draw up a binding agreement. I'm going to start with the easiest one first. Lottie, she wanted you to have all the contents of her workroom. Apparently because you received training from her. Is that agreeable to you?"

I had no desire to become a healer. Yet I knew George and Cecilia would burn everything connected with Francesca's work. All the history. All the techniques and information. All the magnificent leather-bound books. It would be tragic. I swallowed hard and nodded that I agreed to accept the gift. At least I could continue getting the books translated and catalogue any processes contained therein.

There was always room for another out-building at Fiene's Folly. A wee witch workshop. What could it hurt?

"All right. Then let us proceed."

I glanced at Maria and Cecilia. Both sat rigidly in their chairs. George looked scared. My stomach tightened. Conifer read straight through. He finally reached the end. And now for the two main issues. The entity known as Roswell County and land owned by the Loisel and Montoya families as specified in the map and deed located at the bottom of the well."

Conifer peered over his glasses. "That map has been retrieved, I understand."

"It has, sir."

We turned to look at the attorney for the government.

"Very well." Conifer looked directly at me and resumed the reading. "All the land owned by the Diaz family, both that known as Roswell County and all the other land designated in the map that has been passed down, I leave to my dear, dear friend, Lottie Albright, with the binding request that she continue to pursue my case against the United States government."

I took a deep steadying breath, but I couldn't speak.

All hell broke loose.

Maria jumped to her feet. "That snake in the grass. That deceitful woman. As Victor's widow, I should have inherited everything. That vicious witch is leaving me with nothing. I wanted to sell the compound so I can afford to move somewhere else. After all the family is taken care of and George's children's educations provided for, I was going to establish a foundation to assist abused women."

I glanced at Josie. Of course. Of course my stepdaughter would agree to be Maria's lawyer if she were going to help abused women! Elizabeth's life's work revolved around rescuing lost souls.

"You bitch," George said, glaring at Maria. "You conniving bitch. You know Francesca never intended to sell so much as one acre of this land."

"Don't you call me a bitch." Looking like a shocked schoolmarm, Maria hands dove for a pocket in her pants and she pulled out her rosary. She kissed the cross. Out of meanness, I suspected, and quickly established that God was on her side.

The lawyer from the Benedictine Convent looked stunned. Cecilia rose. "How did this happen?" Her voice quavered. "This cannot be God's will that this intruder was allowed to turn Francesca against her own family." She turned toward the sister-in-law she despised. "Maria, I would never, never allow our land to be sold for any reason. You know Victor would want to keep everything intact. I wanted to use the Old House as a haven for unwed mothers and remodel the main house into a chapel."

Her soft voice made her bold words all the

more startling. "We will challenge this will. All of the land will go to the glory of God." The Benedictine lawyer beamed at her.

"And you're a bitch, too," George yelled. "Where will my family go? What will we do?"

"I believe all this is premature." We turned to look at the lawyer for the United States government. "We plan to challenge this bequest. There was no valid claim to this land in the first place. This issue must proceed through the courts."

Until the cows come home, I thought. As it always has done. The government would never acknowledge the Diaz family's ownership. Even now, I was sure there was a platoon of lawyers poring over the language of the Louisiana Purchase. Did Napoleon have the right to sell land belonging to Spanish land grant families? Had the government agreed where the Loisel grant was located?

My blood pressure spiked. "Now wait just a minute here. All this is mine to decide. Gentlemen. Ladies. The will has been read. I have a great many decisions to make. Make no mistake, this is truly Francesca's last will and testament. The discussion going on right now will not alter one single fact. And it should be kept within the family." I whirled and faced the lawyer for the government. "And your presence here today is beyond contempt."

Josie and I left the room.

My cell phone rang a couple of miles later.

"The lawyer we sent just called." Frank Dimon was jubilant. "Talk about an incredible break. We can put an end to a bunch of foolishness in very short order. First off, of course, is to cease and desist with that ridiculous lawsuit. Secondly, since you didn't have sense enough to keep all of this out of the papers, some really big players had shown interest in acquiring some of that land. God, the prospects for development alone stagger the imagination. The government will pay you a reasonable settlement sum with you agreeing to a cease-and-desist order relinquishing all claims and this whole issue will be put to death."

"Over my dead body." I was so angry I pulled over. "The government doesn't have the right to order me to cease and desist anything."

"Be reasonable. You can't go up against the United States government. This is not some little local issue. This will involve state and federal courts. It could go on for years."

"It already has." I hung up.

I stayed home and took walks, listened to music, and mulled over all the ramifications of the will. Margaret had rounded up help for the historical society and Sam definitely was The Man. He tried not to let it go to his head when several sheriffs in Northwest Kansas called him for consultations.

Keith came over and sat beside me on the sofa. "Baby got the blues?"

"Too many blessings. I'm not used to them." I smiled and laid my head on his shoulder. "I honestly don't know what to do. According to the will I'm supposed to continue the lawsuit, but I don't know how I can."

He looked relieved. "I can't decide for you, honey. But one thing is for sure, suing the government would break us."

"Or anyone else. But one family managed to do it for God only knows how long."

"And it caused nothing but grief. You could sell some of the land and give deserving young men a toehold."

"Yes. But according to Elizabeth, even the claim to Roswell County might be shaky."

"While you are working this through, have you thought about setting up a foundation to study Francesca's healing methods and to maintain the plants?"

"That's a good idea. But I'm at the point where I just barely trust anyone to actually serve as officers. But I've come to one decision. I want George Perez and his family to keep living there so the place won't go to hell. Cecilia won't be a problem. I'll bet she moves to a convent by the end of the year."

"Maria?"

"I don't care about Maria. She has no basis for a claim to anything. She has a nice little house of her own."

Keith looked worried.

"Francesca was basically a Buffalo Commons woman. I think deep in her heart she honestly thought not an acre of sod should ever have been broken."

"You know how I feel about that. But even if you form a foundation and appoint officers, they have to be strong enough to take a lot of flak, and if you persist with a lawsuit, you need to find a board chairman with access to power and who is one tough son-of-a-bitch."

"Okay. I just don't want this to work a hardship on our family."

The right person to head the foundation occurred to me in the middle of the night: The Right Reverend Ignatius P. Talesbury. The Catholic priest, turned Episcopal, who had fought his way through double layers of bureaucracy to rescue African child soldiers.

The combined power and wealth of the

Roman Catholic Church and the Church of England. That should do it.

I went out to Saint Helena the next morning. As I had predicted, his ire was raised at once at the thought of someone developing Kansas land. Talesbury had singlehandedly fought off an attempt to thwart a crooked nephew's attempt to lease his land to a wind farm. He understood doing battle against the forces of evil. It only took him the rest of the day to make up his mind.

"But I'll need help," he said when he called. "I'm a man of action, and researching historical documents is not one of my skills. Someone needs to come up with the basis for the land grants."

"I know just the person."

I called Jane Jordan.

"Yes. Oh, yes. It will be a chance to make up for everything my family has done."

"You didn't do those things. You shouldn't feel guilty."

"But I do."

"Put that out of your mind. Just come to the historical society Monday morning and I'll get you started."

"How far back do you want me to go?"

"The Loisel fortune was sort of settled in 1858

in favor of the Loisel Family, but the terms were a mess. The "any vacant lands" were never specified. You'll need to track that down if possible. Then we need to dig up information about the Montoya land grant."

She cleared her throat. "Do you know the first Spanish land grants in Kansas go back to the late 1500s? After the Coronado Expedition in 1541? When we were part of New Mexico? Some of Kansas, that is."

I started laughing. "No, I didn't know." Every schoolchild in Kansas knew about Coronado. There were a number of Spanish artifacts in Kansas museums. "Wow! That's a couple of centuries before the Treaty of Fontainebleau. Coronado. That should keep you busy."

"A lot of those records were burned in the Pueblo Revolt of 1680. Francesca's deed and map would sell for a fortune to collectors, even if the claim is useless."

"It won't be. I'm sure of that."

I would have a chairman with brass balls and a researcher second-to-none. Let the games begin.

It was early evening. Still too hot to go outside. I listened to Keith play, but was too distracted to pay much attention. Josie's words had stung. I couldn't get them out of my mind. I needed to decide. What I did with my life was a choice. It wasn't smart to try to cling to two full-time jobs.

Keith laid down his guitar and reached for his drink. "You're thinking. That's not always good news."

"It is in this case."

Margaret loved running the day-to-day operations of the historical society. The place just hummed now due to unexpected developments. Angie had started helping Margaret while I was lying in my drug-induced haze. My stepdaughter could soothe anyone. She had spent her life doing so. Compared to Angie's husband, Margaret was child's play. She alternated between working at the historical society and tending to the flowers at the compound.

Talesbury knew what to do with injured souls. It was his specialty. Through working with his African boys who were now helping maintain Francesca's elaborate herb garden, Angie was regaining her emotional health. There was always a child trailing after her.

Jane Jordan threw herself into the research and came to the historical society every day. She ran around like a little chihuahua, anxiously watching for affirmation from Margaret.

She was never late. Never careless. Didn't have a mouth on her.

Margaret was ecstatic.

With three other women there every day, the historical society was no longer my private haven. But none of the three were trained historians. I shuddered at the thought of turning Margaret loose to collect oral histories.

Family histories were my specialty and my first love. I would continue to do that and turn over to my eager staff the budgets, politics, publicity, fair booths and floats, grant applications, research solicitation, software problems, and general hassles.

But bottom line, I wanted to stay in law enforcement. For this county. For Northwest Kansas.

"You'll be shocked," I warned Keith. "Like totally."

"Try me. It takes a lot to shock me nowadays."

"I want to proceed with the regional law enforcement center and I want to be the director."

"You're right. I'm shocked."

"I have my own ideas for a regional system. It's a far cry from what Dimon has in mind, but it would work. It would stave off consolidation. Wise old men who keep getting reelected would still have their rightful place. After all, county had just skunked state. Sam Abbott outwitted Dimon and a team of investigators."

"And I could go back to doing what I do best. Vet work and farming."

"You've retired from vet work, remember?"

"Yeah, right."

"I want to begin with a forensics lab and I want you and Tom to design it. Then we'll tackle all the obsolete systems in Sam's office. He will persuade the others to do the same so they will be connected to regional data bases. It's upgrade by stealth. One piece of equipment at a time."

"Sounds like a good idea to me, Lottie. Super, in fact."

I smiled. His relief was all too evident. I was more at home with law enforcement than my husband and I think he knew that. I had an intuitive feel for when to push and when to step back. Keith was more black and white. Right was right and wrong was wrong. Keith thought someone should pay a steep price for breaking the law. But I had been trained by the best. Sam Abbott had a sixth sense about administering justice.

"You're going to be in a higher-risk position than working at the historical society."

"I know. I've thought about that. Are you okay with this?" I watched his face. He was keeping it neutral. I knew it was because he thought he should. The right thing to do and all that. "Honey, you've got to promise not to hover."

He let out a poof of air, looked at me with raised eyebrows and a little half-smile and didn't bother to answer.

"I'll call Dimon tomorrow and tell him Northwest Kansas is planning its own regional center, without the help of Topeka."

"He won't appreciate that. There were a lot of jobs at stake."

I pasted the final story into the first volume of the Carlton County history books. Already, families who had neglected getting material in on time were clamoring for volume two and we had decided to do it. Jane was a meticulous proofreader and indexer. Margaret charged right into publicity and planning, and Angie was a natural for public relations and customer service, and loved the artistic side of creating a book.

They all understood they were not to conduct interviews and collect oral histories. I was just a phone call away.

I locked my office and walked down the stairs. Outside, I looked up at the sky.

There was a good chance it was going to rain.

Author's Notes

Hidden Heritage is the third mystery in the Lottie Albright series. These notes are an attempt to sort fact from fiction because this book is such a curious blend of both.

During my first tour of Sheridan County, led by Evelyn Walden and Marilyn Carder, I fell in love with an enormous cottonwood on the old Twell Ranch. Outside of the California redwoods, I had never seen such a magnificent tree. I later read it really was the largest in Kansas. I was mesmerized by the constant ripples of silver, the peace generated by surrounding cottonwoods, and the creek running through this shaded heaven. I wanted to stay there.

Sears Roebuck houses were real. The package contained everything necessary down to the last nail. They were a godsend for treeless prairie towns. Eastern Kansas has an abundance of timber and there weren't as many sold there.

Surprise! Madstones were real too and I really, really want one. Provided it's from a white albino deer. Madstones are listed in my old huge Webster's dictionary, but not in my new Collegiate Edition.

A good many Americans joined the Ku Klux Klan in the 1920s. At that time the organization was violently anti-Catholic. In fact, I found the old KKK poem at the Kansas Historical Society.

Believe it or not the Regis Loisel lawsuit was real. It went on for three generations. Senator John Ingalls wrote about Loisel and the endless litigation in his extensive personal writings. Ingalls despised Spaniards and believed the "haughty hildago with the sable drooping plume and subtle rapier was the predecessor of the border ruffian, the jay hawker, and the bullwhacker."

Most of the records of Spanish land grants in "Louisiana" were destroyed in the Pueblo Revolt of 1680, but Coronado really did issue land grants in Kansas. Two days before I turned in the final manuscript for *Hidden Heritage,* an old Spanish family sued the government over the very same land grant issues dealt with in my book. Ironically, I had used their name. It is changed in this book.

The Treaty of Fontainebleau was a secret agreement of 1762 in which France ceded Louisiana (New France) to Spain. The treaty followed the last battle in the French and Indian War in North

America. This treaty was kept secret even during the French negotiation and signing of the Treaty of Paris (1763), which ended the war with Britain.

Feel free to visit my website, www.charlottehinger.com, if you have questions or comments about historical issues in *Hidden Heritage.* However, although I learned a lot about herbs and plants I will not recommend treatments and remedies, whether healing or magical.

To receive a free catalog of Poisoned Pen Press titles, please contact us in one of the following ways:

Phone: 1-800-421-3976
Facsimile: 1-480-949-1707
Email: info@poisonedpenpress.com
Website: www.poisonedpenpress.com

Poisoned Pen Press
6962 E. First Ave. Ste. 103
Scottsdale, AZ 85251

CPSIA information can be obtained at www.ICGtesting.com
Printed in the USA
BVOW08s0854250913

332114BV00001B/1/P